# AFTER HANNIBAL

The Partnership
The Greeks Have a Word for It
The Hide
Mooncranker's Gift
The Big Day
Pascali's Island
The Rage of the Vulture
Stone Virgin
Sugar and Rum
Sacred Hunger
Morality Play

# AFTER HANNIBAL

BARRY UNSWORTH

HAMISH HAMILTON · LONDON

HAMISH HAMILTON LTD
Published by the Penguin Group
Penguin Books Ltd, 27 Wrights Lane, London w8 5tz, England
Penguin Books USA Inc., 375 Hudson Street, New York, New York 10014, USA
Penguin Books Australia Ltd, 10 Alcorn Avenue, Ringwood, Victoria, Australia
Penguin Books Canada Ltd, 10 Alcorn Avenue, Toronto, Ontario, Canada m4v 3b2
Penguin Books (NZ) Ltd, 182–190 Wairau Road, Auckland 10, New Zealand

Penguin Books Ltd, Registered Offices: Harmondsworth, Middlesex, England

First published 1996
1 3 5 7 9 10 8 6 4 2

'The Folks Who Live on the Hill': music by Jerome Kern, words by Oscar
Hammerstein II, copyright © 1937 by T. B. Harms & Co. Inc., USA;
PolyGram Music Publishing Ltd, 47 British Grove, London W4.
Used by permission of Music Sales Ltd

Set in 11¼/14pt Monotypye Baskerville
Typeset by Datix International Limited, Bungay, Suffolk
Printed in England by Clays Ltd, St Ives plc

A CIP catalogue record for this book is available from the British Library

ISBN 0–241–13342–4

FOR AIRA

When earth breaks up and heaven expands,
How will the change strike me and you
In the house not made with hands?

Robert Browning, *By the Fireside*

They are called *strade vicinali*, neighbourhood roads. They are not intended to join places, only to give access to scattered houses. Dusty in summer, muddy in winter, there are thousands of miles of them wandering over the face of rural Italy. When such a road has reached your door it has no necessary further existence; it may straggle along somewhere else or it may not. You can trace their courses on the survey maps kept in the offices of the local *comune*; but no map will tell you what you most need to know about them: whether they are passable or ruinous or have ceased altogether to exist in any sense but the notional. Their upkeep falls to those who depend on them, a fact that often leads to quarrels. The important thing, really, about roads like this is not where they end but the lives they touch on the way.

From their landing window, broad and deep-silled, the Chapmans had a view which included a piece of the road, a narrow, yellowish ribbon rising and curving between terraced olives and a field of young maize. They had stopped on the way downstairs to look out.

'Oh, to be in England now that spring is there,' Harold Chapman declaimed. He was at his most exuberant in the mornings. 'Not bally likely,' he added after a moment. 'It was nine degrees centigrade in London when we left, and outlook variable. Seventeen here.' Figures had a talismanic importance for him; who commanded them commanded the world. One of the first things he had done on arrival was to hang his outdoor thermometer on the wall outside the kitchen. 'Look at that sky,' he said. 'Not a cloud in it.' He glanced at his wife, Cecilia, and smiled his usual tight smile, wrinkling his broad nose a little in the doggy kind of way she had always found attractive.

'It's April,' she said.

Harold stared. 'So it is. A shrewd observation, sweetheart. The twelfth of April 1995.' He glanced at his watch. 'Local time 8.43.'

'I was talking about the poem you just quoted from. It's "Oh, to be in England now that April's there." Not spring.'

Harold thought briefly of disputing this. It was not that he believed Cecilia might be wrong; in matters of this sort she never was. Like all intensely competitive people, he had learned to cede land that lay beyond hope of conquest, and he had assigned the marginal territories of literature and art to his wife from the early days of their marriage. Indeed, he was proud to have a wife who possessed such exotic knowledge and expressed it in the accents of the privileged. Apart from anything else, it impressed the people he did business with. But to be caught out, to be corrected, that was a different matter. He glanced quickly at his wife's face. Small-boned, softly moulded, rather squeamish about the mouth, it bore the loving expression it always did when she felt she was making him a gift. She said, 'Browning, the poet's name.'

'Well, I know that much,' Harold lied, and smiled his tight smile again. 'Spring, April, what the hell?'

They were dressed and ready for breakfast, but Harold had paused to admire the view, thus naturally requiring that Cecilia should pause too. He was given to the counting of blessings, which in practice meant the listing of assets, natural enough in one who had made quite a lot of money buying and selling them in the form of residential and office properties in Dockland London.

The view from their holiday villa in Umbria, recently acquired, came under the heading of asset, without a doubt, since a man in some measure possesses what he can see from his house, and also of course it has a bearing on the market value of the property considered as a whole. Harold, partly to assuage the chagrin his blunder had occasioned him, found himself making – yet again – an inventory: there was the curve of the road, the ancient olives, the stiff green shoots of the half-grown maize. Above this the land rose in terraces of vines, bare still between their tall posts. Then the beautiful dipping line of the hills, half-melted in the pale-blue haze of morning, with the walls and towers of little towns nestling here and there among them, places whose names Harold did not know yet, but he knew that some of them had been old already when the Romans came.

Immediately below them there was a peach tree in first flower, the buds a deep rose colour. The plot of ground marked out by Cecilia for her kitchen garden had been turned over for them by a man with a tractor from the nearby village. He had not asked for money yet; Harold was waiting to see if his charges were reasonable before asking him to do anything more. He had already ascertained the going rate for tractor work.

'My God, the peace of it,' he said.

'Heavenly, isn't it?' Cecilia turned to him a face delicately glowing. 'Darling, look at that patch the man turned over for us. It has dried from the deep brown it was at first. It is a reddish ochre now, the true Umbria colour.' She suddenly felt the moment to be a prophetic one. 'It is like us,' she said. 'We will settle into our true colours here.'

These remarks seemed to Harold entirely typical of Cecilia, in that they composed a series, each approaching nearer to the top, the last going over it. Her enthusiasm had always impressed him and roused his irony and restored his sense of authority in more or less equal measure. 'Well, we are not likely to dry out,' he said. 'Not with all this wine around. I should have thought that the true colour of Umbria was umber.'

'Umber is a pigment, not an earth colour. It is just brown really, it has no –'

At this point the peace of the morning was disturbed by the sound of an engine no longer young, a clogged, catarrhal chugging. While they still watched, a tractor of antique design rounded the bend, came into view. Sitting up on it, stiffly heraldic, were an old man in a woollen hat of Phrygian shape, a scowling younger woman of large proportions and a round-faced man in a cap, who appeared to be smiling slightly. They drew to a halt before the house and sat for some moments together while the tractor panted dark breaths from a sort of small chimney.

'It is the Checchetti family,' Cecilia said. 'The ones who

4

helped us with some of our things when we first came here. They are very . . . archetypal, aren't they?'

Harold grunted. It was not the word he would have used himself. 'They charged us plenty for the help,' he said. 'We'd better go down and see what they want. I'd go on my own, but –' He had not learned much Italian as yet, though it was at the top of his list. Cecilia, on the other hand, spoke the language quite well. As a girl she had spent two years at a finishing school in Florence and before her marriage had often come back to visit friends made then.

The Checchetti got down from the tractor in order of authority, the father first, the son-in-law bringing up the rear. The old man was unkempt, his long-sleeved vest stained a rancid buttery colour from the sweats of many summers, his woollen hat stuck through with bits of straw. The daughter, on the other hand, was got up for visiting, in a dress with a pattern of large red poppies, earrings in the form of copper hoops and hair frizzed out round her large head. The husband continued with his hapless smile, which was not really a smile at all but a sort of permanent relaxation of the features. His name was Bruno, Cecilia now remembered. She was on the point of asking them inside, but for obscure reasons decided against it at the last moment.

The daughter began the conversation from some yards away, speaking volubly and with rapid gestures of the hands.

'What does she say?' Harold was impatient. He had been looking forward to his breakfast coffee.

'I don't get it all – the accent is rather tricky. She is saying that life is difficult, money is short, the cost of everything keeps going up all the time, the olives have been damaged by these heavy rains.'

'Same thing in Britain.' Harold smiled his tight smile at the Checchetti daughter. '*Anche in Inghilterra*. Not the olives of course.

5

Surely,' he said to Cecilia, 'they can't have come at this hour of the day just to talk about the cost of living.'

The old man muttered a few words, looking away from them towards the horizon.

'They are upset about something,' Cecilia said. 'The father is saying that what Italy needs is a strong government so as to weed out all the crooks and perverts.'

The daughter made a gesture which might have signified impatience or agreement with her father's words. She began speaking again, with more visible emotion now. Her bosom rose and fell, an alternation which her amplitude of form and the low cut of her dress rendered dramatic. Cecilia listened intently, trying at the same time to suppress her feeling that the Checchetti father and daughter were rather awful people, he with that foxy, feverish look, she with her beefy arms and heavy, ill-humoured face. Bruno seemed less malignant but he was obviously far from bright. She felt guilty at feeling like this about them, as they were *contadini*, peasants, and therefore very authentic people and by definition admirable.

'What does she say?' It galled Harold to be left out of the conversation like this.

'The gist of it is that their garden wall has fallen down.'

'That is tough luck.' Harold nodded his head and compressed his lips to show sympathy. Relations with neighbours had to be put on a sound footing right from the start. 'Tell them we are extremely sorry to hear this and hope that they will soon have their wall back in place again.'

But this was not well received. The daughter bridled. The father turned further away and spoke passionately towards the sky. Even Bruno looked resolute for a moment or two.

'It is the section of the wall that borders the road,' Cecilia said. 'Pieces from it have fallen across the road. They seem to be suggesting that it is our —'

'That is awkward,' Harold said. 'Typical example of Murphy's law. The wall falls down, that's bad enough, but it has to fall just in the wrong place.' He paused, a thought having occurred to him. 'That is our road too, isn't it? They are on the corner where it joins the public road. They have come down here to tell us that the road we share is partly blocked and it may take them some time to clear it. That is really very considerate. Tell them we appreciate it.'

'No, that's not it.' She felt a sudden surge of irritation with Harold. Did he really think that this demeanour of the Checchetti indicated a mission of goodwill? He was so terribly prone to interpret things to his own advantage. Then he would feel aggrieved because he had been wrong, and get aggressive. 'No,' she said, 'it seems they are blaming us.'

Harold's expression changed instantly and a heavy frown settled on his face. 'Blaming us? What on earth has it got to do with us?'

Cecilia spoke to the Checchetti again and father and daughter answered at the same time, each speaking loudly in what seemed an attempt to drown out the other.

'They are saying that the lorries from our building work – the work we had done when we bought the house – were overloaded and caused heavy vibrations and this made the wall collapse. Signora Checchetti says that these lorries, constantly passing back and forth, were a nightmare at the time and now they have caused the wall to collapse. When she protested to the drivers they laughed in her face.'

'And well they might,' Harold said. 'I've never heard such a load of poppycock in my life.'

The Checchetti, understanding that the man of the house was now in full possession of the facts, were looking intently at him. In the silence that descended, he heard the sound of a motor lawn-mower somewhere above them: that German fellow up

7

there again, cutting the grass on his olive terraces. He seemed to start at first light – Harold had been meditating a complaint for some time now. 'Vibrations, is it?' he said. 'That building work was done six months ago. Why should it take their bloody wall six months to register the effect of the vibrations? Ask them that, will you?'

'I'll try.' Harold's swearing always frightened Cecilia a little. She was aware again, as she spoke to the averted faces, of the ugliness and pathos of their visitors. The old man's breath was atrocious, even at this distance. He had a look at once brutish and febrile, as if he might be subject to some disorder of the nerves. The daughter, with her billowing fatness and frizzy hair and bright dress, looked like a sulky troll dressed up for a party. She did not bear the marks of physical toil on her as the men did, and Cecilia wondered if she had some other work. Narrow lives, mean and sordid and grasping. Now they had come here seeking some small advantage. She felt a kind of pity for them as well as repugnance. She glanced at Harold in the hope of finding some similar response but saw nothing on his face except the same look of frowning displeasure.

The Checchetti spoke together again, even more loudly than before. Bruno joined in this time, his voice surprisingly high-pitched. They were addressing their surroundings and one another, like a chorus in a tragedy. The fury that had lain below the surface from the beginning was evident now and there was a new, more threatening tone to their voices.

'What do they say?'

'I don't know. I can't make it out. They are going to turn on us and start shouting any minute now.' She felt helpless. As always, she clutched at her husband's displeasure, his combativeness, as a shield. He was never divided – it was his great strength. 'What shall we do?' she said.

Harold considered. It was something of a facer. Going to see the collapsed wall would not commit them to anything of course; but it might be taken as acknowledging a degree of responsibility. Not going, on the other hand, might have repercussions he couldn't at present foresee. It would be wiser not to make enemies of these people if it could be avoided. 'Tell them we'll come and have a look later on this morning,' he said.

It was the way that the Checchetti greeted this concession that gave Harold his first real intimation of their tactical cunning and formidable unity of purpose. None of them said a word. In silence they turned away, in silence climbed back up on to the tractor. For a few moments the drone of the German's grass cutter was audible once more to the Chapmans. Then all other sounds were overlaid by the throaty coughing of the tractor. After this had rounded the bend it was visible for some seconds more in a space between the poplars that grew along the roadside; and in these seconds it seemed to Cecilia strangely like a war chariot, with Signora Checchetti resembling a bright-robed, snake-haired goddess, urging the men forward into battle.

Ritter, turning off the motor of his grass-cutter in order to clear the back axle, heard the shouting of the Checchetti and the quieter voices of the English people quite clearly. He was high above, on the highest of the olive terraces that rose behind his ruinous house; but the hills made a deep inward curve here, half the shape of a bowl, a natural amphitheatre, and sounds carried for miles – the barking of a dog, a gate closing, songs of small birds.

He knew the English couple were called Chapman because he had once been given their mail by mistake when he called at the post office in the village to collect his own. But he was profoundly incurious about his neighbours, would have preferred it in fact if there had not been any. His was the last house, the road ended with him. Beyond there was no way through, except into scrub country, uncultivated, home to the fox and viper and boar.

He had crouched to clear the twisted grasses from the axle. The grass was long, slightly wet, thickened with alfalfa and chicory and dock. Too much for the machine really, it choked on the thick mush and needed constant clearing. But he persisted. It had started here, on these neglected terraces, with old vine shoots and sprays of wild roses growing up into the branches of the olives, his rage to clear the ground, to bring order.

The grass-cutter, bright red and quite new, stood waiting for him on the terrace a dozen metres off. He must have walked away from it. He could not remember doing this, nor had he any idea what might have caused him to do it. Standing quite still, listening to the chugging of the tractor as it slowly receded, he tried to recollect. Some association of ideas. Something to do with the voices, the sense that though unmistakably human they were interchangeable with any other sound of the morning, something troubling in this, a memory . . . Then he had it: an incident during his life as an interpreter shortly before his breakdown, some Scandinavian city – Stockholm, Oslo? Conference rooms look the same whatever the city. An international conference of industrialists, the usual self-promotion in the guise of productivity reports. He had been working from Italian into German. Screened off in the glass booth, free from any responsibility, any authorship, for what his mouth was transmitting. A mouthpiece . . . A conduit for sewage.

Underlying the statements of corporate philosophy and the statistics of corporate growth there was always the suffering of the helpless. To pay for these suits and briefcases and shiny shoes, people had laboured in remote places, in appalling conditions. Life expectancy among them would not be an item in the balance sheets. But then, he had always known that.

He had done his spell and handed over to a colleague, a woman, and stayed to listen and help if necessary, a procedure quite customary. A young woman, pretty. He tried to remember her face now and couldn't. What he did remember was watching her mouth moving and hearing the words continue, the same dirty stream. He had been gripped then by a kind of dread: the two of them in the booth there, all differences cancelled out, as interchangeable as sewage pipes.

Now and then a pipe gets clogged, needs flushing out. For years alcohol had seemed to do this for Ritter. But there had come a time of fear that drinking only made worse, fear of the words that came with only momentary pauses through his earphones, the panic knowledge that he would drown in sewage if he could not keep up. He would feel the sweat run on his body and hear the loud beat of his heart.

This had ended in fear of all encounters, fear of daylight even – he had stayed alone in his Vienna apartment with the curtains drawn and the phone disconnected. Only a chance visit from his former wife had rescued him from this. She had bullied him into seeking help. And so with time he had emerged from the nightmare, with a certain hesitancy of articulation and an abiding distaste for telephones as main marks of it. But his career as an interpreter was over. He had felt a compulsion to return to Italy, where he had been as a boy, during the war, with his parents – his father had been attached to German Military Intelligence in Rome. With the last of his capital he had bought this ruined house and its three hectares of overgrown and neglected land. He had a disability pension and a small income from money left in trust. For a man with few needs it was enough.

Ritter stayed where he was for some moments longer, looking across to the folds of the hills that rose beyond the plain of Val Lupetto. These days of early April began misty, brightening as the sun pierced through, a process very beautiful in its contrasts, seen thus from above, with the plain still partly muffled in silver drifts and the tawny upper slopes already in warm light. From where he was standing he could see the line of poplars marking the narrow stream that formed the boundary of his land. They were in first leaf now, a haze of green more delicate-seeming than the mist.

He began to walk back towards the grass-cutter, which waited there for him, red and expectant. The terraces fell steeply, curving in a shallow arc. At the furthest point below him, beyond where the road ended, was the tangled gully where the stream plunged down through a mesh of bramble and thorn and festooned willows. Dark-green canes, twice the height of a man, leaned out of this at strange, listless angles. An ancient cherry tree, half-submerged by creepers, raised limbs full of flowers to the light.

Once again it occurred to Ritter to wonder why this little wooded gully had been abandoned so. The cherry might be an accident, a bird could have dropped the stone; but the canes and the willows had been planted there by someone, the canes for supports, the willows for their whippy twigs that were used to tie back the vine shoots after pruning.

A certain degree of neglect was understandable. The old man from whom he had bought the place had been ailing for years past. To live off three hectares means unremitting toil and Adelio had drunk too much wine as he got older, to take the ache from his limbs. His wife was dead, neither of his sons had wanted to work the land. For four or five years he had struggled on. Then God had sent him a crazy German to buy the dilapidated property. But these canes and willows must have been planted in some much earlier time. Adelio had clearly not set foot in there for many years. No one had. No one could now – the gully was impassable, closed off.

Reaching the machine, he stood still again and listened intently. He thought he had heard a faint sweep of wind below, among the drowned trees, although the leaves of the canes were stiff and motionless. And then he knew it for the sound of water; it had been there all the time, a voice that he was used to now and so no longer noticed. Water from the winter snows was still flowing through the stream bed, moving invisible among the close-growing vegetation.

As he bent to take the starter handle, he had a brief glimpse of a small white car travelling in the same direction the tractor had taken, towards the road that led up to the village. He knew the car. Passing on foot, he had seen it sometimes, parked near one of the houses on the road they all shared.

Monti drove carefully. The road was terrible in places. The recent heavy rains had softened the edges and washed away seams of gravel and small stones, making ruts and craters everywhere. He did not like cars but suffered at the thought of inflicting damage on helpless springs.

As he rounded the bend in the road and negotiated the rutted dip beyond it, still puddled from the rain, he glanced up and saw Fabio and Arturo working together on the vine pergola below their house. For some moments, before the slope of the road cut off his view, he could see the weathered tiles of their roof and the descending rows of vines and their two figures raising a long cane, green-gold in this early sunshine. They did not look towards him and in a second more he was past.

He thought about the two as he drove along. For years they had lived together in that house, a devoted couple to all appearance. He knew what he knew of them because of his wife, Laura, who had stopped to speak to Fabio one day and admired the wistaria and been promised a root. When had this been? He sought to fix the time with a kind of troubled intensity, as if there might be evidence in it. But evidence of what he did not know; her leaving could not have depended on such things as this. In October it must have been, soon after their arrival. They had rented the house from September but had not come to live in it until the start of the university term. Laura had stayed less than a month . . .

Laura got on with everyone. It was she who had always determined their social relations as far as these lay outside his

14

immediate colleagues at the university. Fabio and Arturo had asked them to supper not long after this first meeting, perhaps a week or ten days later.

He still remembered the elegance and the attention to detail of this supper, the careful shapes of the salad. They had served their own wine and there had been a vase of flowers on the table, mixed dahlias and chrysanthemums, red and bronze and white. All the elements of the evening were burnished in his mind by Laura's desertion, coming so soon after. The tall, rather severe-looking Fabio had shown himself pedantic in culinary matters and was perhaps so in other ways also – he had described in close detail every step in the making of the *parmigiana*. Monti had glanced during this at the younger man, whose hair was cut close to show his beautiful head and whose lips were everted in a constant slight pout, giving him a look of humorous reproof. There was no way of telling whether he found the account wearisome. What had come over most strongly was the closeness of the two, in this creation of an atmosphere, this occasion they had contrived together. The solemn, courteous Tuscan and the graceful, small-boned Neapolitan had seemed to be celebrating their life together. An improbable life, in a way, for a homosexual couple, here in the Umbrian countryside among people of tra-ditional prejudices.

It was practically the last time that he and Laura had gone out together before she left. All the events of those days, not events even but particular moments, had the quality of a time before loss. He had twice since refused invitations from Fabio and Arturo to come on his own, pleading pressure of work. He suf-fered at the thought of their completeness, shrank from the idea of being a solitary witness to it.

He thought of his wife as she had been that evening. She had worn a dark-green dress of some shiny material. She had carried a cardigan but it was warm enough inside the house for her not to need it. The colour of the cardigan he couldn't remember. She had been animated, full of laughter, perhaps stimulated by a sense of rivalry with the younger one, Arturo, perhaps by some teasing interest in the nature of the men's love. Perhaps only, he thought suddenly, by the excitement of her intention. Already there, the intention of dealing him this blow, returning to Turin and the lover whose existence he did not then suspect, the plan already formed inside her head, behind the bright eyes . . . He experienced the customary nausea, the customary craven desire to restore the time before, the time of being deceived.

As he approached the final stretch of the road, before it joined the broader one that led up to the village, he saw that the garden wall of the house on the corner had collapsed, scattering a rubble of broken cement blocks over the edge of the road. This was the house of the Checchetti, whom people in the village spoke of as a family notorious for quarrelsomeness and avarice and whose bawling converse often sounded across the valley. The man he knew for the son-in-law was standing at the corner, wearing the sheepish half-smile that seemed permanent with him. As Monti was about to emerge on to the broader road, he met a red car just turning in. He pulled over and stopped to allow this car to pass and the youngish man inside it smiled broadly and gave him an elaborate wave of acknowledgement.

As always, he went by way of Lake Trasimeno. The road climbed and then dropped; one came upon the lake quite suddenly and it was always a surprise, always different, obedient to imperatives of light and shadow far more subtle than the eye could register. Today it was vapourish and melancholy, a luminous milk colour beyond the dark green of the reed beds.

He glanced across the water as he drove, past the wooded slopes of the Isola Maggiore, still partly shrouded in mist, to the pale shapes of the hills on the northern shore of the lake, scene of perhaps the most crushing defeat ever suffered by Roman arms. It stirred his mind again now to think of that long-ago ambush, Hannibal and his Carthaginians lying in wait up there, the legions marching into the trap. Though an academic historian and now in early middle age, Monti had retained the excited sense of locality, the antiquarian passion for tracking the past from its surviving traces, which had first led him to the study of history. All his best work had been done on the history of the Central Italian States, ground he knew well and visited often. In the dealings of the long dead and the marks that remained, he had been able to find solace and refuge, even now.

Once again his mind was taken by thoughts of that ancient, murderous encounter by the northern shore of the lake. They had waited up there, on that June morning twenty-two centuries ago, hidden by the early mists, had watched the Roman army under the Consul Gaius Flaminius blundering too close to the marshy verges of the lake, where the footing was soft. What an opportunity for a commander who had always had the eye of a hawk for it. The legionaries caught in a narrow defile between lake and hills, confused by the sun-shot mist that rose from the surface of the water, straying towards the treacherous quicksands. The sudden appearance of the Iberian infantry, looming out of the mist, blocking the way ahead. Then the lightning flank attack of the Libyan light cavalry, descending from Monte Gualandro and the heights around Tuoro, the rout, the floundering troops, the butchery. The place-names still testified to that slaughter, in spite of the recent attempts by Susini to explain them away on etymological grounds. A waste of time this, there were too many for that, too many for coincidence. Sepoltaglia, burial ground, Sanguineto, where the blood ran, Ossaia, place of bones. He could have drawn a map, if asked, accurate in every detail: the configuration of the hills, the ancient shoreline of the lake, the disposition of the Carthaginian forces, the line of march of the Romans. But he could not have told you the registration number of his car, nor could he have indicated the position of his present house in relation to the five others on the *strada vicinale* which they all shared.

The road left the lake, veered eastward towards Perugia. As he drove through the lower city and up towards the university, Monti began to brace himself, prepare an attitude that would get him through the day. He had told no one of Laura's going but in his state of inflamed sensitivity he suspected that somehow the story had got about, that it was known by colleagues and students alike that his wife had left him after only a week or two, returned to Turin and the embraces of her lover. He felt like a wrongdoer; and when he came near to anger it was at the thought of this injustice, that he should feel culpable when the wrong was hers.

Fabio and Arturo had heard the car passing below them but they had not looked towards the sound because at that moment there was a tension of feeling between them and they were both taken up with it. Fabio had just reproached Arturo for his failure to clean a spade before returning it to the rack; it had been returned with clay on the blade and shaft, and the clay had dried and crusted. Fabio had noticed it earlier that day, when he went to the shed for some of last year's onions still hanging up there. Any tool they used should always be replaced in good condition, he had said severely to Arturo. In saying this, he had before him a mental picture of the clean, swept shed, the rack with the shining forks and spades, expensive English ones, bought from a firm in Brescia, the smaller rack alongside this with the trowels and handforks and clippers. It was a microcosm of what he felt their world to be, his and Arturo's, orderly and harmonious and sufficient unto itself. These tools were part of the ritual of their lives, they belonged in the anteroom of the temple they had built together. It had hurt him to see the encrusted spade, like a desecration, and he had felt compelled to speak to Arturo about it.

But Arturo had not accepted the correction, had not acknowledged the justice of it. He had frowned and shrugged and turned his face away. Such a small thing. How can one be expected to remember everything? He did not see the outhouses as the precincts of a temple but merely as sheds where things were kept; and growing daily stronger in him, though not expressed to Fabio, was a distaste for the things that were kept there, things that meant blisters and sweat.

He had felt resentment too, and not for the first time, at the way the other spoke to him. As if I were a child or a servant, he thought. Fabio behaved like a cross between father and employer, when he was neither. When Arturo looked at his partner, at the thick brows and stern, rather melancholy eyes and the slight scar on his forehead, mark of the accident that had nearly killed him and put an end for ever to his career as a racing driver, he could not easily remember the time when he had thought him such a glamorous person, such a splendid protector, so exciting and masterful a lover. I was only nineteen, after all, he thought. Fifteen years of my life I have given this man. How could I have known he would have to give up racing, that we would end by living like peasants? Looking out across the browns and greens of the valley to the long line of the hills, he longed for the lights of Naples again.

They were replacing some of the crosspieces on the pergola with new canes, good thick straight ones that Arturo had cut the day before. Together they lifted the long trailing stems of the vines, one holding them in place, the other tying. It was delicate work: new shoots were pricking from the stems and care was needed not to bruise the sharp, pinkish buds.

When the work was finished, they went in to have their mid-morning coffee. Nothing further was said between them concerning the spade. Fabio already felt regret – his tone had been too harsh. Arturo was sensitive, easily daunted, easily hurt. He was as vulnerable now, to Fabio's mind, and as exotic, as when they had first met fifteen years before in a Naples bar. Arturo had been no more than a *ragazzo di vita* then, a boy for hire. I took him away from that, Fabio thought. He would go himself and clean the spade. It would be a penance for his harshness – and it might serve to drive the message home.

With this resolve he felt that harmony between them was restored. And in fact he saw that Arturo's face showed resentment no longer; he was smiling in the way Fabio knew and loved, at once dreamy and humorous. Nothing in his expression indicated that the words of reproach and self-defence just exchanged between them had been momentous, that they would be kept alive in Arturo's mind quite deliberately, as an active principle, a yeast for his grievances, necessary to a certain kind of plan which he had been meditating for quite a long time now.

Fabio suspected nothing of this. Sitting there at the kitchen table they talked together about the future. Things were getting better. For the past three summers they had had paying guests in the season and this had brought in extra money, though of course involving more work. With their twelve hectares of land they were self-sufficient in vegetables and olive oil and wine. If things went well, in two or three years more they could hope to have a swimming pool installed.

Fabio was contented as he sat there drinking his coffee, eating a slice of the delicious *crostata* that Arturo had made. Their future, their life together, seemed full of promise.

The man who had saluted in so courteous and friendly a manner when Monti gave way to him was an Englishman named Stan Blemish and he was on his way to visit an elderly American couple called Green, who also lived on this road, having bought an old farmhouse some way up the hillside with a view to having it converted.

Blemish noticed the car as by long habit he noticed anything indicative of wealth or status. One never knew what might be useful. A Fiat Uno, pretty basic, with a Turin registration. A man living in Turin, or any sizeable Italian city, would normally not run a big car unless he needed to make an effect, not in that sort of traffic; but there were small cars on the market with more dash than this one. Poverty, indifference? Bespectacled, mild-faced man behind the wheel.

He had made a point of waving acknowledgement because it was a part of his policy of Britishness. Italians did not go in so much for this courteous stuff. The gestures they made at the wheel were nearly always expressive of contempt, or impatience shading into fury. Blemish felt that standards should be kept up. We are all fellow-travellers along life's highway, he was fond of saying. Once an Italian stepped into his car, he shed all sense of common humanity, he acknowledged no limits. Individualistic, some might call it – Blemish called it anarchic and antisocial. So he smiled and nodded and waved quite elaborately at any small-est concession and made a point of stopping to allow cars to come out of side roads or pedestrians to get across the streets, while his fellow-drivers jostled dangerously to take advantage of such weakness, and those trapped behind, furious at having to wait, shouted that he was a shit of loose consistency.

Abuse Blemish did not mind if he felt in the right. He was whistling lightly between his teeth as he drove on. It was a fine morning, the Greens were an excellent prospect. He felt cheerful as he negotiated the scattered stones and pieces of masonry that lay partly across the road at this point – it looked as if the wall had collapsed. These neighbourhood roads were a disgrace anyway, even without walls collapsing on them. Unthinkable in Britain, of course.

However, with a swing entirely characteristic in its suddenness, he was swept now by feelings of violent antipathy for the country of his birth, polluted offshore island, riddled with snobbery and kinky Tories, who would want to live there? Not me, Blemish told the landscape. He would never go back. He had been unfairly dismissed from his post in the Public Works Department of Lambeth Borough Council. Lucky to escape prosecution, they had said. What kind of language was that? *They* were bloody lucky he had escaped prosecution, he could have told a few stories, by God, yes. And they knew it. Anyway, nothing wrong with taking gifts, it was sound business practice. Gifts, commissions, rake-offs, they were what made the world go round. Life was a pattern of giving, receiving, giving again. Like the three Graces. No good saying that to the Lambeth Public Works Department of course – no play of mind there whatever, no culture worthy of the name.

A road like this was in itself a gift for some people, he thought: the people who might come from time to time to level it off, build up the verges, lay some gravel down. All work done by private agreement, they could charge what they liked, especially where foreigners were concerned. His own house was six miles away, on the western side of Lake Trasimeno, a vast ruinous *palazzo* in need of extensive restoration, with twenty-three rooms, most of them presently uninhabitable except for insects and small mammals. He and the companion of his life, Mildred, were striving under difficult circumstances to have the place restored to its former splendour. At least there was a good road to it, well packed down with stone, easily passable in all weather.

He thought of Milly now. She would be in their little greenhouse probably, or in the kitchen garden. She had said she was going to plant out the seedlings of majoram and hissop, her medieval herbs as she jokingly called them – it was their dearest wish, his and Milly's, to convert the whole ground floor of their house into a medieval restaurant with a medieval kitchen adjoining. He could picture her as she went about her tasks, slow of movement, ample of form. An earth mother, he thought, that's what you are. To coin a phrase.

The Greens' house was well above the road, at the end of a rocky driveway. Some way beyond, Blemish saw the roof of another house. Newly laid tiles, he noticed. He had heard that an English couple named Chapman had bought it. Foreigners buying houses all over Umbria now, excellent for business.

The track went round in a curve, climbed fairly steeply for a few yards, levelled off as it neared the house. Both the Greens, having heard him approach, appeared at the top of the external steps that went from ground level to the upper floor – the ground floor was not yet fit for habitation, having long been used, as customary with Umbrian farmhouses, for keeping pigs and cows in. As he opened the car door, Blemish looked up and saw the couple standing side by side, both silver-haired, both the same height, both wearing smiles that seemed closely similar, slightly peering and bemused. There was a symmetrical, emblematic, fairy-tale quality about this, as if the Greens were waiting for the disguised benefactor who would recognize their worth and grant them a wish. Blemish was not a benefactor but he was superstitious in his way and he sensed in that moment that the occasion was auspicious.

He unwound his long-legged frame from the Vauxhall, called up a cheery good morning and took the steps at a fast pace. Shaking hands at the top, the couple were full of apologies for the state of chaos within. Tall and narrow-shouldered and long-necked, Blemish towered above them, blinked soft brown eyes, murmured quite so, quite so, only to be expected.

The interior was indeed cluttered. The Greens had left their furniture in store in Michigan and were making do for the time being with the bits and pieces left by the previous owners. But their clothes and books and smaller possessions were still half in and half out of the various packing cases they had arrived in. They were like elderly castaways, beached up here. There were extensive stains of damp on the walls. 'The water is getting in from somewhere,' Mrs Green said.

They offered him coffee but Blemish explained that he had a hernia and coffee was not good for it. This was quite untrue but Blemish often had an impulse to falsehood, and especially with prospective clients. A successful lie put you ahead psychologically, gave you the moral ascendancy you needed, right from the word go. It belonged to the same order as the briefcase he carried, the tweed jacket, the neat collar and tie.

Herb tea then. They had bought some orange blossom tea, Mrs Green said. They had got it at a wonderful little shop in Perugia, in the Via dei Priori. It was a shop that had just about every kind of dried flower and herb that a body could possibly imagine. 'The scents from it just kind of wash over the street,' Mrs Green said. 'You don't find shops like that back home.'

'This is back home now, honey.' Mr Green went to a carton of groceries still lying on the floor, took a jar and unscrewed the top. 'Just you smell this.' He held out the jar. He had very bright blue eyes, wide and undefended now in the pleasure of imparting something to their visitor. Mrs Green was smiling in full approval.

Blemish declined his long neck and sniffed. 'Wonderful.' He experienced a deep, malignant throb of hostility towards these people. They were condescending to him, treating him as a hireling, someone who could be subjected to random odours on a whim. A professional man like himself. Well, he thought, he who laughs last . . . 'A real scent of the south, that is,' he said.

While the tea was being made and while it was being drunk, the Greens explained their situation. They were in quite a mess with the house, it seemed. 'We got to know about you quite by chance,' Mrs Green said. 'A friend of our daughter's, who is teaching in London, saw your advertisement in the *Sunday Times*, where you offer expert advice to people who have bought houses in Umbria and want to have them put to rights.'

Blemish nodded. He had registered the fact that the Greens had friends, family, possible support. But it was distant; it did not seem likely that they had close connections in Italy. 'Yes,' he said, 'we undertake the management of the whole project from the moment of purchase.'

'We got off to a bad start,' Mr Green said. They had made the cardinal mistake of trying to get the work done while they were still living in Michigan, attempting to communicate by phone and fax, and making occasional visits.

'We were spending a whole lot of money and getting nowhere,' Mrs Green said. 'People made promises but nothing happened.'

Blemish sighed and shook his head. 'Yours is a story we hear frequently. In this country they tell you what they think you would like to hear. That is their way, you know. That is the Mediterranean temperament. One of the most important aspects of our work here is mediating between different cultures, bridging the gap.'

'We could never find out the true situation,' Mr Green said.

He looked at Blemish and smiled. His face was fine-drawn and the smile came slowly, but it was as guileless in its way as the eyes. 'We were beginning to lose trust in folks and that is one mistake we don't want to start making at our time of life.'

Unable to see any meaning in this last remark, Blemish blinked softly and waited. He had a slow, strangely voluptuous way of lowering his eyelids when he wanted to show sympathy.

'We always thought of coming to live in Umbria when we retired,' Mrs Green said. 'We came here for vacations when we could afford it and sort of looked around. Our daughter wanted us to go to Florida, but we always loved Italian art and history, especially the early Renaissance.'

'And the landscape and the light,' Mr Green said. 'The whole deal.'

'All that too.' Mrs Green smiled at Blemish. 'That is the setting, isn't it? I mean, it can't be separated. This is where those wonderful artists lived.'

'Well, of course,' Blemish said, 'it makes the property more desirable, without the shadow of a doubt.'

Mr Green widened his eyes with a sort of gleeful solemnity. 'We came to Italy for our honeymoon, you know.' He pointed at the wall behind Blemish. 'We bought that print in Florence forty years ago,' he said. 'At the Uffizi Gallery.'

Turning, Blemish saw a picture of a nearly naked, long-haired man standing in a stream and another pouring something over his head out of a sort of metal cup. A white bird hovered above with outstretched wings and there were two blue-gowned kneeling figures at the side. 'A highly professional piece of work, that is,' he said. 'Yes, very striking.'

'First thing we did when we came to live in this house was to put it up on the wall. Andrea del Verrocchio. One of the greatest painters of all time. We saw the original all those years ago when we were just married and we never got to see it again.'

'We are saving it up,' Mrs Green said. 'We are saving it till the house is finished. When everything is done and we are really settled in, we are going to make a trip to Florence and stand in front of that picture.'

'We were both art teachers, you know.' Mr Green smiled at his wife with open affection. 'We met at art school. Lucky day for me.'

'A fair number of our clients have artistic leanings,' Blemish said, 'especially in the Trasimeno area.'

'We took the plunge, sold up and came over here. It seems to be the only way to get things done. Then the architect kept revising the estimate – it doubled in the course of a single month. We have got rid of her now.'

They would have had to pay a tidy sum for that too. Blemish felt a pang at the thought of this wasted money. 'You don't need an architect at all,' he said. 'All they know is how to draw up plans.'

The Greens talked on and Blemish listened carefully. These two old people were very confiding – he had no need really to ask many questions. They told him they had sold their house in Michigan. They told him what the architect's original estimate had been, how alarmed they had felt when it had jumped up and jumped up again. They told him the point at which they had realized that they could not continue with the architect, as the estimate had reached a level beyond their resources. By the end of the recital Blemish knew within a few thousand dollars what the Greens were ready and able to spend on the conversion of their Italian house. In other words, and as he put it familiarly to himself, he knew what was in the kitty.

'No, a surveyor is enough,' he said. 'What they call a *geometra* here. A *geometra* will know far more about the practical side of things than an architect. We employ a *geometra* who is quite out-standing. There was a case like yours only a couple of months ago. Their *geometra* kept on taking measurements and asking for more money. No building work was done. In despair they turned to us. We sent our *geometra* in. As simple as that. If you went to visit those people now, you would find them happy and smiling in a tastefully refurbished dwelling.'

'What exactly would you do for us?' Mr Green asked.

'Engage a good and experienced builder. Get him to cost everything and make a proper estimate. Oversee the work, make sure things were done properly and that your wishes were made known to the builder – we speak good Italian.' This at least was true. Blemish had understood very early the advantage of knowing more Italian than his clients. He had embarked on an intensive course while still under investigation at the Lambeth Public Works Department. 'In short,' he said, 'we would carry the project through to its conclusion.'

'And your charges?'

'Forty thousand lire an hour, plus expenses – things like phone calls and petrol.'

'Let's see now,' Mr Green said. 'That is about twenty-four dollars, isn't it? Well, it doesn't seem unreasonable. How soon could your builder be ready to start if we decided to go ahead?'

'We are rather busy just at present.' It didn't do to seem too eager, Blemish knew that. In his way he was a student of business dealings. And when you come right down to it, he was fond of saying, what other dealings are there? The key to the whole thing was to let the others make the running. The Greens must be made to feel that he was doing them a favour, saving them from disaster. 'The builders we work with and trust are all committed at this moment in time,' he said. 'There is no way I would engage a builder I knew nothing about. We work to a very high standard of service.'

'Well, we want to get things moving.' Mr Green glanced round the room. 'Things aren't too comfortable here at present.'

Blemish rose. 'You will need to think it over,' he said. 'It never does to take decisions too hastily. *Patti chiari amicizia lunga*, as the Italians say – clear agreements long friendship. You have the phone number. Remember,' he called up as he inserted himself into the car, '*siamo sempre qua*, we are always here.'

Standing side by side at the top of the steps, the Greens watched him drive away. In the silence following the car's departure they heard the faint drone of a lawn-mower somewhere high up behind them. They remained there for some time, looking at the curving line of the road and the steeply rising terraces beyond. There were remnants of mist in the air, fluffing the lines of the hills, softening the edges of everything. The fig trees below the house were naked still, their pointed shoots dark silver in the sunshine.

After some moments of silence the Greens turned and smiled at each other, sure of each other's feelings, sure that their pleasure in the peace and beauty of the place was shared. Throughout the forty years of their marriage they had always had this communion of feeling, always been completely happy in each other's presence. Mrs Green's eyes were bright. 'We are looking at the hills that Perugino and Piero della Francesca looked at,' she said.

Later they went out together and stood looking up at the house, the ancient broken tiles of the roof, through which the rain came in, the walls where the packing of clay between the stones had crumbled away, the darkness and dankness of the ground floor, where for most of the century farm animals had been kept. There was a lot that needed doing to the house but the form of it was beautiful. It sat there, long and low, dressed in the time-warmed colours of its stone, the outside staircase with its broad terracotta steps leading up to the colonnaded porch. It would be a beautiful house when it was finished – this was something the Greens told each other often.

'This Blemish seems a smart young fellow,' Mr Green said. 'Doesn't know a whole lot about painting.'

'Perhaps he can do something for us.' Mrs Green took her husband's arm and they began to walk back to the house. 'Perhaps this is the turning point.'

'Twenty-four dollars is not so much and we can discontinue with him any time we like – he is not asking for anything in writing.'

'He seemed straightforward enough,' Mrs Green said.

'Funny way with his eyes sometimes,' Mr Green said. 'Kind of sleepy. Why do you think he kept referring to himself as "we"?'

Later that morning a wind sprang up and it began to feel colder. Harold and Cecilia Chapman walked the half-mile or so to the Checchetti house and inspected the collapsed wall. No attempt had yet been made to clear away the rubble that lay along the edge of the road below the house. The width of the road was considerably reduced, Harold noticed; there was room enough for a car to pass and probably a van or medium-sized truck, but nothing any bigger. That faint whisper of alarm sounded again. This was the only way out to the village by car; the road did not proceed beyond the German's place, petering out in vineyards and deeply rutted tracks unfit for motor vehicles of almost any sort. Anyone who wanted to get on to the road leading to the village and the greater world beyond had to go this way.

'Just as I thought,' he said. 'This wall had no foundations whatever. It looks to me as if they laid the blocks down flat, with hardly any digging at all.'

At this point they were joined by the Checchetti, father and daughter, who converged on them from different directions. Of the husband there was nothing to be seen. The two approached rapidly and in complete silence. Then, while still some yards away, they came to a halt and fell to regarding the strewn debris of their wall. This muteness, which had seemed strange at first, Cecilia now recognized as a powerful dramatic device: the Checchetti were hoping that the sight of the wall with themselves standing by it as tragic witnesses would plead their case more powerfully than words.

'Tell them,' Harold said, 'what they know full well already, that their precious wall had no foundation, they built it on the cheap and this heavy rain has brought it down.'

While Cecilia was still struggling to convey her husband's meaning more gently and tactfully, the father retreated to a distance of some dozen yards and began shouting loudly.

'Is he uttering threats?' Harold said. 'I won't proceed on that basis and they had better know it.'

'No, no.' Cecilia paused, listening. 'No, it is his way of discussing things. He is saying, as far as I can make out, that whether the wall had foundations or not is completely beside the point.'

'Discussing things? The man is a complete savage. What does he do when he feels like shouting? How can it be beside the point when –'

'He says the point at issue is not the foundations but what caused the wall to collapse.'

The woman now spoke directly to her father in what seemed an attempt to silence him or tone him down. Cecilia had again the impression that the two of them were acting, improvising from moment to moment, following some instinctive, archetypal pattern.

The father fell silent and Signora Checchetti drew nearer to the Chapmans and spoke more quietly, glancing upwards from time to time as if to take the skies as witness.

'She is saying mainly what she said before, that the wall, which was a very good strong wall and cost them 3 million lire to have built only four years ago, and God is her witness to this, was loosened by the vibrations caused by the repeated passing of heavily loaded lorries.'

'It's a wonder to me the wall stood for so long.' Harold pondered for a moment or two. Money was what they wanted, of course – that was as clear as daylight. It might be better to spend a little money than to get on the wrong side of these people. As neighbours they might conceivably be useful. If they felt wronged they would certainly be vindictive and might find ways of doing harm. One heard horror stories now and again: pets poisoned, fences torn down, wells polluted in the night . . . 'I suppose we will have to accept some responsibility,' he said to Cecilia. 'After all, the road is narrow and the lorries must have been heavy-laden.'

'Oh, Harold,' Cecilia said, 'I am so glad you think that, because it is exactly what I think too.' She was swept by pride at his magnanimity. Harold might seem unfeeling at times but his underlying generosity would come to the fore, however much he might try to conceal it. Radiant-faced, she turned back to the Checchetti.

'Don't tell them what I said,' Harold said quickly. 'Never admit liability, it's always a great mistake. For heaven's sake, Cecilia, think for a minute.'

He stared at his wife in reproof. She really had no idea of the world at all. One did not give ground to people free of charge, one did not render oneself vulnerable, one did not surrender an advantage. Now, as he looked at Cecilia, it seemed to him that this essential lack of grasp of hers found a parallel in the loosely flowing style of her attire, the full-skirted, unbelted blue dress, the pale hair escaping from the confines of her tortoiseshell combs. There came unbidden to his mind a sudden thought of his new secretary, Miss Phelps, blonded and permed, tight-skirted, high-heeled. A woman who was not afraid to look like a woman.

The Checchetti, sensing a turning point, had drawn closer together and maintained now a silence full of expectation. It was they, Cecilia thought, who had controlled the conversation from the very start, with their pattern of rage and appeasement, their calculated clamour and calculated hush. Avarice was written in the lines of their faces and a hostility that no requirement of tact or advantage could altogether mask. She looked over their heads at the hillside beyond, the strange sense of close order imposed by the rows of bare vines strung between pale concrete pillars. Rising steeply in rank upon rank, carefully terraced, the sum of labour they represented was enormous; the yield in money, on such small holdings as these, could not be very great. Little wonder these people clawed for gain.

'Whatever is done will have to be done in legal form,' she heard Harold say. 'I hope they don't imagine we are just going to hand them a lump of money. Tell them we will see our lawyer this afternoon and try to work something out.'

Monti had no teaching until late afternoon. He had some student essays to look at but by eleven he was free for his own work. As usual, he made himself coffee on a small hotplate in his room; he had avoided the common room as far as possible, since Laura's going. He was a stranger at the university, on a visiting fellowship. He had some acquaintances in the faculty but no friends, no one whose kindness he could take for granted; he shrank at the thought of having his humanity reduced, brought down to a single image of cuckoldry and loss.

His nature had always tended to the obsessive and in this period of loneliness the tendency became more pronounced; his studies were not so much a solace to him as a quest for encoded meanings. He was occupied with the relations between the republic of Perugia and the papacy in the fifteenth and sixteenth centuries and more particularly with the rise of the Baglioni family of Perugia, a story marked throughout by the extremest forms of rapacity and violence.

At ease in his small room, with the ancient radiator creaking and occasionally uttering soft hisses, and the smoke from his cigarettes rising up towards the ceiling, he was considering the murder of Biordo Michelotti by the Guidalotti family in the March of 1398, an event which for complex reasons had started the Baglioni on their road to power. He was seeking to establish some degree of complicity in this murder, or at least prior knowledge of it, on the part of the pope of the time, Boniface IX.

An impressive figure, Michelotti, soldier and politician both. One of the most gifted commanders in the history of Perugia. In effect he had been the first ruler of the city, though far too prudent to adopt official titles. Prudent he had been, yes, but not able – as no man of his time was able – to see any real distinction between the fortunes of the city and his own. He had dreamed of recovering for Perugia, and so for himself, those former territories which had ensured to the republic her wealth and power. And he had gone a long way towards succeeding: in a series of brilliant campaigns he had taken Assisi, Castiglione del Lago, La Fratta and Montalto, and subjected them to the *comune* of Perugia.

Such a degree of success brought danger. These were territories that lay within the zone of papal expansion. There was evidence enough that Boniface had begun to find this gifted adventurer an obstacle to his plans.

The leader of the conspiracy, Francesco Guidalotti, was a churchman, Abbot of San Pietro. He had been in Rome in the December of the previous year, only some three months before the murder. Monti had not yet succeeded in unearthing any definite indications of a papal audience, but this must have presumably been the purpose of Guidalotti's visit. The chronicles asserted that he had been promised a cardinal's hat.

With an intensity that gathered and grew in that small room, amidst the complaints of the antiquated plumbing, Monti began to run over again in his mind the events of that distant morning. Michelotti, only five months married, still in his bedchamber. The Abbot arrives, accompanied by his two brothers Anibaldo and Giovanni. They ask to speak with Michelotti on a matter of great importance. He gets up from his bed, dresses, and without arming himself goes out to greet them in the room where they are waiting. *Why so trusting?* This was a tried and experienced soldier, a man accustomed from early youth to the practice of arms. Moreover, he was a man of shrewd judgement, passionate perhaps, but not rash – all his career went to show this. Was it that he trusted in the gratitude of the Guidalotti? They had been expelled once from the city for conspiring against him and in his generosity of spirit he had pardoned them, allowed them to return. Those we have pardoned do we always underrate? Did he not know, this man of affairs, that where there is hatred it can only be increased by favours?

He had walked into the room where they waited. He had embraced Francesco in greeting and, while the Abbot held him in the embrace, the two others attacked him from behind, stabbing him repeatedly with their poisoned daggers, first in the back and then, when he fell, in the chest and throat.

Monti stirred and sighed. It had been a deed of appalling treachery and cowardice, and momentous in its results, bringing back the noble families Michelotti had exiled, the violent and ambitious clan of the Baglioni among them. But in its nature there was nothing particularly to distinguish it from a multitude of such incidents in the sanguinary history of the city. Why, then, did it exercise such a spell on his mind?

Perhaps Biordo had been bemused, softened by his youthful bride. Slackened all the sinews of war. So happy in abandonment that for those moments he saw the world as a field of love. Giovanna di Bertoldo Orsini, his wife of five months. He had risen from her side and walked out to his death. The Orsini were a Roman family, by turns allies and foes of the pope . . .

Monti sat forward. Could the wife have somehow had a hand in it? She could hardly have kept his weapons from him, but a woman can do much in the way of persuasion. He would have been in haste to return to her. He would not have detected the taint of treachery in her kisses. Any more than I did after all the years. She was the same in appearance and manner as she had always been, no less loving, no less kind. The time-hallowed jokes of people who live together – his absent-mindedness, her habit of making lists and drawing up programmes. She had even seemed happy. On her face sometimes a look of remote inquiry, as if she were tracking some elusive thought. This wild thing she had done, where was it to be seen, what intimations had there been in twelve years of wifedom? He knew himself to be often preoccupied, unobservant of his surroundings, subject to habit in domestic matters. There might have been signs that another man would have seen, but he had seen none. She had reminded him to wear his scarf, she had continued to take an interest in his work. Things could have gone on like this for a long time if they had stayed in Turin – it was the move here that had done it. She had come in good faith, she had intended to stay, she had arranged for leave of absence from her teaching job. But the voice of her need had been too strong.

This was his chief suffering now, not the technical act of infidelity but this urgency of her love for another. Following upon this, unavoidable, the anguish of imagining their bodies together. He could not feel anger, only the sickness of the blow. He knew himself to be mild, to be lacking in aggression. None of the Baglioni men would have borne it patiently. Can it be this, he wondered, that draws me so to the story of blood that is Perugia's history?

No one, as far as he knew, had followed up the Orsini connection. He felt a stirring of excitement. Such a line of investigation could lead far beyond that morning of the poisoned knives, perhaps shed new light on papal policy in the period, in all its ruthlessness and duplicity.

The Guidalotti, at any rate, had not profited from their crime. Monti thought about the extraordinary error of judgement that the family had made, more extraordinary in some ways than their victim's reckless trust. They had apparently thought that by killing Biordo they would raise the city in their favour and be brought to power on a popular movement; not seeing, in their arrogance and stupidity, that the murdered regarded by the common people with veneration, as restoring through his conquests the ancient grandeur of the Perugian state.

It was a mistake that cost them dear. A manhunt for members of the Guidalotti family was immediately instituted throughout the city. Perugian manhunts always took the same form: the incensed mob slaughtered anyone they could lay their hands on who was in any way connected with the Guidalotti, including any persons unfortunate enough to be encountered in the vicinity of their houses. The houses themselves were given over to pillage and fire.

Valuable houses on prime sites. Among those who had set on the mob, some would have been interested in political advantage, others would have had an eye on the real estate. Irrespective of right or wrong, causes just or unjust, there were always people in the wings, with their eye on the main chance. And they were always the same people . . .

Blemish had things to attend to in Perugia and it was after midday when he headed back for home. He was pleased with his morning's business and especially with the way he had handled the Greens. They were a promising couple, he had thought so from the start. He saw them now in his mind's eye, standing side by side at the top of the steps, grey-haired, blue-eyed and guileless, smiling in welcome. Once again it came to him that they were like the deserving couple in a folk-tale, the ones who treat the mysterious guest kindly and get the magic goose. Only the simple-hearted could convey an impression like that. Fools, in other words. He felt renewed ill-will towards them. He had gone there on business and they had tried to make him share in their life. Well, this time it would be the mysterious guest who got the golden eggs. They were like Darby and Joan, he thought. The tune of the song came into his mind and he hummed it for a while, then sang the few words he remembered in a cracked baritone:

> And when the kids grow up and leave us
> We'll build a house on a hill-top high,
> You and I,
> Darby and Joan, that used to be Jack and Jill . . .

While still a mile away, he saw the sight that always filled him with pleasure and pride: there it stood, huge, square-fronted, imposing, set on rising ground with low wooded hills behind and the *campanile* of the little town rising beyond it. His house, his and Milly's, someone's nineteenth-century extravagance, now their proud possession, vast, in style ecclesiastic-Gothic, with its narrow pointed windows, dilapidated balustrades, brick-built portico and crumbling terracotta mouldings. There was an arcade of columns running down one side, like a cloister – it was this that had given them their idea for the medieval restaurant. Much of the roof of this had fallen in and the pavement of the walk was cracked and broken. There was a lot that needed doing; they were only at the beginning. But the Greens would make their contribution and with any luck it would be a substantial one.

He found Mildred, the companion of his life, in the kitchen preparing lunch. 'What is it to be today, my love?' he said.

Mildred looked up from her pan. She made a strong contrast in physical type to Blemish, being thick-necked, sturdy and slow-moving, with a habit of lowering her head as if about to charge. She smiled at him now and the light of love was in her smile. 'Green-pea pottage,' she said in her deep, reluctant voice. 'I have used dried winter peas, as they used to do, and coloured it with saffron. It was a favourite dish of Richard the Second.'

'Wonderful.' Blemish gave Mildred two approving pats, one on each of her broad buttocks. 'I think we are in prospect of more *cotto*,' he said. This was a familiar codeword between them. Large areas of their flooring needed to be redone; they had decided on traditional terracotta tiles throughout and so had fallen into the habit of measuring their gains in terms of these.

'New clients?' Mildred said, stirring slowly at the brew.

'I think so. An American couple. I have the strongest of feelings that they will want to enlist my services.'

Mildred smiled placidly. She left business to him. In spite of her bulk and gruffness, she was wedded to the notion of female fragility. Men were the practical ones, the relevant lobes were more highly developed. Women were more creative. She herself, for example, was planning to write a medieval cookbook

42

couched in medieval prose – the sort of enterprise that would never remotely have occurred to Stan.

'Ninety per cent certain in my judgement,' Blemish said. 'You get to know the look on people's faces. Project management is as much a matter of psychology as anything.' He had a way, when pleased, of stretching his neck and raising his chin, and he did it now. 'They are in difficulties with their house. I'll get Esposito for the building. We understand each other – we have worked together before. If all goes well, we'll be able to have the brickwork vaulting in the dining-room restored.'

'That would be marvellous.' Mildred raised a thick-wristed reddish hand to her hair, dampened by steam from the pottage, which she was trying to bring to the right consistency. 'You are so clever, Stan,' she said. 'I know you will do it. That dining-room will be the nucleus of our medieval restaurant.'

Blemish regarded her for some moments. He was touched, as always, by her loyalty, her unswerving confidence in his abilities. 'We will have a fine house some day,' he said. 'I promise you that, Milly. We will have our medieval restaurant. It will be famous throughout Umbria. What am I saying? It will be famous throughout Italy. People will flock to come here, it will be *the* place. They will sit under our magnificent brickwork vaulting, at oaken tables, waited on by jolly serving-men in doublet and hose, eating cabbage chowder and fried fig pastries, and quaffing ale. The floors will be covered with handmade *cotto*. The whole thing will be a vision of the High Middle Ages. We will make a fortune.'

In the afternoon the Chapmans drove into Perugia. Harold had made an appointment to see their lawyer, Dottor Mancini, who had been recommended to them through the foreign department of Harold's bank and had helped them through the various hazards of buying their house. Dottor Mancini spoke English and was visibly prosperous and had shown himself to be wily and wise in the business of the house, and for these reasons Harold had confidence in him.

They were early and so took the opportunity of visiting the Church of San Severo, or rather the fifteenth-century chapel adjoining the church, which they were both keen to see as it contained the only certain work by Raphael to remain in the city. It was still early in the year, there were not many visitors yet, and Harold and Cecilia were alone there. They stood together in the chilly little place and gazed up at the fresco.

'Interesting,' Cecilia said, 'the way it is divided horizontally like that into two sections. It is the upper one that is by Raffaello of course and the lower by Perugino.' She always adopted the same tone when talking to Harold about anything to do with art, not lecturing exactly – her nature was too mild and diffident for that – but gently pedagogic. 'You can see the influences at work though, can't you, when you look at them both together? Perugino was Raffaello's teacher at one stage, you know.'

Harold nodded. He had read this in his book about the masterpieces of Italian art. 'Pietro Vannucci,' he said, 'known as il Perugino. His date of birth is disputed.'

'It must be quite unique,' Cecilia said with a little rush of enthusiasm, 'to see the work of these two masters side by side.'

'One above the other, to be exact.' Harold narrowed his eyes at the fresco. He could not see much similarity between the two, try as he might. 'The colours are similar, aren't they?' he said. 'He was either seventy-three when he died or seventy-eight – Perugino, I mean. Depending on which authority you follow. A good innings either way, considering the times.'

'It is there in the treatment of the draperies,' Cecilia said. 'It is there in the idealizing tendency, which you will see if you look at the faces and the postures. Compare the expression of St Placido in the upper part with that of St Gregory Magno in the lower. Perugino's precise age when he died is really neither here nor there, Harold.'

Harold scanned the paintings anew, the seated figure of Christ in the upper one, hand raised in blessing, white dove with outstretched wings above his head, flanking angels, seated saints on either side. There was nothing much going on in the lower painting, just a row of standing saints, large-eyed and sorrowful-looking, with gold plates suspended over their heads, divided into two groups by a niche containing a statue of Madonna and Child in painted terracotta. He felt resentful with these paintings for their failure to arouse any feeling in him. He wanted to ask Cecilia why she was so interested in the postures of saints when she never even went to church, but he was inhibited because this was art and she knew about it.

He wanted to know about it too. He was eager to see the respective merits of Raphael and Perugino – it was the kind of thing that went with the house. Otherwise they might as well have bought a place in Eastbourne. He was fond of making a kind of litany out of the historic cities of Umbria when talking to people back in Britain. We are in easy reach, he would say, of Assisi, Spoleto, Orvieto, Terni, Todi. Treasure-houses of art and history. He felt as he spoke that by achieving such proximity to these treasures he had come into possession of them. People travelled thousands of miles and spent thousands of pounds to see these things, and here they were on his doorstep. He worked doggedly to profit from the situation but so far had not had much success. However, as a step in the right direction he studied guidebooks and collected as much as he could in the way of facts.

Cecilia understood these aspirations and they made her feel loving, in the way a missionary might feel loving on encountering an amenable pagan. She was given to questioning herself about most things but had not so far made much distinction between loving Harold and wanting to instruct and help him. 'It is not just this Raphael,' she said, 'it is the others one has seen, they sort of reinforce one another. The more of his work you see, Harold, the more you will get to like it. We'll go to the Palazzo Pitti in Florence, they've got quite a few Raphaels there, they've got the Madonna del Granduca and some wonderful portraits.'

She looked up at the frescos again. The rush of happiness that had accompanied this project seemed to have sensitized her anew. The colours worked on her like a familiar incantation, olive, faded purple, gold, rose-pink . . . 'We'll go to the Vatican Museum and see the Raphael frescos there,' she said, turning eagerly towards him. 'Of course, the Perugino is weaker, he is a lesser artist. But you can see the tendency to rhetoric which was so –'

'He was well over the hill when he painted that. It was painted in 1521, so he would have been either seventy-one or seventy-six.'

'So utterly characteristic of the High –'

'Depending on which set of dates you accept. On the other hand, Raphael died young. He was only thirty-seven.' Harold looked back at the fresco and something of wonder finally touched him. 'Just my age,' he said. 'He might have gone on to do great things if he had lived.'

At five to six they were in Mancini's outer office, gazing at the prints of Old Perugia that adorned the walls. The extremely attractive, rather sulky-looking young woman Harold remembered from former visits came to conduct them into the lawyer's presence. Seated there in the spacious and expensively appointed office, they explained the difficult situation that had arisen with the Checchetti.

The lawyer listened quite impassively, looking sometimes at their faces, more often fixing his eyes on the far wall or down on his immaculate desk. When Harold had finished, he nodded slowly but without speaking. He was holding a pencil and he tapped softly with this upon the desk, causing quick reflections in its polished surface.

'It is only a small thing, I know,' Harold said, a little disconcerted by the silence. 'But I thought it best to do whatever is to be done in legal form.'

'That is very wise.' Mancini smiled suddenly. 'Legal form resembles other virtues: when you have it, you don't always need to apply it. Without it there is no form at all, none whatever.'

The smile had been directed at Cecilia and she felt obliged to reply. 'Nothing but a chaos of feelings,' she said. She thought of the hate-filled faces of the Checchetti and of Harold's anger when he thought she was going to admit liability. On his face a certain look. She had wanted to set it down to impatience; like many bouncy people, Harold lacked patience. But it had been dislike really. And not for them, not for the Checchetti . . .

'Exactly, very well said, only a chaos of feelings,' Mancini said. 'Besides, to put it bluntly, big things, small things, these days it is all the same to me.'

It was strangely difficult to form an idea of Dottor Mancini's

47

age. The indications seemed to cancel one another out. The hands that played with the pencil were clear-skinned, quite without freckles or mottles; yet there was an elderly prominence of vein and sharpness of knuckle in them. The evidence of the wrinkles round the eyes and the loose folds of skin at the corners of the mouth was contradicted by the firmness of the mouth itself, the thick dark hair, the humorous shrewdness of the gaze. It was as if he had somehow aged unevenly; or as if certain of his features were periodically renewed. Or, Cecilia thought, remembering Harold's pedantry of shortly before, as if the date of the lawyer's birth were in dispute.

'They live on the corner, did you say?' Mancini asked now.

'Yes, that's right.'

'So they have access to the public road directly from their house, they do not depend on this road of yours, this *strada vicinale*, for deliveries and so on?'

'No, I suppose not.'

Mancini nodded. He was smiling still. 'There is a certain odour of blackmail in this,' he said. 'It was something they thought worth trying with a foreigner. If you had laughed at them, perhaps they would have given up the idea. But you listened, you seemed to be considering the matter. Now you have given their cause life, you have made it real to them.'

'But we promised them nothing.'

'Mr Chapman, these are primitive people. They do not think about all this fair play and good neighbour business. Those are concepts with no meaning for them. They think you are only concerned to keep the road open.'

'If they try to close the road, I will take them to court in double quick time,' Harold said belligerently.

'Double quick time? In Italy?' Mancini raised the hand holding the pencil and made a sweeping gesture round the room. 'Look at those sofas and armchairs. Look at those rugs on the

48

floor, they are Afghan. This office is in the part of town where rents are highest. I have a house in Umbertide and a large villa in Apulia. All this has been paid for by people taking other people to court in double slow time. When I was younger I was glad of this constant and quite useless quarrelling, because it was making me rich. These days I am bored with it and I try to find other ways.' Mancini smiled and gestured again with the pencil. 'Of course, if you want to buy me some new suits, that is all right, I do not refuse. But it would be money thrown away, because these Checchetti will not litigate, they will not pay law-yers' fees, they will wait for a little time then start again, looking for ways, how do you say it . . . ways to do you bad turns.'

'What is there to do then?' Harold spoke brusquely. He had been shocked by Mancini's explicitness about his assets. A man's assets were sacred and not to be spoken of before relative strangers. 'I am prepared to go some way towards helping these people,' he said.

'If you were to offer them 1 million lire towards the cost of materials, I think it would meet the case. That is about 400 pounds at the present rate of exchange.'

'We are leaving in three days' time for England. I have things to attend to there. We'll be away about a month.'

'I will make out a form of agreement. It is important to make it clear that this sum is the limit of your contribution. If you can call in, shall we say the day after tomorrow, you can sign the paper and leave a cheque for the money. I will get the Checchetti here, they will sign the agreement and take the cheque and give me a receipt for it.' Mancini looked from one to the other of the Chapmans. 'And that will be that,' he said.

That evening Arturo cooked for Fabio things he particularly liked: a soup made with lentils and *farro*, a spinach risotto. Both men were rather weary but pleasantly so, having worked out of doors most of the day. It was still cold in the evenings and they had a good fire of logs burning. At supper they drank between them a litre of their last year's red wine. After watching the news and a game show on the television they were sitting now companionably together, one on either side of the fireplace, talking in a desultory way of things that concerned them.

Light from the fire played over the delicate bones at Arturo's temple and cheek and the taut line of his nape as he lowered his head to look at the flames. The right side of Fabio's face was in the light, the slight marks where the skin had been drawn down a little by the surgery needed after his injury. The marks had not disfigured him but they had given a more saturnine cast to the essential melancholy of his face.

He looked across the space between them and even after all these years he felt his heart contract at the beauty of Arturo's lowered head, the graceful line of his neck, the straight, slender shoulders under his close-fitting dark-blue pullover. All Arturo's movements, all the reclinations of his body, had a grace about them that seemed almost stealthy. His dark eyes gleamed in the firelight, rather oddly – he was slightly astigmatic and this lent a sort of dreamy indirectness to his gaze.

Though sitting there together in apparent harmony, the two men were occupied by quite different kinds of thoughts. Fabio was all contentment, glad that the slight quarrel of earlier that day had left no trace behind, happy to make plans. They could charge their guests more when they had the swimming pool, they would be able to take holidays together, something which for years now they had only very rarely been able to afford.

Arturo, while appearing to take a close interest in all this, had been waiting for a moment that seemed opportune and he saw now that it had arrived, here in the warmth and contentment of the fireside. He had a proposal to make, one that he had pondered long and earnestly. The whole property, house and land, was in Fabio's name, which was natural enough as it had been bought with Fabio's money. Arturo had put no money at all into it, which also was natural since he didn't possess any. However, because Fabio was living on a pension and he himself had no income, they would save a lot of money if the property was in his, Arturo's, name because then he could register as a *coltivatore diretto* and so they would receive considerable tax concessions. Not only that, they would be able to get subsidies of various kinds, discounted prices for petrol and for the fertilizers they used on the land. They would be so much better off, they would be able to pay for occasional help, they might even be able to buy a truck and transport their own olives to the communal press at Passignano. Even, some day, they might have their own press.

So much better off, Arturo pointed out, his slightly indirect, dreamy gaze on Fabio, his mouth, in the pauses between speech, set in that humorous, rather self-deprecating pout. There would have to be a bill of sale of course, witnessed by a notary, but that was the merest formality. He took care not to be too pressing, not to seem too insistent. Fabio liked to mull things over, to take ideas and shape them into his own. Please let him swallow this, Arturo thought. Let him digest it well.

The financial advantages were undeniable. Certainly it was something to think about, and before they went to bed that night Fabio had promised to think about it.

There now began a period of anxiety and discomfort for the Greens. Their new project manager presented them with his first bill and it seemed a lot in view of the fact that nothing but damage had been done to their house since he had undertaken to manage the project. They phoned to express their discontent and Blemish called on them to explain matters. He sat at their kitchen table, chair pushed back, long legs crossed to show his paisley socks and trustworthy brogues. His soft brown eyes moved from one Green to another. He had the details of his bill typed neatly on a sheet of paper which he took from his briefcase. He had spent time with the builder, Esposito, and the *geometra*, Signorini. He had been on several occasions, as they themselves knew, to have a look at things.

'It is not that we question the hours spent,' Mr Green said. 'It is that there is nothing much to show for it.'

'Nothing but a leaking roof and this hole in the wall.' Mrs Green pointed to a raggedly gaping hole below the window. 'We had to stuff it with newspaper to keep out the draught. I have taken it all out now, so you can see.'

'A man came about ten days ago, armed with a drill,' Mr Green said. 'He was an immigrant – North African, I think. He spoke very little Italian and no English of course and so communication was difficult.'

'Communication was impossible,' Mrs Green said. 'He came and drilled this hole in the wall.'

'He just came,' Mr Green said, 'and made this hole in the wall and went away again.'

52

'That is for the wiring,' Blemish said. 'An essential first step.'

'Then there is the roof. Two men came and walked about on the roof. They said they were checking what tiles needed replacing. However, since they came the roof has been a whole lot worse. The water comes through now, on to the floor, here in the kitchen and in our bedroom.'

'We have had to move the bed,' Mrs Green said.

'When it rains we have to run with buckets.' Mr Green felt incredulous himself at this, even as he spoke the words. Indeed, a kind of incredulity had been his main feeling since they had engaged Blemish as their project manager. During the night he would wake and would go to make sure the buckets were positioned correctly in case of rain and he would be possessed by a painful wonder. What were they doing there? Had they come all the way from Michigan only to listen to the wind moving over their broken roof tiles? At odd times during the day he and his wife would look at each other without words and in their glances there was a kind of fear.

'We have a feeling of disconnection,' Mrs Green said.

'Well, of course the wiring will need a thorough –'

'My wife is not talking about the wiring, Mr Blemish. She means that the steps that should accompany things are somehow missing. The hole remains there, just a hole. No one comes to do anything further. You get to feel that the hole could stay there for ever, that the roof will go on leaking through all eternity.'

'Nothing much can be done as yet to the roof as such,' Blemish said.

'The roof as such?'

'We are still waiting for the report of our *geometra*, who is a prince among –'

'Yes, you have told us his virtues.' Mr Green's voice held a tone of impatience very unusual in him.

Blemish looked at Mr Green, at the ash-grey, slightly curly

hair, the childlike eyes in the thin face, and he felt a gathering of vengeful dislike. He would make them pay for this lack of respect. 'It has only been a month or so,' he said. 'As Americans that may seem a long time to you, but the scale is different here, the concept of time is different. As I told you, one of our most important functions here is mediating between cultures, bridging the gap.' Even as he spoke, he knew that the moment had come to offer the Greens the security of a written agreement. The timing of this always required a nice judgement: it did not do to seem in too much of a hurry; on the other hand, it was much better to do it before being asked. He sat forward, a slow inclination of the body at odds with his usual rapidity of movement. 'Well,' he said, blinking softly, 'if it will set your minds at rest, I can ask Esposito to give you a contract.'

Not much later, in the cavernous and echoing kitchen of their house, he was telling Mildred about this coup. 'I knew at once from their faces that my instinct had been right. Of course, you need more than instinct. You need psychology, you need shrewd judgement, you need experience. The client's insecurity has to be fostered – that is standard practice. There is nothing that makes people grasp at a contract more eagerly than being left for a week or two with holes in their roof and walls, though the hole in the Greens' wall may well have been a happy accident. Esposito employs illegal immigrants in order to save on wages. So far so good, on one level it makes sense, but the snag of it is that they don't speak much Italian usually and so they get mixed up. For all I know, this fellow should have gone to some quite different house to make a hole in the wall. Still, never mind, it's all grist to the mill.'

'You are so clever, Stan.' Mildred spoke through the steam of her cooking. She was standing at the stove with head lowered, slowly stirring the contents of a pan with a long-handled wooden spoon. It was to be Giant's Eyeballs that evening, a dish Blemish was particularly fond of. He was lovely to cook for, he enjoyed his food so much.

'So we offer them a contract,' Blemish said. 'A casual offer, as if it were the most normal thing in the world, just arising naturally out of the conversation. It will contain the estimate for the conversion and the date by which the work must be finished.'

Mildred was adding now the *powder fort*, her special secret, a magic mix of black pepper, ginger, cumin and cloves. A steam at once fiery and savoury began to expand through the huge kitchen. 'What happens if it goes over?' she said, in her gruff, reluctant-seeming way. 'What if the costs go over the estimate?'

Blemish shrugged. 'That is not the way we look at it, my love. We never take the negative view, it's not good business. What the Greens can't pay for is of no concern at all. It is only what they can afford that interests us.'

He did not, however, go on to explain to Milly the basic principle of estimates, which is that they are based not on what the labour and materials will cost but on what it is believed the punter has to spend. Some degree of professional reserve had to be maintained after all. Besides, while Milly was top of the league as gardener and cook, she had not a great head for business. 'It all depends on what there is in the kitty,' he contented himself with saying now – it was one of his favourite maxims.

He felt well contented with life as he sat there, long legs outstretched, waiting for his Giant's Eyeballs. The kitchen range gave off a cheerful heat, agreeable odours spiced the air, he was on his second glass of Chianti Classico. As always, he was roused to tenderness by Milly's hampered movements about the stove, her gruff voice and that bemused way of lowering her head. 'Yes,' he said, stretching his neck and blinking softly, 'I can see quite a bit of *cotto* in prospect. At this rate we will be able to have a swimming pool into the bargain.'

Mildred rubbed a hand down the front of her apron, a habit

of hers when moved or excited. 'Oh, Stan,' she said, 'wouldn't it be wonderful to have a *medieval* swimming pool.'

'God, yes, with a cloister running round.'

'Marble tiles.'

'Marble might be slippery.'

'Well, then, some sort of plastic done up to look like it.'

'We could have busts of famous people from the Middle Ages.'

'Dante, Machiavelli, William Tell, people like that.'

'We could get plaster casts of them made and put them all round the cloister in niches.'

'No, on stands.' Milly's pale eyes were wide open and full of emotion. She brushed damp wisps of hair from her brow. 'With their names underneath in those Gothic letters.'

During this time Monti heard nothing from his wife and he himself did not write. He had a visit from his landlord, Lorenzetti, a hard-faced, beaky man whom he did not like. Lorenzetti was concerned about the state of the road where the Checchetti wall had collapsed. Nothing much had been done as yet to clear it. There was some kind of quarrel going on with the English couple who lived further along the road. They were away now but Lorenzetti was intending to get to the bottom of the matter. Meanwhile he wanted to assure his tenant that the road would soon be back to normal. It was clear that Lorenzetti was concerned only to safeguard his rent; but he was glancing around, obviously curious, and might have asked about Laura's absence. In a sort of panic to forestall this, Monti spoke rapidly and too loudly. No, the state of the road did not matter to him, so long as he could get out by car, he was not waiting for supplies of anything, he had enough wood for fires in the evening, the gas cylinder was still more than half full. He began to usher Lorenzetti out before the latter was really ready to leave. It seemed to him as they shook hands in parting that Lorenzetti looked at him oddly. As if, Monti thought later, he suspected I had hidden her somewhere or killed her.

He pursued his researches into the history of the Baglioni family with growing absorption. The base treachery surrounding the murder of Biordo Michelotti on that March day six centuries ago continued to hold a strong fascination for him. He had not so far succeeded in tracing any connection between Biordo's bride and the murder; there was no evidence that her family had any political ambitions in Perugia. Nevertheless, he was reluctant to relinquish his notion of the wife's guilt; the politics of the time were complicated; members of powerful families like the Orsini had often followed private aims, not necessarily those of the clan as a whole.

In his weekly seminar he suggested to the half-dozen under-graduates sitting round his room an approach to the dynamics of power in late medieval and early Renaissance Perugia through the chain of property, the process of driving out the proprietors, sacking the houses and then acquiring them on the cheap.

'Consider it,' he said. 'After the murder of Biordo, the Gui-dalotti were driven out of the city and there is nothing to show that they ever came back. Their last sight of Perugia might well have been their own burning *palazzi*. Highly symbolic that, don't you think, their power going up in smoke? After that they disap-pear from the annals, historically they cease to exist. It would be an interesting line of inquiry to find out who acquired those houses and whether they were acting for others. Certain it is who benefited ultimately. The death of Biordo destroyed the power of the *comune* and left the way open for the return of the exiled families – the *fuorusciti*, those outside the gates. They re-entered Perugia, you will recall, in triumph, under the leadership of the great *condottiere* Fortebraccio. And who came in Fortebraccio's wake?'

Monti paused and waited. Among the students there was a reluctant stirring, not readiness to respond but awareness that some sort of response was required. These seminars of his had not been much marked by the free exchange of ideas, or by dialogue of any kind for that matter, and Monti knew that the blame for this was his. He had not encouraged it, he had put up barriers even here. Since Laura's leaving he had wanted only to retreat within himself. When he could not avoid contact, as now, a quality of sardonic detachment came into his tone and the students felt it. They were shy of him and in one or two cases hostile. Perhaps my true nature, he thought now as he waited, the truth of me coming out under this stress, a desire to control, an unwillingness to share intellectual space, to admit the disorder that comes from free and equal converse. It is not because she left that I am like this, he thought. I was always like this and perhaps that is why she left.

'You will remember the name of Fortebraccio's second-in-command?' he said. 'A fateful name for Perugia.'

It was one of the girls who answered, the rather severe-looking one who took notes continuously and never smiled. 'It was Malatesta Baglioni,' she said.

'Exactly. The real power of the family starts here and with it the beginning of the end for Perugia as a free republic. The Baglioni were just a squabbling faction before that, one among many. The first thing that Malatesta Baglioni did on his return from exile, rich from the blackmail of Bologna – the city paid 100,000 florins to escape being pillaged and a good portion of that must have gone to Malatesta . . . What was the first thing he did?'

Monti waited again. 'Establish the power of his family,' he heard someone say. 'Right,' he said, 'but how exactly? What was the first step?'

No one answered this and after some moments Monti supplied the answer himself. 'He did it by acquiring a good part of the site on which the Guidalotti houses had been built. The houses had been destroyed, you will remember, eighteen years previously by the vengeful mob. He acquired the site and set about building his palace there, with towers and courtyards and terraces, all expensively furnished from the proceeds of plunder and rapine.'

Monti sat back and folded his arms. This business of the houses worked extremely well as a symbolic chain of power; he was pleased by the neatness of it. Some sense of this should have been registered by the students too, but he saw nothing much on their faces as they gathered themselves for departure. The young man in the corner, Millucci, was looking at him in a steady way that might have been a prelude to speech. Monti felt an impulse to circumvent this if possible. 'Well,' he said, 'if there are no further questions . . .'

'On what grounds do you say the Guidalotti looked back and saw their houses burning?' Millucci asked.

The question had been abrupt and Monti paused a moment before replying. On the face of the student he saw a certain complacent antagonism and he felt a gathering of dislike within himself, perhaps only for this youthful smoothness and imper- viousness of expression: Millucci looked too young to be vul- nerable, too young to be betrayed. Only those could be truly betrayed who had made a gift of their weakness. 'No grounds at all,' he said. 'Sometimes we can use imagination, or fancy even, to help us make new associations, open up new lines of thought. I wanted to establish the connection between the transactions of power and the transactions of property.'

'In other words, you had no evidence at all for your state- ment.' On the student's face, as he rose, there was an expression of triumph.

'Well, no, but it wasn't exactly a statement, as I have just tried to explain,' Monti said. 'I am sorry if my approach seems ro- mantic to the severity of your youth.' He transferred his gaze rather pointedly from Millucci. 'Next week,' he said, 'we will be taking a further look at the fortunes of the Baglioni – and of their houses.'

When the last of the students had left, he sat quite still for some minutes at his desk, allowing the silence to settle round him. The annoyance he had felt faded quickly. He thought again about Malatesta Baglioni, true founder of the family's power.

Acquiring property on prime sites had not been his only way of marking his return from the years of exile. Among the prisoners taken at the capture of Assisi in the October of 1419 was a certain Gragnuola of Porta San Pietro, who had been present at the killing of Malatesta's brother, Pandolfo Baglioni, in 1393. For this, twenty-six years later, Malatesta Baglioni caused him to be tied to the tail of a horse and dragged from the Due Porte to the Piazza Maggiore of Perugia. He was dead before he reached San Domenico. Pompeo Pellini, in his monumental history of Perugia, declared that the whole of Gragnuola's course was marked by blood. But to Monti, as he sat there in silence, it seemed unlikely that any fresh stains could have showed on those stones, darkened already by so much slaughter.

In the afternoon he drove the thirty kilometres or so to Montone, birthplace of that Fortebraccio who had brought the Baglioni to Perugia in his train. The road wound up from the plain and followed a curving course below the ancient walls of the town, giving wide views over the valley of the Tiber. The cathedral of San Francesco was undergoing restoration and was closed to visitors; but it was the much smaller church, lower down the valley, deconsecrated now, that Monti was interested in.

He could see it from the broad terrace of the cathedral as he smoked in the sunshine and waited for Signor Rossi, a local antiquarian and guide, who kept the keys to the place. It was no more now than one of a jumble of outhouses, seen thus from above, stone-built, with a ruined bell tower. But once it had been the principal church of Montone, then subsequently used as a lazar house for plague victims, run by the Franciscans. Among those victims – and it was why Monti had come – had been a son of that same vengeful Malatesta. Or so at least it was asserted in the chronicles of the time.

As he waited there, however, the sense of an immediate

purpose faded from his mind. The terrace was sheltered and quiet and he was alone there, private and unassailable, with the flank of the church close behind and the ground plunging steeply away before him to the invisible river far below. A feeling of holiday came to him, illicit, unauthorized holiday, such as he had sometimes felt as a boy at school in periods of stillness or inactivity, accidental and always brief – he had been too driven by study, too earnestly ambitious, to enjoy such lulls for long.

The ambition had not been native to him but instilled, he had known that now for many years. He came from generations of small farmers, scraping a living in the difficult mountainous country north of Turin. His father had wanted something more, had set up as an agent for machine tools, failed and ended bankrupt. All his frustration had gone into hopes for his son; and when that son turned out bookish the hopes had intensified.

These thoughts broke Monti's precarious sense of sanctuary. He began to walk back and forth along the terrace, keeping close to the wall so as still to enjoy the sweep of the view. His father had been dead for twenty years. All that admonition, those constant reminders of the seriousness of life . . . Would he have felt rewarded, seeing me now, middle-aged, obscure and far from rich, author of one book and various papers on the history of the Central Italian States?

It had been Laura's great gift, right from the beginning, right from the moment they had first looked at each other and she had smiled at him, in the library of the university they had both attended, to break through the seriousness of his nature, find the sensuous man within. She it was who had made him feel holidays need not be experienced as truancies. What comparable gift, he wondered, had he made to her?

He glanced at his watch, saw that Signor Rossi was some minutes late and fell immediately into a state of anxiety about the appointment. It had happened before, and not infrequently, that he had mistaken things, turned up at the right time but on the wrong day, for example. Or the other way round. Once he had gone to deliver a lecture at the University of Urbino. He had got the right day of the week and the right hour, but had come a week too early. How indignant he had been, at first, to find no room arranged for him, no students waiting . . .

Rossi now arrived, however, and they went together in Monti's car. This they had to leave at the roadside higher up and finish the journey on foot down a narrow track. The man who farmed the land lived in a single-storey house nearby, which had once, Signor Rossi said, been part of the monastic precincts – there had been a community of Franciscans there from the time of the church's foundation and they had stayed to nurse the sick when the plague came, converting both monastery and chapel into a hospice.

There was a coat of arms above the entrance, smoothed by time, indecipherable. Hens scratched in the dust of the doorway, scattered as they approached. The farmer went back into his house without offering to accompany them. Monti felt watched, though whether by this man or by the dead generations he did not know.

He did not know, not altogether, why he was there at all, what it was he hoped to find. The connection with the Baglioni was of highly doubtful authority; and even if Malatesta's son had really died here, what trace could be discovered now? Why was he driven to make these investigations, knowing in advance they were fruitless? In the days of their power, the Baglioni had produced no artists, no patrons of art, no thinkers. None of them had ever said or written anything memorable. They had been men of blood, all of them, arrogant, violent and treacherous. It was not only the habit of research, of leaving no stone unturned, that led him to follow up these dubious leads. There had grown in him a sort of superstition, a feeling that something would be vouchsafed to his senses or understanding, some clue, in the end, that would help him understand the present as well as the past, help him to see – and so accept – through links infinitely small, some vital connection with his own sense of violation and loss. If the history of Perugia was a record of crime – and it was – then the Baglioni were its true representatives, not a dark exception or an unusually virulent strain, but the quintessential stock.

Nothing much remained now, in this place that had seen so much suffering and sacrifice, but the splendid proportions of arches and vaults. His companion pointed out to him the traces of medieval frescos in the apse, the decorative carving on the ruinous altar table, a small recess with human bones in it. The panes of the windows had long gone and the nets placed across them had broken and sagged. Sparrows and pigeons fluttered through the vaulted spaces high above. The whole cavernous interior had the quiet light, the air of hollowness and desolation, of buildings that the winds have long inhabited. The great slabs of pavement were thickly splashed with bird droppings, and tracks of rats went through the dust. Monti saw the perfect skeleton of a pigeon spread on the floor.

He was glad to emerge again into the sunlight. The church was a shell now and meaningless, even as a memorial. Disease had defined its function and limited its purposes. The Franciscans had attended the dying here. When the ravages of the plague subsided, or when there were no longer enough monks surviving, the place had been abandoned. It had mouldered away for half a millennium. There was no trace now of disease or devotion, only the evidence of decay.

They stood for a while at the gate talking to the farmer, who knew nothing of the place's past, only that it was very old. Signor Rossi said that the tower, with its ruined belfry, which Monti had thought an integral part of the church, was in fact much older. It had been a watchtower, Rossi said. Centuries before there was a monastery on the site or any Franciscan Order or any thought of bubonic plague, the Etruscans had looked out from here across the valley of the Tiber.

On his way back, as the road descended, he saw another church, small and rather nondescript, Baroque in style, set back on a level in the hillside. The doors were open and he glimpsed some movement of people, or the shadows of people, inside. On an impulse he stopped, pulled over on to the verge below the church and went up the stone steps to the entrance.

The people moving inside were young women wearing summer dresses in this warm May weather. They were sweeping the stone floors, cleaning and polishing the pews. Two young men were busy fitting up amplifying equipment below the altar. Monti asked the reason for these preparations. The sister of one of the women was getting married, he was told. The wedding would take place in this church. It was disused, no services were held in it these days, but the couple wanted to have their wedding here. 'Just a fancy,' the woman said, smiling. 'They both came to Mass here when they were children.'

All the doors were wide open, letting in swathes of air and sunshine. Monti walked round but there was little to see, the place was bare. Crests of families on the walls, stucco scrolls of blue and white, crudely fashioned marble angels with gilded wings. Nevertheless he lingered. After some time he went out again on to the pavement outside the entrance. In gardens below the walls he saw walnut trees and a cherry strung with ripening fruit. There were wide views across to the hills and the looming grey-blue shapes of the mountains beyond. Monti had a sense of openness, of unimpeded spaces.

Music came from within the church. The young men were musicians, they were trying out the amplifiers with a passage from the *St Matthew Passion*, one playing a hand-organ, the other a clarinet. The noble sounds swelled up without distortion, flooded out to Monti as he stood there at the porch. He had a feeling familiar from childhood, a sense that he must keep still. He wanted to keep everything as it was, in just this combination: the laughing woman, the broad shafts of sunshine, the sense he had of drinking space and distance, the marvellous celebration of the music.

On this afternoon, from which he had expected little, in the course of visiting two of God's houses, he was pierced by a feeling that was both happiness and sorrow. And which of the two was stronger it was impossible to know.

It took Ritter the best part of a month to clear the olive terraces. The ground descended steeply and the terraces were rough and uneven, deeply rutted in places by tractors in wet Decembers of past years during the harvesting of the olives. He could have followed local practice and simply had the ground turned over. This would have cost him something and he was poor, but it was not for the sake of saving money that he decided against it. He wanted to make these terraces into pieces of meadow. He saw them in his mind's eye descending in ranks, scattered with daisies and corn lilies and grape hyacinths, the silver green of the olives toning with the denser green of the grass.

It was a vision that required much labour for its fulfilment. For several seasons now, through the years of old Adelio's illness and discouragement, the tough thick-bladed couch grass had grown up and flowered and died and the stalks had folded over and packed down over the earth in thick swathes, sealing the land off from gentler growths, shutting out light and air. Chicory and bramble and broom had pushed through this rotting mat and were tangled in it. Before these could be cut close, the dead grass had to be raked out and piled up for compost. Up and down the slopes Ritter toiled with rake and billhook and wheelbarrow.

At the end of the day he was exhausted. He would sit in his kitchen with a bottle of the red wine which he bought by the crate very cheaply in the village, grateful for the condition of mindlessness, while the wine relaxed his limbs, stiffened by the hours of labour. It was in the course of these spring evenings, as he sat in the wicker chair he had acquired with the house, and the ancient iron stove on which he cooked his meals cracked and hissed, that Ritter discovered himself to be, though precariously, once again part of the continuity of things.

On the days when it rained and he could not get out to work he read from the small store of books he had brought with him, the poetry of Heine and Montale, some history; but mainly he liked to read about the working of things, the larval stages of dragonflies, the spawning of salmon, the replication of cells. He clung to process as a way of salvation; and his dread was still a return to the stricken immobility of his illness, when the current of time had been frozen.

Part of the price he had to pay for this recovery of time was a certain unruliness of memory. Incidents from the past would come into his mind without warning, without any conscious effort of recall and with nothing in his surroundings that could account for them. In early May, when he had nearly finished clearing the terraces, he stood on the slope above his house looking down at drifting flakes of whitish fluff that came in great swarms from the flowering poplar trees along the stream bank. The day was almost windless but the down from the trees sidled and floated like snow and seemed from where he was standing to fill all the spaces of the air above him and below.

Linnets and thrushes sang through this glinting swarm. Ritter had a momentary sense of screened view, limited perspectives. Then the memory came. A long room with high windows, rubberized tiles on the floor hushing footsteps. He had been down to the body of the auditorium to collect some papers, the texts of speeches perhaps or some programme of events – he could not remember. He was returning, mounting the stairs that led back up to the interpreters' booths, wide shallow stairs, care was needed not to stumble. He had looked up at the row of glass-fronted booths where his fellow interpreters were speaking in languages that ranged from Finnish to Japanese, reproducing the measured hypocrisies of the dark-suited man standing at the podium below. Seen through the glass, with the bumps of the headsets on their ears, they had a remote, strangely robotic or androidal look.

He had stood still and the sensation of nausea and blocked hearing had come to him that he sometimes felt in a plane that was losing altitude too quickly. In these first few seconds of hush he had been aware only of the figures behind the glass. Then fragments of the speech had come from below. Developing nations, benefits of Western technology . . . the world one great family . . . not denying the baleful effects of industrial pollution and his company was foremost . . . anyone looking at their track record . . .

This was coded language, it meant something else. He had stood there, half-way up the stairs, and there was nothing but the words below and the moving mouths above, redundant voices translating a redundant voice. Something of that same hush and sickness came to him now as he stood looking through the glinting, drifting swarm of flakes. Another voice came to him and with it the memory of his father's face, the serious grey eyes, the straight brows, the thin sensitive mouth like a mobile wound. Below this the exact symmetry of the white flashes on the high collar of his uniform. The mouth moved, words came, measured and rhetorical, making no concession to the understanding of a child. *Germany's historic mission . . . heirs to the glories of European Christendom . . . German spirituality, French clarity, Italian subtlety . . . The hegemony of the Holy Roman Empire restored . . . Marxism and International Jewry the great enemies of humanity . . .*

Coded language this too. Could he really have spoken thus to a ten-year-old boy or were these phrases from some other, later time? He had spoken in the same terms afterwards, long after the war, even when he lay dying in an Ulm hospital, but then it had been in tones of disillusion and bitterness. Germany had betrayed its mission, failed in energy. Perhaps on that distant afternoon in Rome, seeing his son's distress, he had spoken more gently, more simply. If so, no memory of it remained . . . March 1944, I was ten and he was forty-three, a former Leipzig school-master, now a captain in German Military Intelligence, explain-ing to me why it had been necessary to take 335 people from their homes, from the streets, from prison, transport them to a quarry on the outskirts of Rome and kill them all with pistol shots in the back of the neck. It was done, he said, in order to safeguard the German civilizing mission.

Ritter began to walk down the slope and with the movement he became aware of sounds again, bird-song, a distant aero-plane, the sound of water flowing invisibly in the gully below. He had not known then the number of the victims or the place they had been taken to or what had been done to them. All this he had learned later, years later – he had made it his business to learn everything he could about this mass killing at the Fosse Ardeatine. He had been too young at the time for abstractions but old enough to understand the meaning of retaliation and he knew that German soldiers had been killed in an explosion in Via Rastrella the day before, the work of the Resistance.

He had known too that these people who had been taken away would never come back again. He had known it because one of them was an uncle – or a kind of uncle – of his one great friend in Rome, a boy of his own age called Giuseppe, who lived in the dark basement of the building with his mother. Giuseppe's mother was the concierge, a handsome woman dressed in black who sat all day in a glass booth knitting and watching people come and go. Father there was none.

When we are very young, Ritter thought, it is others who teach us the modes and management of feeling, behaviour most appropriate whether in grief or joy – a changing expression, the inflection of a voice, a friend seen with tears on his face then never seen again. From that day onward Giuseppe had never come back to play with him. He and his mother had disappeared from their room in the basement and Ritter had never seen them again. And he had known then, as surely as he knew now, that he was to blame for this, that it was he who had betrayed Giuseppe.

When had it been? When had he stood there on the white steps, holding the papers? What year, what city? Through the high windows of that conference room he had seen ornamental cherry trees in the grounds, smothered in pink blossom. Spring, it must have been. That spring of 1944 was cold, the almond trees were late to flower. He used to see them from the windows of the car that took him to school. The wind dislodged the white petals and they floated and drifted and seemed to fill the air. White petals on the desk when he spoke to me that afternoon about Germany's civilizing mission.

Ritter was surprised for the moment – he had not thought of these petals before, had not known they were retained in memory. The white flashes on the uniform, yes, and the whiteness of the room, and the moving mouth. But the almond trees on the way to school, the vase on the desk, the spill of petals, these were things that had lain beyond recall, rescued from oblivion now by the glinting fluff from the poplars. He had not thought about those days in Rome since his illness, nor much in the period immediately preceding it, too burdened with the present, with surviving the hours as they followed in succession. Now, unbidden, unblurred by pain or reluctance, these memories had come drifting back.

He was looking down directly at the tangled vegetation of the gully below him, at the draped trees struggling up from thickets of bramble and blackthorn, opening indomitable leaves again to the sun. It was now that the intention came to him: he would not stop his work of clearance when he had done with the terraces, he would cross the grass-grown track and clear the slopes of the ravine.

With this the world became fully distinct again to his senses, the fading flowers of the crab-apple trees along the bank, the new green on the fig tree above his house, the dipping line of the hills. He was turning away with the intention of clipping some shoots of olive he had noticed growing from the base of a tree, when he saw a man approaching along the track. He descended the slope and began to walk along the track towards his visitor. After a moment he recognized him for the Englishman, Chapman, who had the next house along the road. They had not so far spoken to each other, but Ritter had seen him once or twice in the village shop.

The Englishman waved as he drew near but his face seemed rather serious. 'Harold Chapman,' he said, holding out a hand.

'Anders Ritter.'

'I was wondering if you speak any English?'

'Yes,' Ritter said. 'That is, I used to. It is still good enough, I think.' His voice was soft, without much trace of foreignness in the accent except for the careful distinctness of the vowels.

Chapman's expression relaxed a little with this first hurdle surmounted. 'I wanted to talk to you about the road.'

'The road?' Ritter looked carefully at his visitor. The deranged always assumed that you knew what they were talking about. The Englishman showed no obvious signs of disturbance. He was dressed with rather incongruous neatness, considering the remoteness of the place, in a tie with diagonal stripes and a navy-blue blazer and grey flannels. The blazer, Ritter noticed, had some insignia in gold stitching over the breast pocket. 'Which road do you mean?' he said. 'Do you mean the way forward, the way we should take?'

'I mean the road we are standing on at this present moment in time. The road which provides the only access to your house and mine.' Chapman did not feel very much at ease with this German; the man kept on looking at you as if you were something he had just noticed. 'You must have seen that the garden wall of the house on the corner, the last one if you are coming from this end, has fallen down and partly blocked the road. We left the matter in the hands of our lawyer, but it seems that these Checchetti have refused to sign the papers.'

'Papers? No, I have not seen it. I do not go that way.'

'But it is the only way you can go. You can't get out with a car any other way.'

'I have no car.'

'No car?' Chapman was staggered. 'But how –'

'I go to the village on foot.' Ritter gestured towards the hillside behind him. 'It is a short cut.'

'I see,' Chapman said blankly. This was something of a blow; he had been hoping to make an appeal to their common interests. The situation of being without a car was almost unimaginable to him. He had seen no television aerial anywhere about the German's house either. He glanced quickly at the other's wrist: no watch. This was a man without possessions. A ramshackle house, the ground floor windowless, still with its original earth floor, a broken staircase on the outside, no conversion work in process and none apparently intended. There was something disturbing to Chapman, something freakish, about a man who had so little. However, he was looking for allies and had to begin somewhere. 'All the same,' he said, 'you will want to have things delivered from time to time.'

'It is possible, yes.'

'We have got to present a united front. They are trying to blackmail me.'

Launched thus, he told Ritter the story from the beginning, from the morning that the Checchetti had come to announce the fall of their wall. 'We left the cheque with the lawyer. All they had to do was sign a paper freeing us from further responsibility. We got back from England yesterday, I phoned my lawyer and he told me that they had refused to sign. I don't know the whys and wherefores yet – we'll be seeing him later today – but the reason isn't far to seek, is it?'

Chapman was stocky but not very tall. He had to look up slightly to meet the other's eyes and he did so now in the hope of seeing some reflection there of his own sense of outrage. But the German's eyes were vague and remote, as if the voice that spoke to him, instead of issuing from close at hand, came from some distant point among the hills. After some moments he said, 'Ah, that is a troublesome thing.'

'Troublesome? What it is, you see, they are hoping to get the money without giving any written acknowledgement at all.'

Ritter nodded slowly. 'So that they can ask for more.'

'And more again.' Chapman uttered a short and mirthless laugh. 'I offered the money for the sake of good neighbour relations. Those blighters don't know the meaning of the term. They think I am frightened they will block the road – naturally they only see things from the lowest possible moral perspective. I just wanted you to know the facts. They might come round with a different story, trying to put the blame on me for any inconvenience the people along the road might be caused. But I am getting in first. I intend to call on everyone who lives on this road and tell them the true story. I thought I'd start with you and work my way along.'

Chapman paused. It had not been a very promising start; not much in the way of solidarity could be expected from a man who did not possess a car. 'If there is going to be a war of words,' he said, 'I intend to win it.'

'War of words?' Ritter's eyes were for the first time focused sharply on the other man, who was already turning away. Any folly could carry the day in a war of words: to win, it was only necessary to be believed. The phrase remained in his mind as he watched Chapman's blazered figure receding, as he turned to look down again at the steep and densely overgrown slopes of the gully. Any madness could carry the day in a war of words.

Nothing much had happened since Blemish's offer of a contract to change the situation of the Greens. The hole in the wall remained, no repairs were effected to the roof tiles. A lorry came with bags of cement and then with a load of sand. These were deposited in unsightly heaps immediately in front of the house. The driver was out of temper because he had been obliged to spend some time clearing away pieces of the Checchetti wall that prevented him from passing.

Other than this, nothing. The Greens kept anxiety at bay by making plans. They had always enjoyed making plans together, the element of affectionate conspiracy in it, creating a future, things to look forward to. It was a kind of game played with time, more compelling as one got older. Waiting till the house was finished before going to see the loved Verrocchio painting at the Uffizi was a very smart plan, they both felt. Their whole Italian enterprise was the result of a long-term plan: every month for years now they had put aside what they could afford into a separate bank account, a special house fund. Now, in their un-certainty, they went around the house making plans about the things they would do. They would have a pergola to give shade to the front. They would plant roses and make a trellis for wis-taria. They would have an arch made in the wall between the kitchen and the room that had been used as a granary, to make a large sitting-room.

Then Blemish arrived with a copy of the contract. 'If every-thing is to your satisfaction,' he said, 'Esposito and you can sign it. We will have it witnessed by a notary in Perugia and that will be that.'

He watched them as they scanned the document. The estimated sum was stated there, also the dates of beginning and completing the work. The builder had set a limit of twelve months for completion. 'Rather a long time, isn't it?' Mr Green said.

'Common practice. Esposito has to protect himself against accidents, unavoidable delays and so on. He will finish well within the time.'

'What is *salvo imprevisti*? The estimate is written here and then on the line below there is *salvo imprevisti*. That means "excepting things unforeseen", doesn't it?'

'That is correct,' Blemish said. 'There again, the builder has to protect himself. He might encounter something totally unexpected.'

'Such as?'

Blemish permitted himself a smile. 'How can we say? It can't be predicted – that is the meaning of the phrase. It is nothing to worry about, just a formality. It is the way we operate. It obviously does not include any of the work already discussed, the excavation of the downstairs part, the laying of the floors and tiling, fireplaces and chimneys, the plumbing and wiring and carpentry. All that is included in the estimate.'

'And he will start when he says?'

'Certainly. He can't afford not to, that is the beauty of this document. If you look over the page you will see that the builder is liable to penalties for any delay in starting and finishing. A hundred thousand lire for every day he goes over.' Blemish craned his neck and blinked softly. The Greens were going to buy it, he could tell. 'Quite punitive,' he said, 'but that is the way we operate, our clients' interests come first. We will deploy all our resources in the management of your project. This property will be a bijou residence of striking originality and period flavour.'

Before Blemish left, the Greens had signified their assent and he had made an appointment with the notary on his portable telephone. He hummed and sang to himself as he drove along. The estimate was for 160 million lire, about 65,000 pounds at the present rate of exchange – a sum exactly gauged to the limits of the Greens' disposable capital. Genuine costs of labour and materials for that minimum of work they intended to do might amount to a fifth of this. He would have to keep an eye on Esposito to make sure he didn't exaggerate his costs. How much could be extracted from the Greens before they understood matters was purely conjectural of course, but with any luck it could be as much as 40,000. He would get his share of this from Esposito. Quite a bit of *cotto* there. Then there was his 40,000 lire an hour while all this was dragging on. And drag on it would, for quite a while yet. And the whole thing was legal. In the exuberance of these thoughts he raised his voice in song as he drove homewards, promising to be like the ivy on the old garden wall, faithful and true for ever.

The Greens too felt that there was something to celebrate, a prospect of some action at last. To mark the occasion they made a trip to Assisi to look again at the frescos in the Basilica di San Francesco.

Assisi was a very special place for both of them, a place of pilgrimage. It had been one of the first Umbrian towns they visited on that winter honeymoon of theirs which they had spoken about to Blemish, a visit of undimmed wonder through all the years between. Their love for Italy had been sealed that day and it had become part of their love for each other.

They had borrowed a car and driven from their hotel in Perugia on a morning in early January, a morning of mingled sunshine and mist. They had left the car below the walls and entered the town by the Porta Nuova, passing the Basilica di Santa

Chiara on their left, with its great rose window and arched buttresses and patterning of bleached white and pale-pink stone. On an impulse, instead of going on to the main square, which had been their original intention, they had turned aside and begun to ascend the steep streets towards the upper part of the town. They had followed a series of stepped alleyways, with houses abutting closely on either side, come out finally high above the town at the remains of the fortress known as Rocca Maggiore, twelfth-century stronghold of Barbarossa.

They had climbed the ruined tower and from here had looked back down over Assisi. It was past noon but mist and sunshine contended still and they saw the town in zones of varying distinctness: the lower part and the plain beyond were a lake of mist with buildings and trees and the lines of streets half-glimpsed and half-surmised below the surface as if below clouded water; then a muffled borderland of pale roofs and dark pinnacles of cypress trees; then, immediately above this, clear sunshine, bell towers and bay trees and the blaze of winter jasmin, the cathedral with its leaded dome and Gothic tympanum, the great Basilica di San Francesco lying to the north on its spur of rock, lapped by the mist, freighted with its tomb of the saint. To the east rose the sheer slopes of Mt Subasio thrusting up into sunlight from the obliterated valley below. There was a slight graining of mist still, even so high as this, and the cool scent of the night's distillations still lingered in the air.

That was an experience in the nature of things impossible to repeat. Today they went directly to the Basilica di San Francesco, to the lower church, built as a crypt to house the mortal remains of the saint. By another of those gently conspiratorial pacts which were so much a feature of their life together, they did not enter through the splendid Gothic doorway on the west side but went round to the smaller entrance adjoining the cloister. This way, passing from daylight to the devotional gloom of the

79

interior, one was abruptly presented, at eye level and very close, with the Giotto *Crucifixion* and the Cimabue *Madonna Enthroned* side by side on the wall of the facing transept.

There was a special place where they were accustomed to sit and they made for it now – habits like this were established easily between them, and kept to with a sort of devotion, a repeated affirmation of the fact of sharing. It was almost directly below the cross-vault of the transept, slightly south of the apse. It was a marvellous point of vantage because from here you could look upward at the celebrated allegorical paintings in the broad webs of the vaulting; or straight before you at the Giotto frescos running along the wall – great dramatic images of persecution: *The Flight into Egypt*, *The Massacre of the Innocents*; or – easily seen by turning the head – the Lorenzetti *Crucifixion* with its cloud-burst of weeping angels. Masterpiece on masterpiece, Sienese and Florentine in unique competition, arguably the greatest concentration of genius under one roof anywhere to be found. Sistine Chapel notwithstanding, as Mr Green was fond of saying.

As people do under the assault of beauty, after a while he generalized his feelings, became aware of the minglings of light, shaft of white daylight from the narrow entrance, filterings of ruby and blue from the stained-glass windows, pallid electric light from bulbs slung high above. From somewhere along the nave, out of sight, a guide was speaking in steady monologue, but he could not distinguish the language. Everywhere one looked this extraordinary proliferation of images, ceiling and walls covered with them, haloed saints, cloaked mortals, white angels with rose-tinted wings, meekly inclined heads of martyrs and mourners.

From time to time his attention sharpened, he saw in clear focus the dune-like landscape of *The Flight into Egypt*, blue-robed Mary on the ass, a palm tree bending in worship at her passing, the Gothic sprawl of the bled Christ in the Lorenzetti *Deposition*,

St Francis holding up his hands to be pierced with the stigmata. Nothing in the homely piety of his upbringing had prepared him for the awe he experienced in places like this. He felt the mortal struggle that underlay all this devotion. Fear was just below the surface. Something more than fear . . .

'The dread of faith,' he murmured to his wife. 'Look at those faces, those long brows and narrow eyes swept back towards the temples. You wonder whether they are looking at heaven or hell.'

'Why, Sammy,' she said, 'you know as well as I do that the faces are stylized, there was a convention for brows and eyes.'

But technical explanations never seemed sufficient to Mr Green. He saw cruelty and strife in these looks, both the knowledge of it and the practice. Such faces derived from a time when the weak had small protection in law or custom. Is our time so different? he wondered, as they emerged into the sunlight. Our faces are different, certainly, the stare is masked. There came suddenly into his mind a memory of Mr Blemish's face, blinking softly as he explained the terms of the contract.

His wife had seemed to enjoy the visit to the church in the usual way and Mr Green said nothing to her of his feelings, of how oppressive and even frightening he had found the paintings this time. It was a lapse from the full confidence they enjoyed together, almost like a mild form of betrayal – or so at least he felt it; but he judged it worse to spoil her mood with his doubts and glooms.

On the way back they visited the Church of Santa Maria degli Angeli on the plain below Assisi, not so much for the sake of the church itself – it was too enormous, too grandiose, too lavishly Baroque for their taste – but for the little cluster of much older buildings within it, associated with the life of St Francis and his companions, including the little cell where the saint died. The Greens stood immediately below the vast dome in the very centre of the great echoing basilica and looked at the tiny low-roofed house known as the Chapel of the Porziuncola, improbably preserved among the swirling splendours all round.

'I can never come to terms with it somehow,' Mrs Green said. 'When St Francis was alive this was all there was, this little place, not much more than a hut, with nothing but forest all around, and wolves and bears prowling about. It's not that easy to imagine in these surroundings, is it?'

It had been there more than 200 years already when St Francis came upon it in 1208, ruinous and long abandoned, a small oratory dedicated to St Mary of the Angels. Attracted by the seclusion and tranquillity of the place, the saint had rebuilt it with his own hands, living a life of poverty and prayer here with a handful of devoted companions.

Before leaving through the west gate they turned and looked down the full length of the interior, 115 metres, their guidebook informed them. From here it could be seen how the little oratory so lovingly restored by St Francis had, by a paradox of history, been both preserved and abandoned within the huge and pompous hangar that had grown up around it, built to accommodate the thousands of pilgrims who came in early August for the Festa del Perdono. This elaborate carapace had drained the oratory of meaning; the meaning was all in the opulent decoration of the surroundings: the marble Madonnas and gilded scrolls and trumpeting angels – a display of wealth and power that Francis had sought through the example of his life to oppose. The humble oratory, like the poverty of the saint, was no more now than a quaint survival, reminder of some former, outmoded, perversity or eccentricity. 'St Francis's house,' Mrs Green said and sighed. 'Better if they had left it to the wolves again once he had gone.'

In the evening they went over the money again. They had bought the house on an impulse, immediately drawn to the peace of the place, the warm colours of the landscape and the way the house itself had settled into the hillside and seemed so securely to belong there. It was rather larger than they needed but family and friends would come to stay. The estimate for the conversion was at the limit of what they could afford but when it was done, they told each other, they would live cheaply – they were not materialistic, their needs were simple. They made another of their innumerable planning expeditions round the house. Here they would have the fireplace, set in an angle of the walls so as not to take up too much room; here they would have their bookshelves. There was enough space for them both to have a separate studio and they had already planned the way they would arrange these and the things they would have there.

Later they went out to admire their three rows of vines below the house. The plants had not been pruned while the house stood empty and it was too late in the year to cut them now. They had trailing outgrowths, low to the ground, and thin unproductive shoots growing vertically upward – it would be a poor crop this year. But Mr Green had bought a book on viticulture – in Italian, so he could improve his knowledge of the language and learn about cultivating vines at the same time. These slopes above Lake Trasimeno produced light, agreeable wines and Mr Green was keen to go into things properly and make his own wine and keep his own cellar.

They stood there for quite some time, admiring the small gushes of new leaf that were breaking out all along the length of the vines. Miraculous to see the stems, bare and dead-seeming for so long, begin to produce these fountains of green, the pinkish rosettes of the buds opening from day to day and spreading outwards from the heart in bursts of leaf.

'Nothing could look newer than these vines, could it?' Mrs Green reached out and touched gently the soft, slightly spongy leaves.

The light was fading now and it grew cooler. A nightingale began to sing from somewhere not far away. They listened to the first tuning notes, the sudden loud release of song. Another bird joined in, then another. Any lingering anxiety the Greens might have felt was dissolved in that lyrical nightfall. As they turned to go back indoors, they felt quite certain that they had done the right thing to come here and buy this house.

The following day the Chapmans had two visits, about an hour apart. The first was from Bruno, the Checchetti son-in-law, who had been dispatched with an ultimatum. His round face fixed in its faint, mindless, embarrassed-seeming smile, he delivered his message in the manner of one repeating a lesson – Cecilia felt sure he had been schooled in it. His wife had learned, he said, through her important contacts in the town hall, that the minimum legal width of a neighbourhood road was two metres. At present, throughout the kilometre or so of its length, it was two metres and a half wide. It was slightly less than this below the Checchetti wall because of the rubble along the edge. But not much less, Bruno said. The Chapmans had a week in which to reconsider their position. If at the end of that time they had not paid over in cash, without any interference from a lawyer, the million lire they had promised towards the building of the new wall, they, the Checchetti, would put stakes in the road outside their house at an exact distance of two metres. This would still allow the passage of a car; but vans and lorries would not be able to get through.

There was not much point, both the Chapmans saw, in expostulating with Bruno. He was merely doing what he had been told to do. 'We will not give in to blackmail,' Harold Chapman said, and heard with habitual impatience his firm tones transmuted to the gentle, wavering ones of his wife, which seemed to thin out in the air and drift away. Cecilia was doing her best, he knew, but she did not sound like a woman who would not give in to blackmail.

'We must be firm with these people,' he said as they sat to-gether afterwards over coffee in the kitchen. 'We are coming to a crucial point in this business; it is fatal to show weakness.'

Without quite knowing how she had offended, Cecilia knew that this was an indirect reproach to her. She knew too that any attempt to answer directly, even if in firm agreement, was liable to make him crosser. 'I wonder who Signora Checchetti's important contacts in the town hall are,' she said. 'It is difficult to imagine that a woman like that . . .' Under Harold's indignant gaze she heard her voice falter and trail away.

'I don't know how it is, Cecilia,' he said, 'but you always seem to get led away into inessentials. What matters is not who she knows at the town hall, but whether this two metres business is true or not. I shouldn't have thought that I needed to point that out.'

'It's no good taking it out on me, Harold,' she said with sudden spirit. 'The real point is, what are we going to do about it?'

He thought for a moment, his face settling into the dogged and slightly suffering look which had always made Cecilia feel pity for him, though recently much less. 'I will phone the lawyer,' he said. 'I will phone Mancini and make another appointment. Presumably Italy is a country subject to the rule of law.'

'That's not quite the impression Mancini gives, is it?'

The phone call was no sooner made and the appointment fixed with Mancini's secretary than they had their second visit of the afternoon. This was from a middle-aged couple who introduced themselves as Professor and Mrs Lorenzetti. Cecilia asked them in but they declined. There was a certain stateliness about their behaviour, not unfriendly exactly, but suggestive of grave matters. They had come about the road, they said. The wife seemed not to speak any English but the professor knew a little. He was a stiff-faced, beaky-looking man with small, round eyes like a bird's. She was rosy and plump and her face creased in soft folds when she smiled.

It was soon clear that they had talked to the Checchetti already, because they began by merely repeating the Checchetti view of things. 'You tell this family you will give them money for their wall, then you say you will give them nothing, then you set the lawyer on to them.' The professor spoke as if the lawyer were a dangerous hound that the Chapmans had unleashed.

Chapman looked from one to the other for a moment or two. They were both heavy-bodied and seemed very solid, standing there side by side, united in disapproval. He felt the welcome beginnings of anger.

'They are simple people, not like you and me,' the professor said.

'You and me? How do you come into it? You don't live on the road.'

'Professor Monti, he is my, how do you say it, my *inquilino*.'

'Tenant,' Cecilia said.

'I see,' Chapman said. 'That is your house, the one down the road from us. You are worried about your rent, I suppose. Well, let me explain the true situation.'

He went through it slowly and carefully, as he had done with Ritter. He was word perfect in it now – it was like a lesson he had learned by heart. They were still prepared to pay the money, though patience with the Checchetti was running out. Under no circumstances would they pay anything without proper legal form.

But their visitors were not really listening, Cecilia saw that at once, neither to Harold nor to her when she translated the main points for the sake of Mrs Lorenzetti. She could see it from the air of patience the professor had assumed, from the wreathed smiles of his wife. They had already formed their ideas about the situation, the first and main one being that as foreigners the

Chapmans did not understand the mentality of Italian peasants in general and the Checchetti in particular. This was confirmed when the professor interrupted Harold's story with a short, disagreeably barking laugh. 'These people is very strong,' he said. 'Strong-headed. You do not know them.'

'He means strong-minded,' Cecilia said. She was developing a feeling of dislike for this couple quite at odds with the usual gentle forbearance of her nature. The reverse side of our ignorance, she thought, is their knowledge. The more the first can be stressed, the more the second will come glowing through. They, of course, while superior in rank and worldly endowment, do thoroughly understand the mentality of the *contadini*. The pair of them were positively oozing with self-congratulation.

'Also these people is *furbo*, cunning,' the professor said.

'Well,' Cecilia said, 'We are not *furbi*, but we are not so stupid that we don't know a viper's nest of blackmailers when we see one.'

This was the first time she had intervened directly in the discussion. She had spoken in English and Harold felt cheered and encouraged. 'Yes, by Jove,' he said. 'Blackmail. Tell them that word in Italian, sweetheart, make sure they understand it.'

'*Ricatto.*'

'No, no,' Lorenzetti said. '*Ricatto*, no, it is not a question of money. The Checchetti are unhappy and also *perplessi* . . .'

'Perplexed,' Cecilia said.

'Perplexed, yes. So naturally they ask protection to *la legge*, the law. And *la legge* says two metres.'

'Naturally, eh?' Chapman was silent for some moments. The suggestion was that the Checchetti, being weak and defenceless, were right to protect themselves from the oppression of the powerful in the only way known to them. He looked at Lorenzetti's face, close-shaven, beaky, smiling still with that hypocritical sympathy for the underdog. And as he did so he experienced a fierce joy: for the first time in all this business he had found someone he understood. 'Not a question of money, eh?' he said.

Mrs Lorenzetti, perhaps sensing an increase of tension in the atmosphere, now spoke at some length in Italian, smiling and turning her head coquettishly as she did so.

'What does she say?'

Cecilia's mouth, which tended naturally to turn down at the corners, showed now a marked increase in this tendency. 'She says you have to fall in with their ways. She says she is a teacher but when she comes out here she plays the country girl and they love her.'

'Good God.'

'I know these people,' Lorenzetti said. 'It is not about money, it is about pride. Self-respecting, dignity.'

'So what do you suggest we should do?' Cecilia asked.

Lorenzetti's answer was prompt. 'Do? Give them the money.'

Harold uttered a laugh of genuine amusement. 'So it is not the money that matters to them, it is pride. So we give them the money.' He paused, looked again at Lorenzetti's face, saw the self-interest written there, understood it perfectly, shared it completely. 'I'll tell you what,' he said. 'You are obviously concerned to protect the feelings of these people, these sturdy peasants and so forth, and obviously of course it is not the loss of your rent that concerns you, or fear of losing your tenant, but the principle of the whole thing which makes you come here as an ambassador and sacrifice your time and so on, trying to pour oil on troubled waters, etc. . . .'

The professor had not been able to follow this rather elaborate phrasing and Cecilia translated it as best she could, at once alarmed and exhilarated by the broad sarcasm and by the gleam that had come to her husband's eye.

'And since you don't think receipts are all that important and so on,' Harold said, 'here is what I suggest. With the Checchetti it is not money but pride, with you it is not money but principle. So why don't *you* give them the money and satisfy their pride and your principle both at the same time?'

He saw this register with Lorenzetti, saw the look of incomprehension quickly assumed. The blighter was not going to get away with pretending he had not understood. 'You'd better translate,' he said to Cecilia.

She did so, and as she saw the tightness of rage come to the man's face – the first genuine expression it had shown – she felt a rush of gladness and release. This insolence of Harold's was far beyond her own resources but as interpreter she felt she had shared in it. And it was absolutely right. Harold had cut through hypocrisy to the heart of the matter. These people had been answered as they deserved. She barely glanced at the Lorenzetti as they made their offended farewells. Hers was a nature that needed to admire in proportion as she loved. And for quite some time now – longer, in fact, than she liked to think – she had not been finding it very easy to admire Harold. Occasions therefore had to be seized. 'Oh, Harold,' she said, 'you were really *good* there, with those awful people.'

But Harold's satisfaction had faded quickly. As he watched their visitors walk away he knew that yet another prop had collapsed in his policy of good neighbour relations.

Ritter worked steadily, with saw and billhook and clippers, clearing the bramble and ivy that lay along the crest of the slope. The work was more difficult, more laborious than he had thought. He wanted to clear the whole of the gully on his side of the stream. But the ground was steep, footing was difficult, there were thickets of thorn and scrub oak which had to be sawn off close to the roots. He had to crouch in awkward positions with his short-bladed saw and the thin branches whipped back sometimes and struck him painfully across the face. He could hear the unchanging voice of the water below him, like a message that would be repeated with endless patience until he could understand it. Coded language this too, like the songs of birds round him, the whirring of insects, the dry rustle of last year's thistle and chicory.

A passion for order grew in him as he hacked and sawed and sliced, a rage to clear this stupid and barbaric tangle, to reclaim the land, to offer it again to air and light. This feeling grew as he worked, carrying him beyond his strength, beyond the clear message of his body. Only with the fading of the light did he stop the work and by then he was exhausted. The solitude, the dulling effects of labour, were like a drug to him. Each night he slept for nine or ten hours without moving.

As he scrambled and sweated in the May sunshine, memories came to him, unbidden at first, afterwards sought for with a slow persistence in keeping with the dogged nature of his work. The memories went back to his earlier childhood, before the days in Rome. But they were scattered and wordless. Words began with his father and the white flashes on the collar of his father's uniform. Posted to Rome as Intelligence Liaison Officer almost as soon as Italy came into the war, Captain Ritter had brought wife and child to live with him early in 1941. If he had not brought me to Italy, Ritter thought, I would probably not have become an interpreter at all, my life would have taken a different course altogether. It was contact with another language at this early age. If you knew words you could earn approval, make friends. And both his father and his mother had encouraged him to make friends with Giuseppe.

Ritter paused and sat back on his heels. This cramped work and the difficult footing on the slope made him sweat freely and he felt the prickle of it on his brow and neck where the sun touched him. Yes, he thought, my father encouraged it. He wanted me to learn Italian, he had the sincerest respect for Italian art and culture. He hated no one, no race or people. He was an idealist. Not even the Jews. He simply saw no place for them in the new European Order.

My parents then that gave me this multiple gift – the Italian language, the friendship with Giuseppe, the direction of a career. But the words that poisoned the gift were in German. *A return to the true values of Catholic tradition, German energy and spirituality informing a new hegemony* . . . A dream long dead – nobody talked like that any more. But the poison was potent still, the gripe of it had accompanied him ever since. It was not a question of hypocrisy, still less of lying – that was the stuff of every day. It was a terrible reclothing of reality, something that seemed like madness now to him. His father had believed himself to be explaining important matters to his son when he said that 335 had to be taken and shot in the back of the neck in order to safeguard Germany's high purposes. Not once, not even by implication, had he conveyed any sense that this killing had been done out of panic and revenge.

Which of them, Ritter wondered again, had been the one

Giuseppe called uncle? Doctors, lawyers, priests, army officers, a hundred or so Jews, a dozen foreigners, a boy of fourteen. Taken from the German section of the Queen of Heaven prison or the cellars of the SS Command in Via Tasso, where they had been held for reasons described as racial or political-military. All completely innocent of any involvement in the *Attentat* of the day before.

Almost certainly not his real uncle at all. If there had been a family connection the authorities would have known it. Giuseppe would have never been allowed to come up and play, his mother would not have had the place as concierge. A friend who visited discreetly. Perhaps someone who had lived in the building before it was requisitioned by the military. Someone, in any case, whom Giuseppe loved, who had been kind to him. It had been a well-guarded secret until that afternoon. Ritter himself had had his first knowledge of it from the tears on his friend's face. 'They have killed him,' Giuseppe had said, '*l'hanno ammazzato*' – this first announcement of a death ever made to him had kept the cadence of Italian in Ritter's mind. Then the pause, the tear-stained face, the mouth drawn with weeping and the beginnings of hate. 'It was you that killed him, *l'avete ammazzato voi.*'

It was in the same terms that he had blurted the accusation later, in the room his father used as a study. The desk had papers on it and a vase with a spray of almond blossom; some of the petals had fallen on the polished surface of the desk. White walls, white petals, the white flashes on the collar of the uniform . . .

'Giuseppe says we have killed his uncle.' With the words his eyes had filled with tears, Giuseppe's tears, because he had felt no loss or sorrow himself, only the shock of being accused and the wish to hear his father laugh the thing away and say it was nonsense. Instead there had come this rhetoric of high aspirations and noble aims, this first dim sense of words somehow slithering and twisting away.

Ritter sighed and leaned forward to grasp with gloved hand at the stem of a bramble. Where the earth was loose he was able sometimes to pull old brambles out by the roots and he had made it a habit to try this before cutting them. This one resisted and he searched around for the clippers, which he was constantly mislaying. It had taken him years to realize that his father had known nothing whatever about this uncle. It had not been possible to understand this at the time because his father had made no sign; not a syllable, not a flicker of expression, at least none that a child could recognize. His father's combination of speech and silence that afternoon had been Ritter's first experience of betrayal but the hurt of it had been long delayed. It had seemed then that the only treachery was his own: if he had not spoken, Giuseppe and his mother would not have been sent away.

He had never seen either of them again. That same afternoon they had disappeared from the building. He was told they had gone away – it was all the explanation he ever had. The basement remained empty and the glass cubicle was occupied by a uniformed orderly, who had little to do because all visitors were checked by the armed guard at the door. Kurt was this orderly's name. He was very clever with his hands. Kurt had made him a model Stuka bomber out of matchsticks.

With the passing of the years the interest Mancini took in the psychology of his clients had increased as his belief in the wisdom of the law had declined. As he regarded Harold and Cecilia Chapman, who were sitting on the other side of his large and opulent desk, he thought that he had rarely seen a couple so contrasting in temperament and style. There was the tenacious, terrier-like man, with his stretched smile and his occasional dry laugh, like a cough, and his conflicting appetites for victory and virtue; and the faint-voiced, sensitive woman, with her manner of shrinking kindness and her mouth set in an expression of slight repugnance or distaste. There was a coolness in her gaze, a quality of perception. If I were the husband, Mancini thought, I would be wary of that. But of course he thinks it only exists to support him. 'So they are threatening to narrow the road to two metres,' he said, 'and to mark the width by using *picchetti*, stakes.'

'That is correct,' Chapman said. 'That is what this Bruno, the son-in-law, said at any rate.'

'Well, well.' Mancini joined the fingers of his hands to form a bridge and looked benignly over it at the Chapmans. 'Let us hope they do it.'

For some moments Harold Chapman could not believe that he had heard this properly. He looked at the lawyer's pale broad face with its luxuriant eyebrows and wide-open, curiously impassive eyes. 'What on earth do you mean?'

Mancini sat forward and lowered his hands to the desk. 'Mr and Mrs Chapman,' he said, 'I will confess to you that at the beginning I was not so much interested in your problem with these Checchetti. A little story of a wall that falls down, an offer of compensation in proper form . . . You are my clients, I serve your interests, all the same it is boring, no? But when they refused to sign for the money, everything changes.' He paused, looking from one to the other of the Chapmans. 'From that moment they are in another category. They become criminals, Mrs Chapman.'

As usual when he looked directly at her, Cecilia felt obliged to respond. 'They must always have been like that, they could not have changed overnight.'

'No, of course you are right, they are the same always, but I did not understand it before. After all, a little blackmail, what is that? People see a prospect of gain, they use what means they can. That is the way of the world. But these Checchetti had already succeeded, they had the offer of a reasonable sum. All they had to do was sign for the money, agree to make no further claim. This they have refused to do. I can only conclude that they are intending to use you as a milk-cow.'

With his eyes still upon her, Cecilia felt – ridiculously – that she was beginning to blush. 'Such a mean thing,' she said.

'Yes,' Chapman said, 'they are hardly big-timers.'

Mancini shrugged. 'The scale is not so important, the mentality is always the same. These are not usual country people, they risk something for the sake of something more.'

'What is to be done then?' Chapman said. 'Get the police on to them?'

Mancini sighed. 'Always this haste for police in the Anglo-Saxon people. The Checchetti are ignorant and they have got two things wrong. The first of these concerns the width of the road. The daughter, I have learned, she works as a cleaning woman in the offices of the town hall, she will have seen something, perhaps some old regulations governing the width of the road.'

'That is what Bruno meant by their important contacts in the *comune*,' Cecilia said.

'The width of the road is established by usage. The law accepts the argument of *de facto* and the present width is two and a half metres. The second thing they seem not to know is that while it is legal to put markers on the road under certain circumstances, these must not be raised above the level of the road itself, so these *picchetti* they are threatening you with are entirely contrary to regulations.'

To Chapman's face there had come a broad grin, a thing fortunately rare as it was not attractive. 'By Jove,' he said, 'hoist with their own petard. It is true what the Bard says, "a little knowledge is a dangerous thing".'

' "Learning",' Mancini said.

'I beg your pardon?'

'You have misquoted. "A little *learning* is a dangerous thing", that is what your poet says.'

Chapman's grin vanished abruptly. To be corrected by a foreigner on a point of English literature was really too much. 'Just a minute now,' he said.

'Mr Mancini is right, Harold,' Cecilia said. 'It is a line from Alexander Pope.'

'Well, of course, I knew that.'

'So we wait for them to do what they have threatened to do.' Cecilia spoke mainly in order to give her husband time to recover from his discomfort. 'Then we call the police and report them.'

'That would be one way, yes,' the lawyer said. 'But it would be better to order something, some wood for example. Have you a chimney?'

The Chapmans looked blankly at him for some moments without speaking.

'Not chimney, that is wrong, I mean fireplace. Have you a fireplace or stoves that burn wood?'

'Why, yes,' Chapman said. 'Both, as a matter of fact.'

'And a woodshed?'

'Yes.'

'Good, then you can order a load of wood.'

'But it is nearly the end of May.'

'Never mind, it will be well dried out for the winter. As soon as these Checchetti put in the stakes you order a load of wood. At this time of the year the wood people, they are not busy, they will deliver maybe the same day or the one after. With luck the driver will be prevented by these stakes from passing. It might even be that the Checchetti will threaten to report him if he tries to pass – they are people who easily use threats. He will listen to them, probably, since lorry drivers try to avoid close inspection by the authorities. It is ingrained in them, whether their papers and vehicles are in good order or not.'

Mancini sat back and folded his arms. His face had been impassive hitherto, but now he allowed himself a discreet smile. 'Obstructing the road, using threats, illegally depriving you of your wood. The driver could be called as a witness.'

Cecilia had a renewed sense of something ageless in Mancini, something that had never been young and would never be old. 'Then we have them,' she heard her husband say.

'Then we have them, shrewd observation,' Mancini said. 'They will think at first that the law is on their side, but they will discover their mistake and then they will be frightened. We will generously forbear to press charges, but in view of the in-convenience caused by the delay in the delivery of the wood we will have to reconsider our offer of financial help.'

The lawyer's smile had gone now. His face had returned to its usual impassivity. 'It is beautiful, isn't it?' he said. 'More beautiful than going to the police. These days I am interested in beauty more and more.'

Monti was working at home. He had brought his small table up against the window so as to make the most of the remaining daylight; too much use of the table-lamp troubled his eyes, causing them to smart painfully and run with thin tears.

He glanced up frequently as he worked. It was the time of day that he liked best, the time between sunset and dusk, when for a brief while colours were deepened and the slopes of the hills were visited by a light uniquely radiant and soft. It was this light that he waited for. He had seen it nowhere else but in Umbria. It came suddenly, shortly before the onset of darkness, like a gentle assertion of some value in danger of being forgotten. What was it? he wondered. Certitude, peace, the light of reason? An illusion in any case. What we call beauty or morality no more than the sense of shape, an illusion of design . . .

With some reluctance he lowered his head once more to the page. He was reading among the early chronicles of the city and *contado* of Perugia in an endeavour to trace the course of events which had made the leading members of the Baglioni family, for some half-century or so, before they were finally crushed by Pope Paul III in 1540, the princes of the city. In this mesh of shifting loyalties and incessant intrigue design was difficult to establish. One constant thread was the fertility of the family, the tendency to produce large numbers of male children. Another was the regularity with which these murdered one another, a process culminating on a warm July night in the year 1500, when several of the chief members of the clan had been butchered in their sleeping quarters by a band of conspirators recruited and led by

99

their own relatives. Night of the Great Betrayal, it was called in the chronicles, a phrase that lingered strangely in Monti's mind.

Order he still sought, however, a principle that might seem to give meaning to this bloody welter, something that would work on the past as the evening light did when it visited the landscape. It had come to him increasingly of late that it was some sort of escape route he was looking for; he wanted to be detached from history, rescued.

The earliest reference he had so far found was to one Lodovico Baglioni, who had come to Perugia in 1162 as an obscure knight in the train of the Emperor Barbarossa and stayed on and founded his line, no different then or later, no more endowed with qualities of mind or character than the other great families of Perugia, the degli Oddi, the Ranieri, the Arcipreti. All these had fought for pre-eminence in the centuries following. Then the two most powerful, the Baglioni and the degli Oddi, had become locked in a blood feud that lasted 150 years, following upon the treacherous murder of Messer degli Oddi by members of the Baglioni family in the December of 1331. That killing had been of a type by now familiar to Monti: five or six had lain in wait for Messer degli Oddi and cut him down before he had time to draw a weapon.

The light he had been waiting for came now, falling across the land at a time when there was no longer a visible source of illumination in the sky, so that it seemed like a property of the landscape itself, fulfilling some ancient contract between earth and rock and plant. Tentative at first, it strengthened slowly, falling with a soft blaze of yellow on the flowering broom that lay in swathes on the hillside opposite the house.

He sighed to himself and shifted back in his chair so that he could see higher up, to the crests of the nearer hills. The beauty of the light was in the sense it gave of a visitation. The experience of it was like the experience of understanding something.

He thought of Laura, of the words they had said at different times, their quarrels, their lovemaking. Like a kind of landscape. Their marriage, the years together, his present loneliness, formed a single aspect and this aspect needed a unifying light. Light there must be, he insisted to himself, some key, some guiding principle. Otherwise I am thrashing about in the same blind ditch as the Baglioni, and so is Laura too.

It was with an obscure sense of rescuing them both from such dreadful wallowing that he began now to think of his wife in some of her particular physical expressions, her walk with the toes turning slightly inwards, her habit when puzzled or perplexed of brushing the back of her hand across her brow, beginning at the temple, like a cat washing itself. Laughter came easily to her but her face when unguarded had lines of sadness about the mouth, more than sadness, something like pain; and because of this her laughter seemed like a conquest continually renewed . . .

He sat thus while the radiance faded from the landscape and the accustomed sense of loss grew with the beginnings of the dark. He was roused by a tapping at his door. When he went to open it he found his neighbour Fabio on the doorstep, standing rather close to the wall, as if sheltering there or listening for sounds from inside. Monti was struck by the pallor of his face in the half-light and by what seemed an unnatural stillness about him, a quality of containment. It was unusual that he should visit without a phone call or any warning – they were not on such close terms. However, apart from bidding him good evening Fabio said nothing at all, merely stood there in silence. After a moment Monti asked him in, leading the way into the living-room, where he had been working. At the sight of the papers and books on the table, Fabio began to apologize for the disturbance he was causing, accompanying this with an odd little gesture, almost of helplessness as it seemed to Monti. The bookish recognize the presence or absence of this quality in others quite soon and Monti saw at once from Fabio's manner that he was not a man much given to reading or studying.

'You do not disturb me, I am glad to be given a reason for pausing in my work,' Monti said in the tone of grave courtesy usual with him. He felt the awkwardness of the situation, which was increased by the fact that Fabio said nothing further for the moment, simply stood there tensely, as if containing the desire to break into violent gesture. Monti asked him to sit but with them both seated at opposite sides of the fireplace the sense of awkwardness seemed to grow. Laura would have known what to say, Monti thought. She would have known how to set this man at his ease. His visitor was smartly dressed, he noticed, in a linen jacket and a pale-green shirt and a carefully knotted tie. 'Can I offer you some coffee?' he said. 'Or a glass of wine?'

'Wine, yes, thank you.'

'I have some of the local Trasimeno wine that is not bad.' He went through into the kitchen, returned with the opened bottle and two glasses, poured out the wine. In the face of Fabio's continuing silence he began to talk about his work, to explain why he had been glad, in a certain sense, to be interrupted. Reading Perugian history was cumulatively depressing, often seeming to be no more than a chronicle of crimes. 'Of course,' he said, 'any study of history can seem like that at times, but in Perugia you get it in a concentrated form. Not a concentration of incidents or events, I don't mean that exactly, but it is the constant repetition of a single pattern, power gained by conspiracy and crime, maintained for a certain time by oppression, bloodily yielded in the end to some new gang.'

He raised his glass with a murmured salutation and drank. He watched Fabio taste the wine, watched him move his head very slightly from side to side in the manner of one uncertain about the quality. It was a small gesture and probably habitual but it seemed graceless to Monti, after his recommendation. For a man still relatively young, Fabio seemed too set in his ways, too obtrusive with judgement, even in his present disturbance – that he was disturbed about something was clear enough. There was nothing for it but to go on talking, give him time. 'Some new gang,' he repeated. 'It is the cyclic effect that is depressing. Centuries and centuries of it. Fashions change and modes of speech and styles of architecture, but the murder factor remains constant. There doesn't seem to be much in the way of redeeming features. Perhaps I have been more sensitive to it lately. It makes one feel, you know, pretty hopeless about our human prospects.'

'It is not much different today,' Fabio said. 'Look at Italy. Is this a democracy?' He paused for a moment and his eyes widened under their thick brows. 'Arturo has gone,' he said, 'he has left me, he is in Naples.'

'I see.' Monti rose to fill Fabio's glass. This was it then. He was rather at a loss to know what to say, also troubled by a certain sense of surprise – the two men had seemed so close. But that is how Laura and I would have struck people, right up to the moment she went . . . 'When did it happen?' he asked, an odd query, as he at once realized, inappropriate; desertion was not an event in itself, merely the culmination of an obscure process – his own experience had taught him this.

'I had a phone call from him this morning. He went to Rome two days ago. He said he wanted to go alone, he was tired, he needed a break.' Fabio's lips twisted at the falsehood of this. 'I let him go. Then he rings me from Naples to say that everything is over, he is not coming back.'

'I see, yes.' Monti nodded, putting as much comprehension as he could into it. A bare understanding of the words was all he could offer, at least for the moment; he did not know enough to attempt more. He had noted the phrase about granting

permission. It had seemed authoritarian to him, rather disagreeably so; but then, he was an outsider.

'We had a little quarrel before he left,' Fabio said. 'Nothing
much, a few words. He went to buy some chicken breasts for
supper and instead of going to Ellera he went to the little shop
here. We always go to Ellera to buy our meat. I had told him
never to buy anything in that shop.'

'You mean the butcher in the village? I always get my meat
there.'

'You are making a bad mistake. I wouldn't put my nose in
there, they don't keep the place clean.'

'Well,' Monti said mildly, 'I haven't noticed any dirt there, but
I often don't notice things.' He paused for a moment and some
sense of the other man's intolerance had sharpened his tone
when he spoke again. 'I've been going there for four months now
and no symptoms of poisoning so far.'

'Stop while you are in time,' Fabio said. 'You think it is nothing but for me everything has to be done in the right way, it has
always been so. Besides, we had agreed together not to go to that
shop. And still he went. I have been at home all day, working
outside. When it began to get dark I could not stay there alone. I
came here.' He hesitated for a moment then went on, in a tone
of deeper feeling, 'There is no one else living nearby, no one who
would understand . . . I remembered your visit to us with your
wife, how well we got on together.'

'That was a very pleasant evening.' He was relieved that Fabio
had not yet remarked on Laura's absence. Tact perhaps – or
perhaps he was too stricken to notice. Monti reached for the
bottle. 'Some more wine?'

'I do not want to intrude.'

'No, you were right to come here.' Fabio had not been able to
bear the thought of night falling and himself alone in the house.
He had come to seek company. An impulse quite contrary to

mine, Monti thought. Since she left I have avoided everyone, turned in upon myself. Nothing so much marks people out as these reactions. Fabio had dressed for this visit to a stranger, changed out of his working clothes into pale-green shirt and dark-red tie and linen jacket and stone-coloured jeans. This punctilio in the midst of distress was touching to Monti, disturbing too, indicating a mind that ran in grooves. 'We are in the same situation,' he said. 'My wife left me last November, not long after that evening when we came to you. She went back to Turin.'

It was the first time he had made this admission to any living soul. He had expected to feel, and in the moment or two before speaking had actually felt, a sort of preliminary shrinking and shame; but the words when they came brought an immediate feeling of liberation. 'She has somebody there,' he said, going a stage further.

'I am sorry.' Some colour had come back into Fabio's face, either from the wine or the kindling of these confessions. From something in his tone and look, Monti had the impression that his visitor was rather put out by this intrusion of a rival sorrow and he felt an obscure resentment at the injustice of this. Unhappiness strengthens our prejudices, including those we are not always aware of or willing to admit. Monti could not say what he privately felt, which was that wives counted more in the scale than homosexual companions. 'Laura and I have been married for twelve years,' he said in a tone of slight reproof.

'Arturo and I have been together for fifteen.' Fabio paused a moment, then turned his head aside. 'There is more than just the leaving.' He swallowed with a pronounced movement of the throat. 'He has taken the house.'

'Taken the house?' In the competition of loss that had been developing between them, Monti was compelled to recognize this as a winning move. 'Just a minute,' he said. The bottle was now empty and he went into the kitchen to get another. 'How could he take the house?' he asked on his return. 'Isn't it owned jointly?'

Fabio shook his head. 'It was in my name. It was my money that bought it. But I signed it over to Arturo, we made a deed of sale, a legal document signed and witnessed.'

'But why?'

'It was a way to save money, or so I thought.'

Monti listened while his visitor explained the matter. Various concessions would have become available to them . . . Reduced taxes, increased subsidies. He went on at some length, describing the advantages, perhaps in an effort not to seem too much duped. But no hoped-for gain could cover the error of judgement, only make it seem grosser. Perhaps becoming aware of this, Fabio said, 'It was a blunder, yes, but I trusted him. Now he phones me and says he has already been to a lawyer and started proceedings to gain possession of the house.'

The habitual severity and melancholy of his face had softened with hurt as he spoke. Monti listened aghast. Arturo must have planned the whole thing in advance, not just to desert Fabio, not just to secure his own share, but to rob his partner of his home, to take everything from him, all the years of work, all the security of the future. It was hard to think of a worse treachery, taking someone's love and using it against him.

'It denies the time we had together,' Fabio said. 'If he could do that, it is hard to think he could ever have cared for me. That is what hurts so much, this poisoning of the past.'

They were well into the second bottle now. Wine and sorrow were combining to make Fabio less guarded than he would have normally been in talking to a man who was not gay. And now, for the first time, he showed a closeness to tears. 'I gave him everything,' he said. 'He had no future, a low-life character, hanging round the bars, part-time waiter, part-time whore. I took him away from all that, I brought him to live with me, and this is how he repays me, he schemes to take the roof from over my head.'

Gifts are two-edged, Monti reflected, as he looked at the other's face, so convinced of betrayal. He had brought this youth from the bars of Naples to the rural depths of Umbria. In making gifts we think that we cancel all that is negative. Everything is irradiated by the simple act of giving, like the light he had just waited for and watched, all-enveloping, as beautiful on the barren hillside as on terraces and orchards. We think – as Fabio obviously thought – that it is a light renewed every day. But how had Arturo experienced it, this gift? From day to day, how had he felt it? The scheming to take the house was treacherous and base; but the leaving Monti thought he could understand. Fabio did not seem to him very flexible or imaginative; it might become intolerable to be trapped in such a man's vision of things. Perhaps Laura too had felt in some way imprisoned . . . 'My work was perhaps too important to me,' he said. 'I am obsessive about work, I always have been so. Perhaps I did the same, made what I thought were gifts into a form of oppression.'

'The same?' Fabio frowned slightly. 'I did not make him many gifts, I bought him occasionally something, a silk scarf, a tiepin, little things.'

'I was speaking figuratively,' Monti said. 'Have some more wine.'

'Take a beautiful car,' Fabio said. 'Everything perfect, the engineering, the bodywork. I always loved cars, I loved racing. When I heard that I could not race any longer because of the damage to my hand, I wept.'

This recalling of another loss brought tears to his eyes now. He paused and swallowed, then after a moment went on again. 'As time goes by you get scratches, the paintwork dulls, the undercarriage suffers from corrosion. You do not feel the same about the car, there is not that sense of perfection any longer. It becomes a different relationship. What I want to say is that with Arturo this never happened.'

'Bodywork still perfect,' Monti said rather vaguely – he cared nothing for cars and could not imagine having a relationship with one. He thought of Laura's body, past its youth now, the dearer to him for that. The comparison was somehow typical of Fabio; but it was through a house, not a car, that he had been cheated and betrayed, the house he and Arturo had lived in together, a thing of stone and mortar, yes, but also an abode of spirit, a shelter from the world in a sense more than physical. Even this rented house where I am sitting now, he thought, drably furnished, still unfamiliar. While she was here with me it was a dwelling place, when she walked out she left it gaping open.

'I am not so interested in cars,' he said. 'People who live together, it is not in a car that they live. People who live together build a house around them day by day. But the house –'

'I will kill him,' Fabio said. 'He will not take everything from me and live to laugh at me with someone else.'

He uttered this threat quietly but with complete seriousness and Monti felt sure he meant it. The eyes of Fabio had a hunter's steadiness about them; they were the eyes of a risk-taker. His own were mild and evasive, eyes of one who submits. Why do I always slide away into speculation? he wondered. I want to tell this man that I look at the things she left behind, a belt, an evening bag, a piece of jewellery, I take these things and look at them and want her back. The reason I don't speak of it is that I am afraid of his contempt . . .

The wine was working on him now. He was on the point of braving this imagined contempt by telling Fabio that there had been times since her going when he had taken articles of Laura's clothing and held them closely pressed against him. He was saved from the confession – a rescue for which afterwards he was profoundly grateful – by a tapping at the door. The windows were unshuttered still and when he glanced up he saw wavering arcs of torchlight in the darkness outside.

He opened the door to find the figures of a man and woman, both vaguely familiar, standing at the threshold. 'Chapman, Harold Chapman,' the man said, extending his hand. 'This is my wife, Cecilia.'

'Ah, yes, we are neighbours.' Monti read English easily but spoke it badly, with a strong Italian accent. 'Please come in.'

Inside, the Chapmans were introduced to Fabio, who, by contrast, did not read English and had no idea of grammar but spoke with a passable accent, picked up during his years on the motor-racing circuit.

'I hope we are not intruding,' Chapman said.

'But no, not at all. You will take a glass of wine?'

This involved opening a third bottle. Chapman, without being very sensitive to others, was observant in certain ways. He had noted the empty bottles, the vinous atmosphere, the sense of close colloquy, the absence of women. Had he stumbled on a pair of poofs? His attempts to enlist support for his battle with the Checchetti had been marked by difficulty from the start. First the demented German and now these two. 'Well, here's how,' he said, raising his glass. '*Salute*. I am making a point of going round and seeing everyone. Everyone that depends on this road, I mean. So far I've only been able to see the German chap at the end, Ritter. Now the situation has been complicated by the fact that the Checchetti are threatening to put these stakes in and narrow it down to two metres.'

This would not have been very clear to his listeners, even in Italian. Chapman always assumed more knowledge than those he spoke to could possibly have. Cecilia had to spend some time explaining things, which she did quietly, with a faint, defensive smile. She was wishing she had found the resolution to refuse to accompany Harold on this outing.

She was not feeling well disposed towards Harold in any case. They had been that day on a visit to Città di Castello, an ancient and beautiful Umbrian town set among green hills above the valley of the Tiber. They had lunched in a small trattoria, spent an hour in the medieval maze of streets and squares enclosed within the city walls, and afterwards gone to see the collection of paintings in the municipal gallery.

It was here that Harold had shown a side of himself not at all attractive. Up to then things had been all right, more or less. Harold had studied the guidebook and was well fortified with facts. He knew the town went back to remote antiquity, had been a centre of the Umbri and then of the Etruscans, that it had been a Roman municipality, that Pliny the Younger had owned a villa in the region, that the ruling family in the fifteenth century had been the Vitelli, that the city had come under the control of Cesare Borgia and thence passed into the hands of the Church.

All this he knew and a good deal more. But when they went to visit the gallery, which – as Cecilia informed him – housed the most important collection in the region after the National Gallery in Perugia, something got into him, some spirit of perverse resistance. He showed himself unwilling to accept Cecilia's judgements about the paintings. He made disparaging remarks about paintings she loved. When they stood before the huge painting of *The Madonna and Child with Six Angels* by the anonymous Maestro di Città di Castello, instead of seeing the otherworldliness of it, the way all the faces seemed dazed and stricken with the power of spirit, he scoffed at the diminutive monk kneeling in prayer in one corner. 'The whole thing is completely out of proportion,' he said. When they looked at the painting by Giorgio di Andrea di Bartolo, which shows the Madonna giving suck to the Infant Christ, Harold sniggered at the total roundness of Mary's left breast and the way it was detached from the rest of her clothed and composed body, like a pale, round fruit which the Child holds up between them in both hands. 'Good catch!' Harold said. 'Well held, sir!' At that ribald moment the missionary in Cecilia had understood that Harold was hardening his heart against her, that he wanted to hurt her with his unbelief.

But it was as they were about to leave the gallery that the real offence was caused. They were in the last room, which was rather small, with a long, curtained window and some paintings of the late sixteenth century on the walls, classical themes, not very distinguished. As they were turning to go, an attractive young woman, one of the gallery attendants, had come towards them and begun to relate in English a legend associated with this room.

The gallery, she said, was originally a mansion belonging to the ruling Vitelli family, lords of the city in the fifteenth century. One Alessandro Vitelli had owned it but had lived there hardly at all. He had been a soldier of fortune and followed the wars, leaving the vast house empty save for a few servants and a former mistress, a courtesan, past her first youth. The window of the room looked down over the street, which was just inside the city walls – the attendant raised the curtain to show them. Left alone here, the woman had enticed young men of the town, lowering ropes of silk so they could climb up to her chamber. When they had pleasured her she killed them. There had been a secret door – the attendant showed them the outline of it in the wall. Through this the slain lovers had been bundled, landing by means of some kind of chute outside the city walls. 'So she escapes the bad fame,' the attendant said, smiling. Her English was not perfect but it was fluent enough – Cecilia could see that the girl had told this story to visitors quite often before, that she was trying to add something to their visit, to make it more memorable.

Harold, however, had not seen it in this light. He had, with

III

what Cecilia could only regard as gross vulgarity, appeared to think that this story had been told for him alone, that it was in the nature of an advance on the part of this attractive young woman. He had wanted to dwell on certain details, in particular the sexual energy and Messalina-like properties of the courtesan. 'Maybe she gave them such a good time it was worth dying for,' he said, with something close to a leer. 'She should have found a man who could satisfy her and keep his mouth shut.' And he had smiled that stretched smile of his and looked rather deeply at the attendant and it had been obvious to Cecilia that he saw himself as this well-endowed and discreet fellow climbing up the rope and the attendant as the lady at the window. Worse still, terribly shaming, it had been obvious to the young woman too. Her manner had changed, become more distant. Her smile had disappeared. As they left the gallery together Cecilia knew that to her dying day she would not forget the ugliness of spirit that her husband had shown in the beautiful town of Città di Castello.

'We want to make it clear that it is not our fault,' he was saying now. 'If they do put the stakes in, that is.'

'But the people doesn't believe the Checchetti,' Fabio said, when he had understood. 'Everybody knows them. In the time I am living here they quarrel with everyone, they have no friends.'

'That doesn't surprise me,' Chapman said. Nevertheless he was somewhat put out. This general distrust of the Checchetti rather undermined the value of his campaign and the worth of the victory that would ultimately be his. But nothing could affect his underlying euphoria, inspired as he still was by the masterly boldness of Mancini's plan. 'I just want you to know that the situation is well in hand,' he said. 'That blackmailing crew are about to overreach themselves.' He would have liked to go into it further, explain the beauty of the trap, but he was afraid of ruining things – it might get back to the Checchetti. So he contented himself with praising the author of the scheme. 'We have this marvellous lawyer,' he said. 'His manner is a bit unusual but in my opinion he has a touch of genius. He is an absolute wizard, believe me.'

'What is his name?' Fabio asked. 'I think I am needing a lawyer myself very soon.'

It was during this period, while the Chapmans were waiting to see whether the Checchetti intended to carry out their threat, that Blemish and his chosen builder, Esposito – a curly-haired, smiling man with a gold crucifix round his neck and a mobile phone constantly to hand – decided to start closing the trap around the Greens. A certain delicacy of touch was needed for this and Blemish was worried that his partner might somehow bungle things. Esposito was not much endowed with that ability to look ahead and take thought for the morrow which Blemish regarded as one of the fundamental requirements of civilization. Esposito took a short-term view of things. Get what you can while you can more or less summed up his philosophy. Blemish was afraid he might show too much crude haste and put the Greens off in some way.

Both men knew that a point could be reached, a psychological point of balance, at which the client realized that his control of the situation was slipping away, that he had laid out too much money to begin over again with another builder, that there was no alternative – short of walking away from the house altogether – but to go wading on in the hope of somehow ending up with a home beautifully restored along the lines agreed. By the time he came to see the vanity of this hope and refused further payment, he would have been relieved of a good half of his disposable capital.

This of course was the model operation, conducted under optimum conditions. Things did not always go so smoothly. But it was something to aspire to, as Blemish said, it was the kind of thing to aim at. Above all, it required patience. These things he tried to explain to Mildred, the companion of his life, while he was waiting for his supper of Dragon's Teeth and decorated meatballs in their cavernous kitchen. 'Extraction,' he said, 'that is the name of the game. It is a process of extraction.' He stretched his neck and blinked softly, watching Mildred's lumbering yet purposeful movements about the stove. 'You need finesse for it. You need professionalism. That is why Esposito will never amount to much.' He paused to drink some Chianti Classico from his long-stemmed, goblet-type glass – they had recently bought a set of these in Perugia, attracted by the medieval shape. 'I am what you might call a gradualist in business dealing,' he said. 'You have got to keep yourself above it, you have got to take an overall view. I am talking about detachment, Milly. The true professional is always detached. Without detachment there is no mobility, there is no play of mind. The Greens aren't detached at all, you see. They have set their hearts on a piece of converted residential property.'

Mildred turned towards him, ladle in hand. 'But dearest, we have set our hearts on something, haven't we? We have set our hearts on a medieval restaurant and swimming pool.'

'True, my love, quite true, but that is at a remove, it is not in dispute, not at risk. For us the Greens represent just a few square metres of *cotto* more or a few less. We can afford to wait but they can't.' Blemish paused and his narrow mouth tightened with disapproval. 'The Greens are old,' he said, 'but they cling to this idea of a future. That is what the house means to them, a future. It is quite different with Esposito, he doesn't believe in tomorrow, he wants everything now.'

In the event Esposito spent most of the time talking on his mobile telephone. The Greens had returned home in late afternoon to keep the appointment, having spent the day at Sansepolcro. Their life during this period was a strange alternation between beauty abroad and chaos at home. The first phase of the excavation work on the ground floor had been completed but bags of cement and heaps of gravel and sand and broken masonry lay everywhere about. There were still holes in the walls waiting to be filled in. The roof had not been repaired yet. Pipes had been broken here and there in the course of the work and a pervasive smell of drainage hung about the house.

To escape from all this, and from the dust and noise of the work itself, the Greens devised a game of visits to the ancient towns of Umbria and Tuscany. Like most couples who live very closely together over long periods, they were given to private pacts and accustomed jokes and time-honoured observances. They were also – what is perhaps less usual – quite prompt to add to the existing stock according to circumstance and situation, sometimes in self-defence, sometimes just for the fun of it. It had been like that when they were looking for a house to buy. Those they couldn't afford they had pretended for a while to own and made a game out of the changes they would carry out. Now, in these days of discomfort and anxiety, they began to make each other gifts of towns. Naturally they would go to see the town together so the gift in the end was mutual. It was Mrs Green's idea; she thought it funny, with their house in such a state, to pretend to have whole towns to give away. She began by giving her husband Cortona and he responded with Spello and so it went. On this particular day the town was Sansepolcro, a particularly good choice as it was the birthplace of Piero della Francesca, one of their very favourite painters, and neither of them had ever been there before.

They were late in starting, it was nearly midday when they arrived and the churches were closing. They visited the imposing, long-fronted house where Piero was born in 1410 and the little garden opposite with its pine trees and eighteenth-century statue of the painter. They walked down the main street, where noble buildings, Gothic, Renaissance, Baroque, followed one another in unbroken succession.

The experience of walking around in a town like this is deepened by the number of times you have done it before, and the Greens had done it often. Like all such small and ancient towns in Italy, Sansepolcro is undemonstrative, unclamorous – it makes no very loud or evident claim on your attention. It exists in its own right, in its venerable and richly layered past and harmonious present. To the Greens, as they wandered through streets and squares, even the sunlight seemed part of this ancient existence and the pigeons and the flowers on the window-ledges. The stucco was peeling, some courtyards of palaces were sombre with decay; but the noble proportions of arches and vaults, the beauty of mouldings round windows and doorways, these were there still and open to view.

After lunch they went to the Civic Museum, main object of their pilgrimage, and gazed for long at Piero's painting of *The Resurrection*, alone on its wall in pride of place, Christ not emerging from the tomb but fully emerged, motionless. No ballet dancer this, but a being whose power was expressed in utter stillness. The knowledge of torture and death in his eyes still, he has supped with horrors. He rests one foot on the sarcophagus, now the pedestal of his conquest. The guards sleep below, in the grossness proper to sleep, bodies sprawling, faces slack. There has been nothing to rouse them, no violence, no struggle of escape. The lid of the sarcophagus is still in place . . .

The splendour of this virile Christ was still present to their minds when they returned but it did not long survive the encounter with Blemish and Esposito. It was going to be necessary, Blemish explained, to dig a trench a metre wide and a half-metre deep all the way round the house and fill it with concrete. 'We will have to secure the base of your house,' he said. 'Mr Esposito has come to this conclusion and I must say it makes sense.'

Hearing his name, Esposito nodded and smiled. He had a quantity of gold about him in addition to the crucifix – a ring, a bracelet, a watch with a thick chain of gold links. His car, an electric-blue Alfa Romeo, was parked at the side of the house.

'Yes, I must say it makes sense,' Blemish said. 'The interests of the client come first with us. That is part of our philosophy, it is the way we operate. This is an earthquake zone. Extra precautions have to be taken.' He was in best British gear for this crucial meeting, in hairy tweed jacket and corduroy trousers, despite the hot and rather humid weather.

'Why was this not discussed beforehand?' Mr Green said. 'How come we only learn about it now?'

'It was assumed that the house was resting on a shelf of rock. In our experience the majority of houses in the region south and east of Lake Trasimeno make use of the limestone base as a means of ensuring protection against earth tremors. With your house this is not the case. Esposito, who is a very good and experienced builder, will bear me out in this.'

He turned and spoke in Italian to the builder, who smiled and shrugged and seemed about to reply when a call came through on his mobile phone. He strode some distance away and spoke loudly into the instrument.

'Esposito is very busy,' Blemish said fondly. 'He has several projects on hand. When you get a good builder that is always the case. No, you see, this need of a band of concrete to secure the house at the base, it could not have been foreseen at the outset. Even Esposito, with all that expertise at his command, could not have foreseen that. There are things you can't know until you start digging.'

There was something, some inflection in the way this was uttered, that caused Mr Green to look at his project manager rather sharply. 'Work not foreseen. Is that what is called an *impre-*

*visto* in our contract? It is charged extra to the estimate we had agreed?'

'That is so, yes. It will give you a band of reinforced concrete –'

'How much extra?'

'I think we can keep it down to 20 million lire, including the cost of materials.'

Silence followed this announcement. Esposito had retreated to his car, where he sat talking on his mobile phone. There was a steady sound of dripping water. Somehow or other Esposito himself or one of his North African workmen had pierced a pipe leading from the kitchen. Water ran down an inside wall and fell drop by drop on to the newly laid concrete of the ground floor.

'We'll fix that pipe in no time,' Blemish said. 'Once we have got the other matter sorted out.'

It was to occur to both the Greens, in the light of later events, that a sort of threat was contained in these words. But at the time they were too busy grappling with the sum of 20 million lire.

'That is something like 12,000 dollars,' Mr Green said. 'We will have to think it over.'

'Of course. Bear in mind that you will have a band of reinforced concrete a metre in width encircling the premises, holding them in a grip of steel.' Blemish was carried away into poetry by his desire to get the Greens to agree. 'Firm against tempest and storm,' he said. 'Steadfast and sure while the billows roll. I don't know if I mentioned this but we are proceeding on the advice of our surveyor, what they call a *geometra* here, whom you haven't met as yet, I think, but he is very aware of safety precautions in this area, which as we all know is an earthquake zone. He is a real stickler for safety, our *geometra*. Of course, Esposito, I dare-say Esposito would accept it if you said you didn't want this work done, but we might run into trouble over the planning permission and then the work would have to be suspended while they went fully into things.'

Blemish paused, looking from one Green to the other. 'That can take time in Italy. It would be very uncomfortable for you, apart from anything else.'

On this note he took his departure, leaving Esposito still talking to his phone. It had been a good exit-line but as he drove home a mood of self-doubt descended on him. It was not often that Blemish admitted weaknesses or fallings-off, even to Mildred; but when he got home again after this interview with the Greens he felt obliged to acknowledge that he had talked rather too much.

'I am pretty sure they will agree to have it done,' he said. 'When it comes to foundations people tend to pay up, nobody likes to think that his property is liable to subsidence. It isn't that, it's the lapse in professionalism that bothers me. I went on too long from the business psychology viewpoint, and just at the wrong time, just when they said they were going to consider it.' He brooded for some moments, then said with deepened self-abasement, 'It has always been a tendency of mine to gild the lily. When people say they are going to consider something, you show quiet confidence, you don't start urging them, not at that point, it looks like weakness. These Greens somehow bring out the worst in me. I must say I don't like that couple, I don't find them *simpatico* at all.'

Seeing that her man was downcast and in need of reassurance, Mildred came padding towards him. 'You are just tired, my love, that's all,' she said. She nestled against him and he smelled her warm body-odour and the mingled aromas of baked meats that came to him from her gingham apron and the steam of sauces that got into her hair. 'I am quite sure you handled it all perfectly,' she said. 'I wouldn't think about those silly Greens a moment longer, they don't sound the sort of people we would care to know.'

To take his mind from things she nudged him gently with her pelvis. Blemish felt a stirring in his loins. 'Shall we dress up tonight?' he said.

'Oh, yes, do let's.'

First they had one of Mildred's medieval dishes, one which she was trying out for the very first time, sweet-sour spiced rabbit. This was a rich dish, containing a quantity of pork dripping and currants and red wine.

'Delicious,' Blemish said, swaying his head on its long neck to show a sort of hypnotic bliss, like a charmed snake. 'This will be a popular one with the customers. I'll get fat if you go on feeding me at this rate.'

She regarded him fondly. 'You'll never get fat,' she said. 'You are always on the go, morning till night, working to get the money together so we can have our dream house and our medieval restaurant just as we want them. No one could be a better breadwinner than you are.'

'Well, Milly, I do my best,' Blemish said.

Afterwards they dressed up. Blemish had always gone in for this, even before meeting Mildred, when he was still living alone. He had loved being in costume as a child and could still remember every detail of his outfits of those days, his pirate eyepatch, the tasselled fringes on his cowboy holster, the shiny buttons on his fireman's tunic. Later it had become a need of his nature, feeding fantasies of success and achievement. By good fortune, in Mildred he had found an enthusiastic convert.

They had donned quite a variety of costumes in their time together. In the London days, Blemish had spent a fair amount of money at the shops of theatrical costumiers. There had been a military phase, with Blemish as a guards officer and Mildred as a sort of regimental girl mascot in a pleated skirt and high boots. In their sporting days Blemish was a high-scoring striker in Liverpool colours and an excitingly constrictive jockstrap, while Mildred had worn a lacy Wimbledon get-up with a sort of ballet skirt and white satin panties. They never transdressed; Mildred was traditional in her views and could not have respected a man who made himself effeminate.

Now of course, since the idea for the restaurant had come to them, everything was medieval. Blemish's long legs were encased in stretch-nylon hose and he wore a skirted tunic and sported a codpiece – he had given up the jockstrap with reluctance. All these items had been fashioned by Mildred, who was good with her needle. She herself wore a tight-fitting, low-cut bodice that drew her breasts together and the sort of hooped skirt called a farthingale. This last was rather out of period but Mildred liked it as she wore nothing underneath, which gave a stimulating sense of air and freedom to all her lower parts.

As Blemish pursued a squealing Mildred round their double bed, finally brought her down, searched to disencumber her broad behind from the plastic hoops of the farthingale, as he manoeuvred her into the position of readiness for the mode they both preferred – doggy-fashion they jokingly called it – as he felt himself more than filling out the medieval codpiece, triumph of conquest and restored commercial confidence caused him to put more than the usual emphasis into the ritual abuse he now heaped on his partner and to enjoy more keenly the ritual whimpering with which she answered it.

Ritter had reached the grove of canes some two-thirds of the way down. The canes grew close together and the older ones were more than twice his height. As he crouched among them they obscured his view of the sky, enclosing him in a world of stems and roots and thickets of undergrowth. They leaned in all directions, snared and dragged down by thick ropes of bramble and creeper and wild vine. Streamers of bryony and honeysuckle laced through them.

It seemed to Ritter strangely silent within this enclave, among the burdened stems and the tuberous roots that showed here and there, pale and swollen, monstrous-looking, like the knuckles of some buried Titan. In the very heart of it, through the debris of leaf mould and dead vegetation, new shoots of cane were thrusting up, a fresh and vivid green. The root system of canes was like the industry of spiders, about which he had been reading: aspects both of the terrible tenacity of nature. He thought for a while of this blind, silent struggle of plants. The struggle of animals was not a silent one, for the most part; but only man had the language to clothe his in abstractions.

His father's face followed close upon this thought – these days, since he had started on his work of clearance, it lay in wait for him at every turn. He saw again that thin, sensitive mouth moving with words and the white petals on the desk and the white patches on the collar of the uniform. The fate of the hostages had been an abstract matter for his father. The essential truth of it did not lie in the killing by shooting of a randomly collected group of human beings and covering the bodies over with an explosion of dynamite. It lay in the Nordic Spirit combining with the tradition of Latin Christendom to make a New European Order.

The mouth moving, the words coming, his face . . . What was the expression of his face? Ritter could remember only two faces for his father: the one he had known in childhood, calm, close-shaven, vaguely kind; and the other, the face of the nursing home in Ulm, gaunt and staring. But the shape of the mouth was always the same, and the shape of the words. He had known, even at ten, that the shape was wrong, that his father's words could not be the right ones, not because he detected flaws of fact or logic but because they bore no relation at all to Giuseppe's tears or to the beginnings of hate in the lines of his friend's face.

He crouched among the canes and began to reach into the ancient ramifications of bramble and blackthorn so as to cut them away at the base of the stems. It was his intention, before he stopped work that day, to clear all this undergrowth, free the canes, let air and light to them. Those that had rotted or been dragged out of shape by the creepers – some were bent almost into hoops – he would cut out, so allowing the new ones to grow straight. It was hot there in the hollow and the shade of the canes was too thin to give much protection from the afternoon sun. Ritter sweated heavily and his back ached from the squatting and reaching; but the discomfort was a fuel to his resolve, creating a steady rage against the obstinacy of life opposed to him, creating at the same time a vacancy of mind in which what he had learned and what he had already known, the things that proved the wrongness of the words, were repeated again, in dogged and familiar sequence.

The afternoon of 23 March 1944, the anniversary of the foundation of the Fascist movement. Rome was under German occupation. Badoglio had made a separate peace. The Allies had landed in Sicily. I was ten years old and a pupil at the German

School and I had a great friend called Giuseppe, who lived in the basement with his mother, the concierge. Giuseppe and his mother were sent away because of me.

On that afternoon a detachment of German security police was marching as usual towards the Viminale along Via Rasella, a street lying between the Quattro Fontane and Via del Traforo, in the heart of the city. SS troops of the Bozen Bataillon. The Via Rasella has a steepish slope to it. Someone in the guise of a street cleaner waited half-way up with the kind of covered handcart used for collecting rubbish. In the handcart was a steel box containing twelve kilos of explosive and a package with another six kilos, attached to a short fuse. As the troops began the ascent someone below made a signal. The man waiting above lit the fuse and walked away. The timing was perfect: the cart blew up just as the troops drew level with it. Total deaths – from the explosion itself and from the grenades thrown down from windows at the fleeing survivors – thirty-three.

What happened then had very little to do with the founding of a New European Order. The Germans were frightened by the scale and boldness of the attack. There had already been some assassinations of Fascist officials and on the first of that same month several hundred thousand Italian workers downed tools in Turin and Milan, bringing production to a standstill for a week. There was fear of a general uprising. The authorities decided upon reprisals. The only question was how many to kill. Settlement of this question involved most of the key German military and diplomatic officials in Italy. My father among them. My father knew, before he spoke to me that afternoon, he knew about the panic, he knew that Marshal Kesselring's headquarters had informed Hitler, who had wanted at first to have fifty Italians shot for each German policeman killed. He knew that in subsequent phone calls this had been toned down to a ratio of ten to one.

Ritter paused in his work and the silence of the place, which had been held off by his own small movements, descended on him. Somewhere below, near the stream, a bird sang briefly. My father knew all the time, he thought, with the same naïve surprise he had felt when this had first come home to him, in the years after the war, when it had become possible to learn about such things. My father knew that Kesselring had been told by the SS chief in Rome, Kappler, that there were enough people already under sentence of death to make up the required number. He knew that this was a lie, that people were taken at random, that in the haste of rounding up the victims the quota of 330 had been exceeded by five. My father knew this because his Italian colleague, the police official Pietro Caruso, with whom he was on close terms, had been responsible for selecting the victims . . .

This knowledge on his father's part, unsuspected at the time, never referred to since, struck Ritter in retrospect as the most monstrous thing of all. A pervasive sense of treachery had gathered around and within it, deepened over the years by his sense of there being a pattern in the business, a pattern that was neat, symmetrical, universal. He repeated it to himself now: *I betrayed Giuseppe and his mother by knowing something my father did not; my father added this knowledge of mine to his own much greater stock and betrayed me with it.*

As his own knowledge of the killings at the Fosse Ardeatine had increased, so had this shape of treachery filled out, a development that had its own strong colouring of irony to his mind and one that during his career as an interpreter, seeing the power of words to conceal and distort, he had come to regard as a fact of life: whatever knowledge we achieve, it is always at the expense of faith.

There had of course been another kind of knowledge in his father's mind at the time and this too Ritter had not realized until years later. It was the knowledge possessed by the German military command in that March of 1944. Even while the mouth moved and the words came and the almond blossom stirred on the desk, his father must have known that the war was as good as lost. The break-out from Anzio was only six weeks away. In little more than two months Kesselring had abandoned Rome without a fight. The German headquarters staff, including his father, had been transferred north to Milan and he and his mother, together with other dependants of serving officers, had been sent back home to Germany.

Within a year Germany had surrendered, the war in Europe was over. The family moved to Argentina, where his father had connections. Here Ritter had continued with his Italian and added Spanish to it. He showed an unusual aptitude for languages, not merely an understanding of grammar and syntax but an ear for pitch and intonation and a natural mimetic faculty; even while still a schoolboy, he had understood that the way to knowledge of a language is through imitation of those whose native tongue it is, the gestures and modes of thought, that complex of habit and assumption that distinguishes one people from another.

They had not returned to Germany until 1953, when things had settled down. By then he was nineteen and virtually trilingual. It was this that had determined his choice of career, sent him to a school for interpreters at Heidelberg. A fortuitous accomplishment, seeming so natural to him as not to be much valued, except that it won praise. Certainly it had never been accompanied by any sense of esteem on his part for the profession itself, any sense that it was useful or contributed much to the well-being of his fellows. How could he have felt this, who had no belief even then in the power of words to convey truth? There had been the glamour of travel about it, that was all. He had taken what seemed the easy way but it had got harder and harder, until in the end it was no way at all.

He took refuge from this in a renewed sense of his father's duplicity. Those resounding words had been no more than a cover for the rage of the defeated. *You must have known*, Ritter said to his father's second face, the one where death showed already beneath the skin.

Blame and pity blended and became diffused among the stems of the canes, the beauty of their colours. These formed a subtle register of age, going from green through paling yellow to dark ivory and bone white. To several were still attached the dead vine tendrils of some old cultivation, pale brown in colour with a faint purplish tinge, hue of their death. They had curled round and clung and died in this clinging, the ultimate expression of their being. Now they were hard and brittle, like thin bone, impossible to separate from the stem.

He continued to hack and clip at the tangle of growths that bound the canes. Many were beyond saving, they had rotted in this long embrace; others were permanently disabled, twisted out of shape. But the younger shoots, freed from the cables that held them, swayed upright with slow rustling sounds that seemed like gratitude or relief

They were bordered lower down by a dense and ancient screen of bramble spiked with dark-red thorns two centimetres long and needle-sharp. The stems had to be clipped away close to the ground and pulled out, difficult work this as they were meshed with other vegetation and interlaced among themselves. Ritter persisted, despite his aching back and the numbers of small black flies that came with evening and showed a persistent interest in the exposed parts of his skin. The sun had already set when he was brought up short by a sudden falling away of the ground, a hollow running almost at right angles into the slope of the ravine. It was still partly obscured by the last of the brambles; but when these were cleared away he found himself looking down into the sides of a cave with a narrow ledge at the entrance. There had been some fall of earth further inside but the roof, roughly a metre in height, was held up by the arching roots of a tree stump and these, smoothed and polished by age, had kept the opening free.

The cavity was natural but it had been enlarged. Walls had been hollowed out into the bankside. There was a small, square-shaped recess some way in, with a litter of fire-blackened stones. If the fallen earth were cleared there would be a good two metres of sleeping space. It was clear to Ritter that he was looking at what had once been the den of a man.

'There is an irony in it,' Monti said, glancing round at the students assembled in his room. None of them looked as if they cared one way or another. The faces were turned to him, except that of the young man from Bologna, Millucci, who always kept his face turned away, as if reserving judgement; but they were quite unexpectant. 'Yes, a strong element of irony,' he repeated.

At this one of the girls, Rosa Bellafante, made a brief entry in her notebook. Monti thought it probable that she had written just that one word, 'irony'. 'When you consider,' he said, 'that Perugia throughout almost her entire history as an independent state, and particularly in the years of her greatness in the fourteenth century, was faithful to the papacy, she was a consistently Guelph city, through all political vicissitudes, and this was the more remarkable in a period when warring factions and shifting alliances were the order of the day in the Central States of Italy, when you consider this it seems ironical that she was to fall at last under a papal tyranny even more unjust and oppressive than the rule of the Baglioni family that had gone before.'

He paused on this, in the hope that some response not directly solicited by a question might be forthcoming. None came immediately and he was about to resume when the pale, quiet girl with beautiful legs, whose name he thought was Maria and who spoke rather seldom, said, 'I think it is only ironical, I mean it can only be called ironical, if the republic of Perugia kept faith with the papacy out of principle and not for selfish reasons.'

'Selfish reasons?' It was touching to Monti, this childlike phrase applied to a period characterized by the extremest forms of arrogance and self-seeking and ambition. All the same, there was a point there. 'Yes,' he said, 'I see what you mean. If it was purely a matter of expediency that kept Perugia on the papal side, she was simply paid back in her own coin when the time came. But I think it is a mistake to consider the matter on a moral plane. The policy of states then as now is dictated by considerations of power and commercial advantage. The language of morality is used to conceal this, but when we go into things we will generally find self-interest to be the determining factor.'

He hesitated for a moment and his mind shifted. When he spoke again it was in a tone less dispassionate. 'If Perugia had acted out of pure devotion to the papal cause, then her subjection by the papacy would go beyond irony, it would amount to the tragedy of betrayal.'

It seemed to him that his voice had faltered on this last word and he wondered if something in his face had changed. He had the impression that the students were looking at him oddly. The silence that followed was broken by Millucci and for once Monti was glad of the intervention, though it was motivated as usual by the desire to undermine the discussion rather than contribute anything.

'I think the whole question of irony is beside the point,' Millucci said in his slightly nasal voice with its Bolognese inflections. 'After all, the people involved did not think in those terms, they were reacting to situations that we can only have an approximate idea of now. What is the point of using words that belong to us, not to them?'

'That is the great privilege of those that live after,' Monti said. 'That is the vantage point that history confers on us. We lose immediacy but we gain perspective. We see connections not possible to see at the time. The sense of irony can only be cultivated in detachment.'

But Millucci was studying the wall again. 'Take a look at Gibbon's *Decline and Fall* some time,' Monti said. 'You will see the uses that irony can be put to.' To mitigate the sharpness of this, he added quickly, 'An eighteenth-century English scholar writing about ancient Rome, a period as remote to him in its manners and morals as the time before the Flood. Detachment could not be more complete and Gibbon makes brilliant use of it.'

He waited a while but no one spoke. 'Good,' he said, 'let us take a particular series of events. Arbitrary, I know, but it can be helpful to see patterns. In the June of 1424 Fortebraccio, Lord of Perugia, dies beneath the walls of Aquila. The people of Perugia hail his bastard son as the new Lord. But the Pope of the day, Martin V, has other ideas. He is eager to re-establish the authority of the Church in Perugia. In Malatesta Baglioni he finds an instrument ready to his hand. You will remember Malatesta, the great expropriator and refurbisher of houses, he who tied his enemy to the tail of a horse and had him dragged through the streets of the town. Malatesta is not in a very good bargaining position at the moment, being in a papal prison. He realizes that the way to gain his liberty and keep his family in power is to make a pact with the Pope. He persuades his fellow citizens to accept papal authority in exchange for the backing of the papal troops in case of trouble. And so it comes about. Perugia retains a nominal independence but she has lost her essential freedom and she will never regain it. From now on liberty under the Pope will be her highest ideal.

'Now let us jump seventy years or so. It is 1495. Malatesta is long dead but the Baglioni have gone from strength to strength, building their great houses on the Colle Landone, laying out orchards and gardens in their spacious grounds overlooking the Pianura Umbra. They were great people for houses, the Baglioni. I don't know if any of you have thought further about the connections between houses and power in the history of the

Baglioni family . . . No? Well, 1495 is a year of great triumph for them. They have succeeded in expelling their greatest rivals, the Oddi family. Their cause has been espoused by the Medici – there is work still to be done on the relations between the Medici and the Baglioni in the fifteenth century, perhaps a postgraduate thesis for somebody? The Medici use their influence with the Pope of the day, who confirms the outlawing of the Oddi by official decree. I wonder who took over their houses . . .'

He saw Millucci look towards him. 'Yes,' he said, 'I know it is speculation, there is no way now of unearthing these property deals. But speculation is one of the pleasures afforded us by the study of history. Like the exercise of irony, eh, Millucci?'

Quite unexpectedly, Millucci's face broke into a smile, the first that Monti could remember seeing in any of these sessions. The others were smiling too, as if aware of some release of tension. Monti's spirits rose. It mattered to him, as it always had, that he should succeed with his students, succeed in sharing his enthusiasms. And he had thought he was failing with these.

'Well,' he said, 'let us go to the third event in the series. It is May 1540, a half-century later. Fifty years of Baglioni misrule and civil disorder and incessant quarrelling with the papacy. But the Pope now is Paul III, a very different man from either of the two others we have mentioned today. He is far-seeing, relentless, constantly in need of funds. He wants total power in Perugia and he knows that this is not possible without first destroying the Baglioni. He is not really interested in doing deals with the family, though he may at first pretend to be. He is interested in getting rid of them altogether. He is helped in typical fashion by the family itself: six years earlier Ridolfo Baglioni and some of his people have waylaid the Papal Vice-Legate and stabbed him to death in the street.

'Paul III bides his time. Early in 1540 he publishes a bull

increasing the price of salt by three *quattrini* a pound. The people of Perugia, suffering from a series of bad harvests, rise in revolt. Paul sends his troops in. The Baglioni attempt resistance but they are easily defeated. By the end of May it is all over, the city has capitulated.'

Monti paused a moment for dramatic effect, looking straight before him. 'Three events then, and three Popes. Covering 120 years. There is a kind of pattern in it, or so it seems to me, and I would like you to think about this before our next meeting and try to decide how far it is a typical pattern, how far it expresses the nature of the period considered as a whole. Who lives by the sword perishes by the sword, so the saying goes. Certainly the Baglioni made good soldiers for generation after generation – it was perhaps their only virtue. But they lived by intrigue and extortion and these were the weapons Pope Paul III used to destroy them.'

In speaking he had felt some self-mockery at his own rhetoric; but he had caught the students' interest, he could see it from the faces. Something had happened in the course of this session, there had been a shift towards sympathy, the recognition of shared endeavour, something difficult to define but definite, ir-reversible. 'One last thing,' he said, 'and it forms part of that symbolism of property we were discussing. Perugia surrendered to the papal forces at the beginning of June 1540. One of the first things their new master did was to appoint demolition experts. Within a month the towers and turrets of the Baglioni were falling, their splendid palaces were being razed to the ground. On this prime site, the finest in the city, a single gigantic build-ing rose, the Pauline Fortress, named after the new Lord of Perugia. It was destined to hold the city in subjection for three centuries to come.'

When the students had filed out Monti lit a cigarette and went to the window. There was nothing to look out at but a flat roof with a low parapet on which dishevelled pigeons sat. This time, he felt, the hour had gone well. Of course there were pitfalls in this game of patterns; one tended to lose the sense of their provisional nature, to believe they expressed a settled truth. Patterns were imposed on the flux of events, they were arbitrary and creative, they reordered the world. It was good if this re-ordering cast light, but vital that it should soon be discarded or modified or merged into something else. All the great pattern-makers had held on too long – Hegel, Marx, Darwin, Freud. A rigid insistence on patterns was the mark of an arrested mind. I should have stressed that more, he thought.

He had not been free of the vice himself – perhaps no one was. And it did not apply only to views of history or human society. All relations sustained over long periods tended to fall into patterns of one kind or another. He thought again of Laura, what he had expected of her, what she had expected of him, the habitual demands, the selective vision, the ground shared and unshared. Patterns of behaviour are formed by some law that may relate to love but they are not necessarily informed by love itself and they can harden into a framework strong as steel. Somehow the shape thus formed had been the wrong one for Laura. She had discovered it to be wrong and she had gone away.

What we call betrayal, then, no more than the breaking of a pattern, the doing violence to settled assumptions . . . But what when it is betrayal itself that is the pattern? His mind moved to the Great Betrayal of the Baglioni, 15 July in the year 1500, the night of the Red Wedding, as it had been called, when the clan, not content with oppressing their fellow citizens and murdering members of rival families, had turned themselves.

In the principal branches of the family there were too many male children and all of them were given to violent quarrel.

There was not space enough for all this squabbling brood. Most were scarcely literate. The only profession they knew was that of arms.

He fell to imagining that summer night five centuries ago, the sun setting, that last radiant visitation of light that he waited for himself in the evenings. A luminous deepening of colour, the stubble fields below the city walls deep gold, the green of distant trees darkening and shining, the line of the mountains hazing violet. Then quite suddenly the fall of night, the fireflies on the slopes of the hillside below the grand houses on the Colle Landone, the chorus of crickets filling the spaces of the gardens, the splash of fountains.

The killers would have heard and seen these things as they made their way through the night. Grifonetto, the nephew of Braccio Baglioni, Filippo, a bastard of the Baglioni house, numerous others – there was no shortage of men hopeful for advancement or resentful of neglect.

Four of the chiefs of the clan were killed that night: Astorre, Guido, Simonetto, Gismondo. And all with the utmost ferocity. Filippo entered the bedchamber of Astorre Baglioni and killed him in full view of his young wife before he had time to seize a weapon. The chronicles were unanimous in asserting that his killer tore out the heart.

Before the eyes of his wife . . . It was like the killing of Biordo Michelotti 100 years before, whose murder had brought the Baglioni back to Perugia and founded their power. There was a similarity here that went beyond coincidence: both the men had recently been married, Astorre only eighteen days before, both to women of illustrious families and both in circumstances of pomp and splendour and dazzling display. At the wedding of Astorre Baglioni triumphal arches were erected in the streets, there were processions, the wedding gifts were displayed to public view – gems, gold ornaments, rich brocades. At the wedding feast, held in the open in the Cathedral Square, Astorre's brother, Simonetto Baglioni, who like the groom had only eighteen days to live, threw basketfuls of sugared almonds to the populace from a loaded cart.

A pattern here too, of a kind: in each case a display of wealth and good fortune had shortly preceded – and certainly provoked – the murders. And behind the pattern a raw truth: hatred there is always, it waits only for a goad.

True to their word, exactly seven days after delivering their ulti-matum, the Checchetti drove short stakes into the surface of the road below their house at a precise distance apart of two metres. Harold Chapman had made a point of reconnoitring the ground daily and he saw the stakes himself. 'Just below that wall of theirs,' he said. 'They are about six inches high. We must phone immediately and order some wood. I'd do it myself but you know what my Italian is like.'

Cecilia's usual response to this was the loyal assurance that he was making great strides. This time, however, as she took up the phone, she said nothing, obscurely repelled by her husband's glee.

'They don't know what they are doing,' he said. 'Those who God wants to destroy he first makes blind.'

Cecilia paused, phone in hand. 'Mad,' she said, 'not blind.' But he didn't seem to hear this or at least to take it in, and she did not repeat it. It came to her now, with a sort of muffled shock, that she did not really care whether Harold misquoted things or not. She spoke to someone at the other end and ordered the wood. 'They say they will come later on today. Some time late in the afternoon.'

Chapman rubbed the palms of his hands together. 'I was afraid the Checchetti would think better of it.'

Mad they may well be, Cecilia thought. It was more than an attempt at extortion, more than mere stupid greed. Some pas-sion had entered the business. The Checchetti seemed to have suspended their rational parts. They must know that various other people used this road, that whatever by-laws they had unearthed they could not simply block it by unilateral action. Probably they were hoping that the others would take their part against the newcomers. But this was mad too . . . It was hatred, or something like it, that had trapped the Checchetti in this blind alley. Hatred for foreigners, for people who came and went, who had a life beyond these hillsides with their steep terraces of olive and vine, who had a silver-grey BMW, who could afford to buy a house only for holidays. This hatred was waiting for us, she thought. It was there before we arrived. It was not lessened by our offer of help with the wall. What made it active and malignant was the simplest and most ordinary of requests: we wanted a receipt for the money, we wanted to do things in legal form.

'I must say Mancini is a brilliant chap,' Chapman said. 'I had my doubts at first, I don't mind admitting it. His manner is strange at times and he tends to wander a bit, but he came up trumps with this one. Late afternoon, the wood people say? I'll take the binoculars out and go up the hillside behind the house a little way. There is a point up there from which you can see the turning at the corner where the lorry will come in.'

His eyes were bright and his whole being had become charged with joyous energy. With a dispassion that had some shadow of despair in it, Cecilia noted these signs in her husband and felt the beginning of that desolation we feel when what we have thought familiar betrays us by its strangeness. It was a stranger who stood there with his stretching smile and wrinkling nose, talking of binoculars and observation posts. It couldn't be the money, it was a relatively small sum and they were quite well off these days. No, he wanted to punish these people, he wanted to give them the equivalent of a black eye or a bloody nose. She was tempted to ask him if he didn't feel in some way, however slightly, sorry for the Checchetti; but she knew this was the wrong question, that he would think it sentimental. In a way it was presumptuous too: she had no job, no income, no particular abilities or skills; before getting married she had worked part-time in an art gallery run by a friend of her father. It was all Harold's money, money he had worked and schemed to get. And now these people were trying to take some of it from him.

'How old do you think Mancini is?' she said.

Chapman stared. 'No idea. I've never thought of it. Somewhere in his fifties, I suppose. Why?'

'I get this feeling about him that he isn't any particular age at all.'

'Everybody is a particular age.'

'Yes, I suppose so.'

'I thought I'd walk along and have a few words with the American couple. They are the only ones left who I haven't explained the situation to. It doesn't so much matter now of course, but for the sake of completeness, you know. I have always believed in finishing the job. It's a moral question really. Once you have set your hand to the plough . . .'

He paused, looking for some sign of approbation for these sentiments. None came, however. Cecilia was looking strained and tired, he thought, with the downward pull of her mouth more pronounced and that expression of sad steadiness that came into her eyes at times. He felt a rush of annoyance, which, however, he took care to conceal. Why could her mood never match his own? A man had a right to expect his partner in life to share in his moments of triumph or success. His new secretary, for instance, Miss Phelps, he felt sure she would have rejoiced. Cecilia was a death's head at the party, no other word for it. 'Well,' he said, 'we've got a couple of hours before the wood man can be expected. I thought you might like to come with me to see these people.'

'If you like.'

They walked the few hundred yards to the Greens' house in

silence. There were poppies along the verges of the road among long grasses burdened with flower, and there was a profusion of vetch and chicory and wild geranium in the banks of the terraces above them. It was warm and still, with a hum of insects in the air, presaging summer.

The Greens' house was between their own and Monti's. As the road curved round towards it they came upon a scene of considerable desolation. It was not just the piles of sand and gravel and the litter of broken bricks in front of the house and the heaps of rubble along the edge of the road. These they had seen before in passing. But what was not evident unless you approached on foot was the trench running along two sides of the house, half-filled in with concrete. And there was now a sizeable hole in the roof where a section of tiles had been moved. This was covered only by a square of plastic held in place by stones.

'Good God,' Chapman said. 'The place looks as if it has been blitzed. First good bit of wind and that plastic sheet will be lifted clear off the roof.'

Cecilia called up as they approached. 'Anyone at ho-o-me?'

After a moment or two the Greens appeared side by side at the top of the external staircase. Silver-haired, small-boned, closely similar in appearance, they stood there for a brief while in unnatural silence. It was immediately clear to Cecilia that she and her husband had arrived at a moment of crisis. 'I hope we are not intruding,' she said.

Mr Green uttered a sound that might have been a laugh. 'We have got beyond being intruded upon. You'd better come on up.'

At the top of the stairs introductions were effected. Cecilia saw now that Mrs Green's eyelids were swollen as if she had been recently crying. She wished that they had not called at such a time and began to seek about in her mind for a way of indicating to Harold – never very sensitive in these matters – that they should not prolong their visit. 'You are probably busy just now,' she said. 'Harold and I can –'

'I was just saying to my wife, you look as if you've been in a blitz,' Chapman said.

'Do come in,' Mrs Green said. 'Things are a bit in a mess, I am afraid.'

This, it was immediately clear to the Chapmans as they looked around, was no more than the truth. It was not just a matter of disorder, though this was considerable; there was a quality of ruin about the inside of the house as there was about the outside – it seemed a place that people might have lived in once but had long since abandoned.

The schooling of manners, natural warmth, the traditions of her hospitable nation operated on Mrs Green now. 'Can we offer you folks a cup of coffee?' she said.

'That would be great,' Chapman said, before Cecilia had time to demur. 'What on earth has happened to your fireplace?'

All that was left of this was the exposed back wall of the chimney, charred and blackened by a century of smoke; all the front part of the hearth had been wrenched out.

'We wanted a smaller fireplace,' Mr Green said. 'The one that was here before was huge, very fine in its way but all the heat went up the chimney. We discussed it with this man Blemish, who has been acting as our project manager. They came and took the fireplace out but nothing further has been done.'

'The draught is worse than ever now.' An inveterate optimism lightened Mrs Green's face. 'Of course,' she said, 'it doesn't matter so much in this warmer weather.'

Chapman stared for some time longer at the black gaping hole that had once been the fireplace. 'Looks as if someone has thrown a bomb down the chimney,' he said. 'I wanted to bring you up to date with the latest developments in the road situation.'

'Road situation?'

'Yes, the Checchetti have now driven stakes into the road at a distance —'

'Harold,' Cecilia said, in a voice considerably firmer than usual, 'Mr and Mrs Green have troubles enough of their own by the look of things. I don't think they want to be bothered with our little squabbles.'

This belittling phrase seemed to Chapman extremely disloyal and he resolved to take it up with Cecilia later on. For the moment, clearly enough, the way was blocked. He waited for some moments in the hope that the Greens, their curiosity aroused, might ask for further details. But they showed no interest whatsoever. Old people, he thought, self-centred, set in their ways . . . 'What have they been doing to your roof?' he said.

This question seemed to act as a precipitating factor for the Greens. They began to speak eagerly, supplementing each other's account, their voices often blending in a single tone of bitterness and woe. From the very beginning there had been problems, but the real trouble had started with this ditch round the house, the builder had begun to dig a trench all the way round and fill it with cement so as to secure the foundations.

'The house is not built on rock as they expected, you see,' Mrs Green said. 'It was an *imprevisto*.'

'They filled one side in and started on another,' Mr Green said. 'Then they asked for some money.'

'We paid it, there didn't seem much alternative.'

'Then they told us we would need a *cordolo*.'

'That's an *imprevisto* too.'

'What is a *cordolo*?'

'It's a kind of concrete reinforcement going all the way round the house, just below the roof.'

'Why do you need one?'

'Well,' Mr Green said, with a reasoning air about him that Cecilia found strangely touching. 'This is an earthquake zone, you know.'

'I know that,' Chapman said. 'But we have had our house converted without needing one.'

'No, you see, it's because they are putting this band of concrete round the base of the house. This *geometra* they have, that's a kind of surveyor, he says he won't be able to sign that the house is soundly built unless they put in this reinforcement below the roof.'

'I am sorry,' Chapman said, 'I am not following you.'

Mr Green felt a certain increase in authority at being in a position to explain this technical matter. 'Well, you see, otherwise all the stress would be on the upper half.' He raised both hands and extended the fingers to make the shape of a square. 'If the base is gripped tight and there is an earth tremor, all the shock is transmitted to the upper part, there is no give.'

'No give?'

'None at all.'

In the silence that followed upon this, they could hear the light, continuous rustling of the plastic sheet above their heads. 'But they must have known,' Cecilia said. 'They must have known from the beginning that if they put the concrete round the base they would have to do the *cordolo* too.'

'Mr Blemish says they didn't know how the *geometra* was going to react. The snag seems to be that he is such a stickler for the regulations, so kind of meticulous that he won't go over the line by even the slightest degree.'

This sounded improbable to Cecilia, but she could see from the faces of the Greens that they wanted very much to believe it and she could understand why: to cease believing in the good faith of these people would be a nightmare worse than the one they were going through. They were much older than she was, but they struck her now as sorely in need of protection, not on grounds of frailty – they were both active, wiry-looking people – but because of this tenacity in maintaining the bonds of faith, their own, other people's. Bonds of faith that hold the world together, she thought. They had probably put nearly everything they possessed into this house. 'That's a beautiful picture,' she said, pointing at the wall behind the Greens. 'Verrocchio, isn't it?'

'Verrocchio's *Baptism of Christ*,' Mr Green said. 'We bought that print forty years ago, when we came here on our honeymoon. First thing we did when we got here was hang it up on the wall. It is kind of symbolic for us, that picture.'

'We are saving it up,' Mrs Green said. 'We are waiting for the house to be finished, then we are going to see the original. It is sort of like a present we are making each other. Perhaps you folks do that, give each other presents, things you do together?'

'No, not really,' Cecilia said.

'You know, to celebrate. It's in the Uffizi Gallery in Florence. The kneeling angel, the one on the left, that was painted by Leonardo.'

'He was apprentice to Verrocchio, you know, when he was about seventeen or eighteen,' Mr Green said.

Both the Greens had brightened up considerably, Cecilia saw, with this change of subject. 'You can see it is Leonardo's work, can't you?' she said. 'It is less three-dimensional than the other figures, more in plane with the picture surface. Do you see what I mean, Harold?'

'Verrocchio was a sculptor too,' Chapman said, dredging up a fact remembered from his reading.

'That's right,' Mrs Green said. 'He did that wonderful equestrian statue, the one in Venice.'

'Yes, I know the one you mean.' Cecilia looked for some moments more at the picture, at the beautiful congruence of the figures, the outstretched arm of the Baptist making an arch, the dipping chalice and the hovering dove at the apex. 'Baptism of a standing figure, it's like a coronation too, isn't it?' She was touched by the way the Greens had confided their love for this picture to more or less complete strangers. It came to her again that they needed sheltering somehow. She wanted to say something comforting to them, something reassuring . . .

'Sounds to me as if you have been taken to the cleaners,' Chapman said. 'They have started messing about with the roof before the trench is filled in. That doesn't promise well. Who is this Blemish anyway?'

'He is our project manager.' Mrs Green's voice quivered a little saying this and Mr Green put a hand on her shoulder. 'This house was habitable when we bought it,' she said. 'It was primitive but it was habitable. Now it is getting impossible for us to live here. We go to the bathroom and look up to see this plastic sheet where the roof tiles should be. It rustles and flaps all the time.'

'Come and have a look for yourselves,' Mr Green said.

The Chapmans were taken to look at the bathroom and then at the internal staircase, one of the few pieces of work Esposito had actually completed. Huge vertical cracks had opened up on either side of the landing.

'This is the latest development,' Mr Green said. 'There were no cracks here before.'

Chapman stepped up close and inspected the cracks. They ran down in jagged lines from the corners formed by the angle of the staircase with the ceiling. At their widest they were over an inch across. 'They have opened the whole house up,' he said. 'Have you got any kind of contract? Well, if I were you I would have it checked by a lawyer. It so happens that I know of an excellent one. I'll give you his name and number, if you like. He has been very helpful to us in our dispute with the Checchetti family, which far from being a little squabble is a fundamental issue of principle. They are trying to blackmail us, you know. Do you know what they have done today?'

'Signor Chapman, Harold Chapman, gave me your name,' Fabio said. 'He recommended you very strongly.' He watched as the lawyer tapped lightly with a pencil on the desk before him. It had been a struggle for him to come here; it meant admitting fraud on the one hand and foolish credulity on the other, more or less in equal measure. The lawyer would be accustomed to these things of course; but they would normally be represented in separate persons, whereas Fabio felt that he embodied both and the feeling made him uneasy. The habitual melancholy of his face deepened as he sat forward in one of Mancini's luxurious armchairs and began his story. His difficulty was made strangely greater by the fact that a thin shaft of sunlight was slanting through the Venetian blind at the window and falling across Mancini's shoulder and the side of his head, dressing his hair in radiance and obscuring the upper part of his features in a bright haze.

He did not try to conceal anything. He told the lawyer how he and Arturo had made out a bill of sale by mutual agreement, how in this way the house and land had passed from his ownership to that of his partner. A paper transaction, he repeated – no money had changed hands. But the deed of sale had been drawn up and witnessed by a notary, it was legally binding.

Mancini nodded and laid the pencil carefully down on the desk. 'What did you set the price of the house at?'

'Two hundred million with the land and outbuildings.'

'Yes, I see. About half its market value. You naturally wanted to keep the tax on the sale as low as possible.' Mancini smiled. 'Fictitious sales are still subject to taxes,' he said.

The smile had seemed to Fabio more a motion in the brightness lying round the lawyer's face than an actual movement of the features. 'It seemed to make sense at the time,' he said. 'I get a pension, you know. I had a career as a racing driver before my accident. It is a reduced pension because I took as much as I could in cash to help me buy the house. Even so, it prevents me from getting the tax concessions you are entitled to if your income is derived solely from direct cultivation of the land. Now Arturo, you see, has no pension, no income of his own at all . . .'

'I see, yes. And of course by selling the house rather than simply making it over as a gift, you saved on transfer tax. In certain cases a gift of that kind is counted as the realization of an asset by the donor, who might then be liable to capital gains tax on any increase in its value since it was originally acquired by the said donor. You have had the house for several years?'

'Yes, ten years.'

'In that case the increase in value would be considerable. No, you were right to do it as a deed of sale.'

'Right?'

'Entirely right, I think, yes. A shrewd move, Signor Bianchi.'

Fabio narrowed his eyes to get a better look at the lawyer's face, thinking this might show something sarcastic or derisive in it. 'Shrewd? But it was disastrous, it was entirely stupid, I am going to lose the house because of it.'

'That is an entirely different issue.' Mancini leaned forward out of the light and now his head and face were clearly visible to Fabio, the full gaze of the wide-open eyes, the luxuriant sweeps of hair on either side. 'We must distinguish,' he said. 'Making distinctions is one of the most intensely human of our attributes. The actual transaction you entered into with your partner was not stupid at all. On the contrary, it was very reasonable under the circumstances, reasonable, I mean, in the sense that it was designed to save you money and there are not many things more reasonable than that. Saving money, or increasing your stock of it, is an activity everywhere regarded as normal. In the whole of Italy there would hardly be a dissenting voice. Of course the transaction was fraudulent in that it was designed to deprive the state of its rightful dues and there are penalties for that if it comes to legal process. But as a private arrangement with limited aims, it was, as I say, eminently reasonable. The use your partner is trying to put it to, that is another matter altogether.'

Fabio found it hard to endure such a calmly objective way of looking at his loss. He felt a spurt of anger towards this man behind the desk who talked so smoothly about other people's troubles, took a view of such Olympian detachment. All the years of warmth and companionship, the struggles to make ends meet, the labour of every day, their physical joy in each other. Not just mine, he thought – I can't be deceived in that. But he had always known there was a difference. He had singled Arturo out, taken him up. Arturo had responded to the promise of protection and would do so again . . . What had Monti said on that evening of the visit, of which Fabio was now ashamed? People who live together on close terms build their house around them day by day. This house Arturo had already taken from him because the fabric of it was love and trust. And now here was this man before him, talking so reasonably, so dispassionately.

But it was not only resentment that he felt: there was some quality in the lawyer, some emanation of personality, that made one want to secure his sympathy and understanding. Fabio wanted him to understand the enormity of what had happened, to realize that these quibbling distinctions were as nothing compared to his sufferings, the desolation of Arturo's treachery. But there is no language for pain. He could only repeat the facts, seek to magnify the injury. 'He has left me alone,' he said. 'He has deserted me after all these years. I took him to Verona for the opera season at the arena, every year without fail, tickets in good places for all the operas. One year I took him to Egypt to see the first performance of *Aida* against the background of pyramids, a historic occasion. We are both fond of opera . . . Now he does this to me, he tries to take the roof from over my head.'

'Yes, this attempt to dispossess you, that is the heart of the business. His going away, that is neither here nor there, if you will forgive me, it is merely a matter of emotions. I suppose he became, you know, disenchanted. People change, things form and dissolve. That is the way of the world, Signor Bianchi, do you not agree? I used to be more interested in emotions than I am now. These days it is the machinery that interests me more. But I understand how you feel. This attempt to deceive you and cheat you is very wrong, it is a great treachery your friend has been guilty of.'

'Machinery . . .' Fabio felt moved by this expression of sympathy. 'He has brought everything there was between us down to machinery,' he said. 'A car is more than an engine. It is bodywork, it is upholstery, it is beauty of design. He plotted it all beforehand, in cold blood. After I had done so much for him.'

Mancini nodded but made no immediate reply. It seemed to him that his new client was rather too absorbed in the role of wronged father. This companion had perhaps grown weary of being taken here and there. Perhaps this bid to dispossess his benefactor, steal his habitation, had been no more than that, an attempt to annihilate the grounds of a generosity long resented. What better way of asserting independence than taking over the presidential palace? 'Yes,' he said, 'I agree, quite despicable. Italian law as at present constituted encourages such tricks. It makes no provision at all for the rights of men who live together and then separate. In law your partner is entitled to nothing, not a single lira. If you had been a married couple the one leaving would have been able to claim compensation for the years of work and service. He or she would have been entitled to share the value of the house.'

'I suppose so, yes.' Neither in face nor in voice was there any indication that Fabio felt this as an injustice.

Mancini waited a moment then sighed and shrugged slightly. 'Be that as it may,' he said, 'he has wronged you, so much is certain.'

'What can I do? Take him to court for fraud? I know that would mean admitting my share in it, but perhaps we can get the deed of sale annulled.'

Mancini shook his head. 'That would be a thorny path indeed. In my younger days I insisted always on the letter of the law. I applied the law with devoted consistency and I prospered, because the law applied with devoted consistency enriches lawyers to the same degree that it impoverishes their clients. Then I saw that justice rarely resulted from this and at the same time I began to feel bored. The due process of law is mainly a tedious rambling, Signor Bianchi. He would deny fraud, of course. We would have to try and show that his income had not been sufficient, that he could not have disposed of such a sum of money. For this we would need documentary evidence, in the nature of things rather difficult to obtain. No, my advice to you would be different.'

He stopped and leaned back in his chair. Fabio saw him close his eyes, or at least surmised he had done this – the shine of the eyes ceased as if eclipsed by the sunlight that still lay about his head. There was silence in the room for the space of two minutes or so. Then the lawyer's voice came again, rather deep in tone, unfaltering and unhurried. 'Two acts of deception have already taken place. The first is the fraudulent transaction by which you two sought to evade the proper taxes by making a fictitious deed of sale. The second is the application of this fictitious deed by your companion as if it were not fictitious at all. A trick within a trick, we can call this. So we must now use a third trick to defeat him – or rather a series of tricks arising rather beautifully from within it, like the petals of a flower. However, as preliminary condition, it requires a third party, a man completely honest. Not so easy to find. Have you got a friend of such a kind, someone you can trust without reservation?'

Fabio was silent for a moment or two. Then he said, 'Yes, I think I have. There is a man in Carrara, we grew up together, we were like brothers. We don't see each other so often now but I know he would be ready to do me a service – and I would trust him.'

'Well, an element of risk there must always be. This finding of an honest man is the first hurdle and in a way the most important. He will present himself, on oath, not as your friend but as your relentless creditor, pressing for repayment of a largish sum.'

'But I don't owe him any –'

'Bear with me a while longer. This debt we are speaking of was contracted *before* you made the agreement with your partner. Obviously the house, as your principal asset, acts as security. Now the debt has fallen due, you cannot pay, you fall into a panic. Do you begin to see? We will present the court with a *cambiale*, signed by you and made out to your friend in Carrara. This is a document containing a written promise to pay a stated sum to a particular person, or sometimes to the bearer, either at a date specified or on demand.'

'I know what a *cambiale* is,' Fabio said.

'In that case, you will know that it is a standard document and that they are issued in batches and the year and the number of the issue are printed on them. They come in different denominations. We will need enough of them to cover the sum your partner is claiming to have paid for the house. They will have to be dated well before you made the bill of sale, let us say three years ago.'

'Do you mean backdated?'

'The date when the debt was contracted will be written in ink in the space provided. But the document itself will bear the authentic year of issue, which also of course constitutes evidence of the year of signature. In other words you will have to find old ones. Three years old, to be precise. There is always a certain quantity of these forms in circulation, blank of course but with the original year of issue on them. As I am sure you know, they are made available to the public through stores with a licence to sell tobacco. Some of these may have stocks of old ones lying around. But it is more probable you will get them through a bank. Perhaps you are on friendly terms with a tobacconist or someone who works in a bank? It is always better to do things through people you know. In any case, with a little patience you will find them.'

'I dare say that is true,' Fabio said, 'but I don't see –'

'You will,' Mancini said. 'In a short while you will.' He regarded Fabio with smiling benevolence for some moments; then he raised his head and his smile merged with the light. 'We will obtain the *cambiali* and we will ask your friend in Carrara to act as the creditor. That is to say, you will sign and date a document bearing in its watermark the year 1992, promising to repay your friend, within three years, a certain sum, fairly substantial but not too improbably large, say 220 million lire, just a little more than the price of the house. In other words, this promissory note has now fallen due. Are you beginning to see the pattern, Signor Bianchi? It has a certain beauty, as I think you will agree. We will be invalidating a fictitious sale by means of a fictitious debt. The note has fallen due, you cannot pay back the debt, you panic, you enter into a false sale of the house, you admit it is false, you throw yourself on the mercy of the court. Why did you do it? Not to avoid tax, not to evade your responsibilities as a good citizen, no and no again, you did it because you were afraid that this creditor would take the house, which you have offered as security for the debt, leaving you and your partner without a roof over your heads. The judge may not altogether believe it, of course.'

'But in that case –'

'I mean as a private person he may not altogether believe it. But the papers will be in order, your friend will be there as witness, he will have a lawyer to present the *cambiali* on his behalf, which will really be on your behalf, though it will not seem so. Naturally you will have to pay the fees of this lawyer of your friend, you could not press friendship so far as to expect him to pay them. Have no fear, Signor Bianchi, we will carry the day.'

'And afterwards?'

'Your friend will not hold you to payment, naturally. When everything is settled he will tear all those pieces of paper into much smaller pieces and throw them to the wind.' Mancini paused, tilting his head slowly, first to one side, then the other. 'That is, if he is the man you think him,' he said. 'If he is not, then of course he will say you have defaulted on the debt and perhaps he will try to take possession of the house. In that case we would probably have to declare these *cambiali* to have been fictitious documents and try to invalidate them by declaring the existence of some genuine document antecedent to them. In theory there could be a whole series of such documents stretching back into the past, each invalidated by the one before.' The lawyer chuckled, an abrupt and rather startling sound in that quiet room. 'That would give them something to think about,' he said. 'It won't be necessary, of course.' He spoke almost with regret.

155

'I certainly hope not,' Fabio said, rather sharply. 'It would cost me more in legal fees than the house is worth.'

'A regression of falsehoods and deceptions going back through all the generations to the original agreement, God's pact with Adam. The money hasn't been minted that could pay the fees for that. No, we will prevail in this matter, Signor Bianchi, never fear. Of course, you may find yourself facing a charge of fraud in the end, but that is better than losing your house, don't you think? The law is on our side, you see.'

'On our side?' Fabio felt his head beginning to spin a little. There was something unsettling in the way Mancini unfolded his thoughts. He seemed to look at everything in the light of the universal.

'I mean in the sense of the law's delays.' Mancini looked at the man seated before him, at the strong, still-athletic frame, the pale scars, not unbecoming, on the cheek and forehead, the deep-browed face at once melancholy and saturnine. Before this business of the house was over, long before, there would be another young man, another dependency, seeds perhaps of another betrayal. 'Well,' he said, 'I have looked at the deed of sale that you and your partner cooked up, so to speak. It is made out in proper form, there is nothing to get hold of there. But there is one thing strongly in your favour and that is the clause giving you usufruct of house and land. It was very wise of you to include that, otherwise you could have been turned out of the place at once, bag and baggage.'

'If they had tried to do that,' Fabio said, 'I would have burned the house down. The usufruct clause was the notary's idea, not mine – I trusted my partner completely.'

'Whoever's idea it was, it is a very fortunate thing for you. You will have the right of continued residence and the enjoyment of all produce and income and any other advantages derived from the house and land until the case is settled. And the case will take long to settle, Signor Bianchi. Cases like this in Italy take many years. With the hearings concerning the *cambiali* and the hearings concerning the legitimacy of the sale and the disputes arising from these, it will be well into the next century before we get even a preliminary ruling. Then if it were unfavourable, which I think highly unlikely, there are various appeals procedures . . . No, I think we can safely say that the threat of dispossession is very far from imminent. Meanwhile there is the situation of your former partner. He has no money, as I understand it. He has no profession. Now, effectively, he has lost his house. He may find, may have already found, a new protector, if I may so express it. But he is ageing, as we all are. Protectors will get scarcer. It seems to me that he is considerably worse off than you are.'

'I would not have him back,' Fabio said, and this was not altogether true but would become so. 'Not if he came begging. Why did he do it?'

'You have no idea?'

'None at all.'

Mancini regarded his client in silence for a moment. It was quite extraordinary, the evasions people were capable of, the way they would armour themselves against the lance of blame. Even a blunted lance, even minor blame. He smiled and placed his hands flat on the desk before him as if about to rise – it was his way of signalling that the interview was over. 'Perhaps some lawyer talked him into it,' he said.

From his vantage point on the hillside Harold Chapman kept watch with his binoculars on the stretch of road that included the Checchetti house. From here he could see the junction of the road with the broader one that led down from the village. The lorry would come this way.

It was quite hot, even here in the shade, and the flies were bothersome. But it did not occur to him to abandon his post. When you have set your hand to the plough . . . Somewhere below him he heard a snatch of bird-song, abrupt and lyrical, with a melancholy dying fall. Some kind of warbler. He had originally bought the binoculars in order to do some bird-watching during his stays here in his holiday house. He knew little about birds but they were on his list of leisure activities for Italy, like learning more about art. He had always, since his boyhood, made lists of things to be accomplished; but the lists changed with circumstances. Quite often, looking back, he could not understand the importance he had attached to some of the items. Getting Cecilia to marry him had headed the list once . . .

He brought the binoculars to bear on the stretch immediately below him, where the terraced land levelled out to the road, pale clay colour now after the recent spell of dry weather. The poplars along the road were in full leaf and they fluttered in the light breeze. It was a complex interplay of branch and foliage that the binoculars showed him, arbitrary to the point of hallucination, full of movement and shadow and gloss, with depthless spaces here and there, leading him through the leaves into some radiant world beyond. There was no sign of any dark lump that might have been a warbler.

He moved the glasses in a long sweep over the silver gleam of the olives on the rising ground beyond the road and the rows of vines above them. Perspectives were confused by the nearness of things, the vines and olives meshed together in an intricate trellis of silver and green. At the far edge of vision, on his left, he saw Ritter emerge on to the track, walk a few paces, then stop suddenly and stand quite still with his head lowered. Dangling from his right hand a hooped blade, bright in the sunshine. It was a billhook, Chapman decided after some moments. Ritter must be doing some clearing of the ground.

This sudden, inexplicable immobility confirmed Chapman in the distrust he had felt on first meeting the German. He remembered the vague eyes, the strange absence of possessions. The man was standing there, as if transfixed. What could you make of a man who stopped like that, for no apparent reason?

Chapman moved the binoculars away, reinforced in his sense of his own normality, his solidarity with the great majority of the human race. Lying there on an early summer day, under a vast and cloudless sky, dabbing at flies, clutching binoculars, he felt himself to be entirely reasonable. He was waiting for the defeat of his foes. Some were winners in life, some losers. He knew himself to be a winner.

The returning swing of the binoculars gave him a section of the Greens' roof with the edges of the plastic sheet curling and rippling in the breeze. The Greens were losers. He focused again on the junction of the roads. The lorry would turn off, begin to descend, be brought up short by the stakes half-way down the slope, just below the Checchetti house. Chapman had not seen military service but he felt now like a commander, waiting in ambush with his troops. Hannibal, somebody like that. He had read in his guidebook about that long-ago battle on the northern shores of Trasimeno, how the Carthaginian commander had waited in hiding in the hills above the lake, watched while the Roman troops blundered into the trap. Just as he himself was waiting and watching now. Admittedly the scale was different, the Checchetti could hardly be called an army, except as stragglers from the shadowy host of those who had tried at one time or another to get the better of him, do him down, deny him his rights or his gains – two things often confused in his mind. But the feeling was the same, that elation Hannibal must have felt, he, Harold Chapman, was feeling now, the sense of commanding the heights, like an eagle. Of course, looked at another way, both he and the Checchetti were no more than little coloured flags on the spacious map of another's mind. Mancini was the Supreme Commander. But as he lay there Chapman was content with his role. He would be in at the kill, like Hannibal. He was well provisioned: there was a bottle of white wine and a cheese sandwich in his knapsack. He would lie there and think his thoughts and wait for the prophecies of the amazing Mancini to come true.

Ritter stood still for several minutes, holding the billhook loosely against his side. He had clambered from the gully to get his rake, which was lying some distance away at the edge of the road. But the act of emerging from the tangled slope to the fuller light and uncluttered space above had somehow stilled him, like an exposure. And in the first moments of this stillness a memory from his interpreting days had come to him. A conference in Singapore, ten years before, in the mid-1980s. He had gone as interpreter to the official dinner on the last evening of the conference.

Consecutive interpreting, not simultaneous. Perhaps that was why the memory of it had sprung to his mind so suddenly, coming with the sense of exposure he had felt on emerging from the gully. Consecutive interpreting, when one is alone and unscreened and in full view, speaking for two or three minutes at a time, had always given him a feeling of being over-exposed, too much in the open; and this had intensified in the years just before his breakdown.

A private room in a tall building, high up. One wall was plate glass, through which you could look down on the lights of the city. Someone was speaking after dinner. Which one was it? He could remember the people at the table only in their official functions: representatives of the Relief Agency, the pharmaceutical company, the Singapore government; and their jewelled, bare-shouldered wives. The faces of the men were all one face, benign, calmly prosperous. The words too were the same, whatever the mouth that uttered them, full of friendly sentiment. Heartfelt thanks to our hosts of the Relief Agency, who have made such dedicated efforts . . . If we had in places of trust more people of this calibre, I venture to suggest . . . Hear, hear! General euphoria and congratulation. And the reply from the agency chief, Singapore Chinese – Ritter remembered his face now, shallow-set eyes, full mouth. See it as a privilege as well as a duty . . . But the true philanthropists are those who like my friends here are ready to accept financial loss in order to make these drugs available to the countries of the Third World . . .

One of the drugs was called Soronex. He had remembered the connection at that moment, while the Chinese was speaking, like the detail of a dream recalled unwillingly, wrenched into focus by some doleful sensation or event. Soronex. A medical conference in a grey northern city on the other side of the world, some six months before, the briefest of references. Under investigation, deleterious side-effects, possible interference in the supply of sugar to the brain. Under investigation – that meant automatic suspension of marketing in countries where controls were enforced. But these were not the countries the Chinese was talking about.

Ritter thought again of the faces around the table. He had glanced aside at that moment of unwilling recall, seen a sudden scatter of raindrops across the glass wall that divided them from the darkness outside. Every evening during his stay in Singapore the rain came just at this time, as if seeking still to nourish the roots of the lost forest buried beneath the great complex of banks and hotels and shopping precincts that is the modern city.

Well-fed and well-satisfied humanitarians sitting at the long table. The drug would be available at a much lower price. Quite frankly we have accepted substantial cuts in our profit margins. In India, for example, where gastric disorders are endemic, Soronex will be of great, of inestimable . . .

Nothing official yet, of course: tests on suspected drugs take a long time. But an unfavourable response expected. No further manufacture, naturally. A smooth switch in marketing to sell off stockpiles in the Third World. Some few at that dinner would have known; most would have guarded their ignorance carefully. Perhaps one or two genuine innocents.

Ritter began to move forward again, as if that possibility of innocence had released him. A medical conference in Brussels, a celebratory dinner in Singapore. Quite different people, no connection; but interpreters are wanderers, they move from conference to conference over the face of the earth, sometimes they see connections that were never intended to be seen. He had thought himself a mouthpiece for these people and others like them. But since his breakdown and illness he had understood that they too were merely conduits, that the stream had been fouled somewhere higher up, nearer the source, by other people making other speeches, or no speeches at all. His father too, he knew it now, nothing so dignified as a spokesman, a mouthpiece only.

He took the rake and returned to the gully. The cuttings he had made below the mouth of the cave had gathered into a mound, blocking his way; they had to be raked back before he could proceed further. When this was done he was able to see into the cave more clearly. It went some two metres into the hillside, deep enough for a man to sleep in shelter. Leaf mould lay thickly over the mouth; but when this was swept away he discovered the ground to be clear and level. There was an old wine bottle, cracked at the neck, among the mould and loose earth at the entrance.

As he stood there with the bottle in his hands it seemed to him that the water running in the stream below sounded suddenly louder. He was near it now, there only the final close-growing barrier of bramble and blackthorn, then the leaning, smothered poplars that lay just above the stream. He could see nothing of the water yet, the level had fallen in this drier weather, the course of the stream was still invisible.

He was in a green twilight here. Wild clematis had clambered up through the branches of the poplars to a height of ten or twelve metres and they mingled their darker leaves with the foliage of their host, shutting out the light. The trunks of the trees were ragged with ivy. Ritter saw great clumps of it, thick with dark berries, bending the upper branches with their weight. The new shoots of the parasite, higher up, showed a delicate tracery of leaf and a beautiful spiralling growth of the gently adhesive creepers; but the reality of the ivy, to Ritter's sense at least, lay in the ground-roots, dense and hairy and hideously matted, like a thick pelt round the base of the tree. Cutting through this dealt a mortal blow to the whole: it withered there where it had clambered and triumphed, high up in the sunlight. But the ancient cables of the ivy were embedded, they could not relax their grip, could not be removed without death to the host. Strangle-marks that would never be healed, they would stay there on the tree till the tree died . . .

Late in the afternoon Harold Chapman's patience was rewarded. Through his binoculars he saw the approach of the lorry, saw it turn off into the *strada vicinale*, saw it halt, saw the driver accosted by three gesturing figures. He made out the slack-faced Bruno, the rancid-looking woollen hat of the Checchetti father, the powerful bosom of the daughter, whose hair today was a mass of newly permed Medusa curls. He saw the driver get down from his cab.

A lot depended, of course, on the character of this driver. He might choose the path of least resistance, as Mancini had shrewdly thought, preferring not to risk any brush with officialdom. On the other hand, he might be a quick-tempered man or by nature intransigent, he might kick the Checchetti stakes out of the ground and so ruin everything.

Chapman watched with bated breath. The colloquy was not protracted. After perhaps two minutes the driver climbed back into his seat. Chapman saw the lorry reverse away up the slope and turn back towards the village.

Clutching the binoculars and his jacket and the knapsack in which he had brought his picnic provisions, he scrambled down the hillside and made his way round to the back door of his house. He found Cecilia making herself a cup of tea in the kitchen. 'They have turned him away,' he said. 'It has worked out just as Mancini said it would.'

Chapman's usual mode of showing pleasure or satisfaction was a wide stretching of the lips with the mouth remaining closed; in moments of particular glee, however, he had a grin which changed the look of his face altogether, the upper lip rising well clear of the teeth, which were widely spaced and sharp-looking. The grin was in evidence now as he said, with a rather hissing emphasis, 'Now we shall see, now we shall see.'

Cecilia paused for a moment in the act of measuring out the tea into the pot to look at the triumphantly grinning person before her. More strongly than ever before there came to her the feeling that she had somehow opened the wrong door, entered the wrong hallway, as she had once done years before in England in a street of terraced houses, houses closely similar on the out-side, strangely different within. The umbrella stand in the hall, the colour of the walls, something different in the smell . . . 'See what?' she said.

'For God's sake, Cecilia. We shall see these bloody people get their come-uppance.' Chapman was rendered more downright than usual by his immediate irritation at his wife's vague and distrait manner and by the loose-fitting, lilac-coloured smock she was wearing, a garment that seemed, in its paleness and shape-lessness, to sum up Cecilia's perpetual inability to exert a grip. 'I am going to phone Mancini and give him the news,' he said.

But he had some tea first and before he had finished this there was a further development. A knock came at the door and when Chapman went to answer it he found a man in blue overalls and a state of considerable rage, who immediately began to speak loudly to him and make gestures towards the hillside. Chapman had not the remotest idea what he was saying, but after some moments it came to him that this might be the lorry driver. 'Just a minute,' he said. 'I'll get my wife.'

Leaving the man at the door, he went back through the house to the kitchen. 'Come and interpret,' he said to Cecilia, resolving yet again to press forward with his Italian as speedily as possible – he could not go on having all his vital experiences mediated in this way.

Cecilia came and listened and after a while said, 'It is the man who came with the wood. He has left his lorry up there somewhere.' And she too gestured towards the hillside behind them.

'Up there?' Chapman was bewildered. 'Why should he do that?'

'It seems that the Checchetti told him there was another road to us, one that goes up behind and circles round.'

'But that's not a road, it's no more than a track, you would need a jeep to go up there.'

'The Checchetti's idea of a joke perhaps,' Cecilia said. 'In fact the driver has got stuck half-way down. Loaded as he is, he can't go forward. He wants us to come and look and tell him what to do.'

The Chapmans looked now in silence for some moments at the lorry driver and he returned the look. Then he spoke again, but less crossly.

'He says he hasn't got a lot of time, he has to make another delivery today.'

'We'd better go and have a look.'

By Chapman's watch, a high-precision instrument of which he was very proud, incorporating a compass and an atmospheric pressure gauge, and guaranteed waterproof at any depth, it took them eight minutes and thirty-six seconds to reach the lorry, though they had sight of it considerably before that, perched in lonely prominence on a downward slope of the rutted track.

Himself an experienced driver, Chapman saw at once that the man had spoken no more than the truth. The track, bad enough already, grew conspicuously worse below where the lorry had stopped. It was not only the narrowness and the rutted surface; the edges of the track were loose clay and on one side the ground fell away steeply.

The driver spoke again, addressing Chapman from rooted

167

habit of male speaking to male in time of crisis, though by now he knew it was the *signora* who understood Italian.

'He daren't take the risk of going forward with such a heavy load. He wants to know if he can dump the wood here.'

'Here on the track?'

The Chapmans looked at each other and then at the lorry driver and for some moments, under that blue sky of early June, with birds singing nearby and the drone of a tractor faintly to be heard, the three of them seemed suspended in some impalpable net. Three strangers, Cecilia thought, forced into temporary communication by the strangeness of this stranded lorry. She felt the sun hot on her head and wished she had remembered to wear a hat. 'He doesn't want to take the wood back to the depot and unload it all again,' she said.

'Can't he take our wood to the people he has to deliver to next?'

'It seems that the logs are cut to the wrong size for them. Harold, this is not his fault, is it? We can't expect him to lose several hours of work because of us.'

'I suppose not. He'd better dump the wood here then.'

There was a level piece alongside the track a little higher up, wide enough to take the wood. The Chapmans saw the deck of the lorry tilt sharply up, saw their logs come down with a long, growling crash, saw the lorry draw away and tip again to clear the last of the load. In a hurry now to leave the scene, as if he had assisted in a crime, the driver shouted a promise that a bill would be sent and began to reverse away up the track. Long after the lorry had disappeared they could still hear the sound of the labouring engine. They stood there while this sound faded, looking at the lonely mound of logs standing so improbably there on the hillside.

Silence settled round them and Cecilia thought how strange it was that she and Harold should be standing here, so glum and divided, among these ancient hills where the pleasure-loving Etruscans had grown their grapes and pressed their wine. 'These were the heartlands of the Etruscans,' she said. 'They made their wine and danced and had their games and celebrations all around here. You can see it in the paintings on the walls of their tombs. They were a very hedonistic –'

'Etruscans?' Harold looked at her with a sort of angry wonder. 'This is no time to be nattering about the Etruscans, Cecilia. What are we going to do about these bloody logs?'

This time Cecilia felt no alarm at her husband's swearing. She shrugged in a fashion calculated to annoy him further. 'I haven't the foggiest idea,' she said.

They returned home in silence. Once there Chapman went immediately to the phone. The sulky secretary put him through and Chapman related the latest developments. 'This dumping of the wood complicates the issue,' he said in a tone of accusation. 'It wasn't foreseen in the strategy you recommended. Now there is this great heap of logs up there and I am responsible for it.'

There was a short pause at the end of the line. Then he heard Mancini's voice, oddly remote and metallic-sounding. 'When the initial idea is truly sound, further developments can only enhance it. These people have played into your hands. Because of their interference in your lawful pursuits there is now a heap of logs half-way up a hillside. They have caused it to be there, not you. They will bring the logs down to you and stack them neatly in your woodshed.'

'Bring them down to us? How can they be made to do that?' These questions came from Chapman in a strangely involuntary way, not so much driven by a need for specific answers but because he was, he discovered now, reluctant to let the conversation end. There was authority in that detached, impersonal voice and Chapman felt he needed it – felt he had always needed it. The fancy came to him that Mancini's voice was pre-recorded – as if the lawyer had known in advance that he would phone, anticipated the questions he would ask and recorded the answers. 'They won't do it, they will refuse,' he said.

'No, they will not refuse. Mr Chapman, there is a time for waiting and a time for acting. The whole secret of life lies in the management of these two times. Now the moment has come to bear down on the Checchetti, to let them know they have been proceeding illegally, that they have been wrong from the very beginning in the matter of these stakes, that their illiterate faith in outdated regulations has lead them into serious error. They may not believe it at first but they will make inquiries and they will find that it is true.'

'By God, yes,' Chapman said.

'We shall tell them two things. First, that all talk of a contribution on your part to this wall of theirs must now be suspended. The possibility is still there but it becomes more remote. Second, that unless the logs are brought by them to a point specified by you and stacked there to your satisfaction within forty-eight hours, you will issue a writ against them for damages. You see the beauty of it, Mr Chapman? The only certainty they have is a negative one. If they do what we ask they may get some money or they may not. If they don't do it, they certainly will not and moreover they will be sued.'

'By God, yes. This will teach the beggars to try their blackmailing tricks on me. All three of them will have to take part, not just the men. And I don't want them ploughing over my land in a tractor. They will have to do the last bit with wheelbarrows.'

'That is outside my province. It lies in the area of your private arrangements. As also whether you choose in the end to give them the money. Better to give it, you will have kept your word. Generosity has a value, Mr Chapman. Not to make you less hated but to give you the upper hand.'

Chapman put down the phone and turned to Cecilia. 'That man is a genius,' he said. 'It will take the three of them a day of continuous labour to get that wood down and stack it. We shall see now whether that fellow was right.'

'What fellow?'

'You know, the one who came here and told us it was a question of pride not money but we should pay the money all the same.'

'Lorenzetti,' Cecilia said, keeping her eyes averted from the spectacle of her husband's triumph.

'Lorenzetti, that's right. We shall see whether it is sturdy peasant pride or the desire to get their hands on the money that wins the day. Like to take a bet?'

That afternoon Monti drove out to Tordandrea, a small village on the plain below Assisi. There, in the Church of San Bernardino, in the dimness behind the altar, there was a painting he wanted to see, a *Presentation of Christ at the Temple* by Andrea of Assisi. It was said – though Monti had not found certain authority for this – that Andrea had included portraits of some prominent members of the Baglioni family among the figures assisting at the scene.

Alone in the church, Monti went up close and peered at the canvas, craning his neck one way and then another in an attempt to avoid the obscuring shine of the varnish – there had been at some time a misguided attempt to restore the picture. However, the spirit of devotion that had inspired the painting had survived. There was a charged, hieratic stillness about the scene, as if intensity of awe had frozen the figures in symbolic attitudes, the hatted priest, wrinkled Simeon holding the baby, the holy parents on one side, the devout spectators on the other, bearded and robed, heads reverently inclined. They were all men, all richly dressed.

This opulence of dress, the damask and velvet, the trimmings of ermine, gave some substance to the belief that these were portraits of wealthy, powerful people. The artist might have had a patron among them; he would have wanted to show them in a flattering light. However, there was not much attempt to make a difference in the faces. All were presented in profile, narrow-eyed, sombrely attentive.

It was just one collective face and this was appropriate in a way, Monti thought, if they were the Baglioni, because it was a single mask they wore here in the church, the lines of arrogance smoothed out by piety. The picture had been painted towards the close of the fifteenth century, perhaps not long before that night of the Great Betrayal, the July of 1500. But it was useless to seek among these faces for killer and victim, for the beautiful, treacherous Grifonetto, for the bridegroom Astorre, whose heart had been torn out, for his brother, Simonetto, who had distributed the sweets at the wedding feast, for Giovan Paolo, chief of the clan, who had escaped the killers, fleeing over the rooftops in his nightshirt. The faces were interchangeable, as were the roles.

Monti stood before the painting for a long time, staring up until the faces seemed to run together. He did not really know why he had come, what he had expected to learn here. He had thought much about the Baglioni since Laura had left. Now it was as if these dignitaries in the temple had clambered up from some pit in which they had their daily being, crawled out and washed the bloodstains off, groomed and perfumed themselves and dressed in their most sumptuous clothes for this important ceremony, to which, as close associates of the Holy Family, they had been invited. When it was over, when the little cut had been made in the flesh of the Saviour of the World and the two doves offered on the altar, when St Simeon had asked God to let him depart in peace, the Baglioni would put on their killing clothes and descend again into the reeking pit ... Monti was glad to emerge into the sunlight, the quiet square, the customary life of early evening.

On the way back he was in time to call at the post office and collect his mail, which consisted of a single letter, addressed to him in his wife's handwriting.

He returned to his car and sat there for perhaps half an hour holding the letter in his hand. Then, very quickly, with the last of the sun on his face, he opened the envelope and took out the one sheet. He disregarded the opening and closing phrases, had eyes only for the body of the letter:

I have been wondering how you are, alone there, with only the ghosts of the Baglioni for company. But perhaps you are not alone any longer. It seems to be a common fact of experience, and so at my age it shouldn't surprise me, but somehow it does, to do something with a conviction of rightness and after what seems reasonable thought, only to find that you needed to do it before it was possible to know whether it was reasonable or not. I am finding that it wasn't. I hope this doesn't sound too muddled. I should like to come down and talk things over, if you agree. Perhaps you will let me know.

'We have decided to take the contract and show it to a lawyer,' Mr Green said. 'We thought it only fair to tell you that.'

Blemish nodded. His usual softly blinking look, the misleading air of sleepiness, was quite absent now. He had the wide-eyed expression of a creature threatened. 'That is your right,' he said. 'But let me give you just one word of warning. Lawyers can be dodgy in this country, very dodgy indeed. It is one of the things we have found to be very different from what obtains at home. Lawyers in this country will often set out to fleece you if they humanly can.'

Mr Green looked rather closely at his project manager's face: it had a look of total sincerity. 'The lawyer has been recommended to us by a neighbour. A fellow countryman of yours, as a matter of fact.'

'An Englishman? They can be dodgy too, highly so. I say it as shouldn't, but they haven't all got our standards. This neighbour may well be in receipt of financial inducements. Nothing surprises me in this country. Corruption is widespread, it has its tentacles in the most unlikely places.' Blemish gave a nervy hitch to his sharply creased navy-blue trousers and sat forward. 'Now we have a really outstanding lawyer,' he said. 'We always deal with him in any matters affecting our clients. He has never let us down yet. I could recommend you to him, if you like.'

'No, I think we'll stick with this one.'

There was a distinct sense of strain in the air. Blemish had arrived to say that the builder was asking for more money, another 10 million lire. By way of response the Greens had taken him on a conducted tour, shown him the half-filled trench outside the house, the flapping plastic, the charred and gaping hole where the fireplace had been wrenched out, the wide cracks that had appeared on either side of the internal staircase.

'The floors that Esposito laid downstairs are not even,' Mrs Green said. 'My husband went out and bought a spirit-level.'

'In the room below this, the one we are hoping to have as our sitting-room.' Mr Green paused and uttered a sound between a grunt and a laugh, narrowing his eyes at Blemish as if aiming. 'Seventeen centimetres. From wall to wall there is a difference of seventeen centimetres in the level.'

'The internal staircase gets narrower as it comes down,' Mrs Green said. 'You don't need an instrument to measure that, you can see it with the naked eye.'

'We have given the builder 60 million lire already. That is well over a third of the total estimate for the conversion of the house.'

'And now he is asking for more,' Mrs Green said.

Mr Green gave Blemish the same close-observing kind of look as before. 'What is it for exactly, this 10 million lire?'

Blemish was finding this atmosphere of suspicion unsettling and he had difficulty in sustaining the American's very direct and unwavering regard. But to look people in the eye was a basic principle of business practice and so he did his best. 'Well,' he said, 'it seems that in excavating downstairs at the back, where you are planning to have your guest room, they have encountered rock. They will have to drill it out before they can lay the floor.'

'Let me get this straight,' Mr Green said. 'They didn't find rock where they were expecting to find it and so they had to dig this trench round the house and fill it with cement.'

'Which they haven't done yet,' Mrs Green said. 'And that was an *imprevisto*, something not foreseen, and we had to pay extra for it.'

'Then, because of the trench, they had to make this *cordolo* under the roof and that was an *imprevisto* too and we had to pay extra for that.'

'That is correct,' Blemish said. 'Believe me, in the end you will have a house that will withstand anything the elements can do to it.'

'And now they have found rock after all and they will have to drill it out and unless I am greatly mistaken this too will be an *imprevisto*.'

'That is correct. The rock is in an unexpected place.'

'It's crazy,' Mr Green said. 'It's like a bad dream. You told us that each phase of the work was to be paid for when it was finished.'

'That is the way we usually operate. But in your case, for technical reasons, it was found necessary to embark on various phases all at the same time.' Blemish leaned forward with a gesture of philosophical resignation. 'That is the basic problem,' he said. 'Everything will be all right in the end, of course. We have seen it happen again and again. The various pieces will fit into place, you will find yourselves in possession of an extremely desirable country residence, all these teething pains will be forgotten.'

He packed all the sincerity he could into this assertion. A house was more than a simple acquisition, it was a dream of the future, he knew that; by pointing to the future you could generally persuade people to put up with what was unsatisfactory in the present. Especially gulls like these two . . . 'Elegant and spacious,' he said, 'standing in its own broad acreage, with extensive views across to the foothills of the Apennines.'

He felt no sympathy for the couple before him, had no real sense of their perplexity and distress. The fellow-feeling that would have been needed for this had not been included in the sum of his endowments. They were dupes, they belonged in the contemptible herd of the cheated and deceived, the dumb providers of *cotto*. But for these two he felt more than contempt, he felt a malignity that threatened to disturb his judgement. As he looked from one to another he saw despite himself the decency of these elderly people, their efforts at forbearance even now, their affectionate closeness in this time of trouble. He had controlled and outsmarted them from the very beginning, he had been superior in both strategy and tactics, he had watched them blunder into the trap. Yet they contrived somehow to deny him his just reward, the customary surge of power that sweetened his profits.

He glanced aside for a moment, shifting his feet in their suede desert boots. The trouble of course was the old one, Esposito's incompetence and carelessness. You would think that with an easy 25,000 or 30,000 pounds in prospect, clear profit, he would take some elementary care with the staircase and the slope of the floor. Those cracks he had opened up looked really dangerous; it was obvious that he had not properly supported the walls . . . 'I will have a word with Esposito,' he said. 'I think he can be persuaded to wait for his money. I mean, if it is put to him as a question of cash flow.'

'It is not a question of cash flow,' Mr Green said in louder tones. 'The sum that we agreed to pay for the conversion of the house is immediately available. It is a question of being overcharged for work badly done or not done at all. My wife and I have thought things over and we have decided to suspend operations with this Esposito.'

'Suspend operations?' Blemish regarded Mr Green and saw what, if he had not been distracted by his own malignity, he might have seen earlier: the blaze of rage in the American's bright-blue eyes, an anger open, direct and very strong.

'What I mean is,' Mr Green said very distinctly, 'that we are not going to shell out another cent to anyone until we have had some legal advice. And that applies to you too, Mr Blemish. In that sense, it is very much a question of cash flow.'

Blemish retracted his narrow head sharply on its long stalk of a neck in the rather snake-like gesture usual with him when he felt threatened. 'But you owe me for twenty-six hours of project management. That is 1,040,000 lire. I'll knock off the 40,000 – let's just say a million.'

'We don't really feel that you have done a good job as project manager,' Mrs Green said. 'In fact, if there is anything to be said about this project, it is that it has lacked management altogether.'

'As far as our interests are considered at least.' There was anger still on Mr Green's face. 'It may be that you have managed Esposito's project better.'

Blemish did not feel resolute enough for the moment to demand an explanation of the innuendo he sensed to be contained in these words. He had been caught off guard by the quietness, the lack of bluster or threat, with which the Greens had reached and announced this decision. His mouth felt dry. With an effort he relaxed the posture of his body. Were these dummies actually going to do him out of his earnings? 'We have the bill all ready in our briefcase here,' he said, reaching down.

'Until things are sorted out,' Mr Green said, 'it better stay right there.'

Blemish pulled himself together. He must try to put the frighteners on these people. It was sooner than he would have liked but the situation demanded it. 'You are making a terrible mistake,' he said. 'If you discontinue with Esposito at this stage, he will be the one to go to a lawyer. He will institute proceedings against you.'

'On what grounds?' Mr Green did not look worried, merely slightly angrier.

'On the grounds that he has been denied his legitimate expectations. You offered him the job of converting and refurbishing your residence and he accepted. With his experience and expertise he might have been offered other jobs. Those other jobs are lost to him for ever. Now you are threatening to withdraw from a signed agreement before he is half-way through the work.'

'He has been overpaid already for what little he has done – and even that was done badly.'

'He would dispute that – it would be a matter for the courts. But the quality of the work is not the point at issue. Mr Green, Mrs Green, Italy is a country in which the process of the law is subject to a great deal of delay. The mills grind slowly. It could take years before your case was decided. In the meantime, while the matter was pending, no new contracts could be made with anyone else, no further building work could be undertaken on your property, which would remain in its present state, incompletely converted and exposed to the weather. It would not be possible for you to continue to live on the premises. By the time the case received a ruling, the house would be in a ruinous state. Then if it went against you, as it is 90 per cent certain to do, in addition to your legal costs you would have a large sum to pay in compensation to Esposito. You could find yourselves in the evening of your lives sitting on a heap of stones unworthy of being called a residence and facing a bill for a quarter of a million dollars. I advise you to think again.'

Afterwards, when the Greens talked about the matter together, they discovered that for both of them it had been the inflection of this last remark of Blemish's that had stiffened their resolve. There had been an unmistakable quality of menace in it. Blemish, while endeavouring to sound like the trusted family adviser, had not been able to keep from his voice a slightly snarling, intimidatory note. And because he was an artist in his way and this interview and its outcome were part of a shaping creative vision in which the Greens would realize they were trapped and go on with Esposito hoping for the best until they had no money left, because of this he was not so alert to their state of mind as he might have been and noticed nothing of this hardening of attitude, which he now made considerably worse by saying earnestly, 'Mr Green, Mrs Green, listen to me before it is too late. I am telling you this for your own good.'

Mr Green stood up rather abruptly. 'No point talking about this thing any more,' he said. 'We intend to call a halt until we have had legal advice. You can tell Esposito that.'

Bitterness possessed Blemish as he too rose to his feet. 'You will regret this,' he said. 'You will find that contract you have signed is more than just a piece of paper.'

'I advise you to take yourself off.'

Mr Green's voice was marked now by that throb of absolute sincerity which often preludes some violent physical act. The American was short but he was compact. He moved lightly for an elderly man . . . Blemish took up his briefcase and retreated with dignity down the steps and across to where his car was waiting. The Greens stood together at the top of the staircase and watched him. 'I will advise Esposito to sue,' he shouted up to them as he drove off.

As a parting shot it lacked power, he could not help feeling, especially after he had been ordered so ignominiously off the premises. He drove home in a mood of discouragement. One worked and planned and this was what it came to. He had received his share of what had already been extracted from the Greens, except for the last payment, which Esposito still owed him. Whether he got any more, any share in the final settlement, would depend on whether he could make the builder believe that he would be included in further projects. As for the management side of things, the Greens had cheated him out of the money due for his twenty-six hours. Sweated labour, he said to himself bitterly. He would be lucky to clear 2,000 pounds when he had hoped for three times that much.

He found Mildred, as usual at this hour, in their vast and cavernous kitchen. She was preparing an assortment of medieval snacks. Bare-armed beneath her pink and white apron, she was occupied, when he entered, with fried fig pastries. It was typical of Mildred's endless inventiveness that she was trying now to quieten down her special savoury spice mix, *powder fort*, which was rather explosive, by adding cinnamon and sugar, so as to achieve an experimental spice base of *power fort-doux*. Being eager to explain these culinary details, she did not at first see how downcast her man was. But when she heard him sigh heavily and saw him glance gloomily around, she was quick to ask him what the trouble was.

Tersely Blemish told her of the Greens' defection. 'In my experience,' he said, 'and it is considerable, once people have been to a lawyer, the project is at an end, it dies a natural death. There is no further scope for management, you see. Esposito will ask for a lump sum of course, and he will certainly get something. That is only natural, it is his name on the contract, not mine – I never sign anything, Milly, as you know.'

Blemish brooded for some moments, hunching his narrow shoulders. 'That is the way we operate,' he said. 'Strictly speaking he should give me 5 per cent of whatever he gets, but he is not an honest man, Esposito, and I can't be sure he will keep his word. We have made something out of it, but it will not buy as much *cotto* as I had hoped.'

Mildred wiped her hands on her apron. 'Never you mind, dearest,' she said. 'Don't fret about the money. You are so clever and you always try so hard to make a beautiful home for us. I never had much of an opinion of those Greens, not from the moment you first mentioned them.' Mildred smiled and brushed wisps of hair from her forehead. The hairs on her sturdy arms were lightly flecked with some glistening substance like melted butter or egg yolk. 'Someone else will come along,' she said.

'That's true.' Blemish was cheered, as always, by this thought. 'Foreigners buying houses all over Umbria. Especially Brits and Americanos. What with Tuscany being so expensive these days and the coast getting so fouled up, people are coming here in droves. The green heart of Italy, home of history and art. The competition is growing, of course. Well, naturally it grows at the same rate as the volume of profit. That is the law of progression, Milly, we are very familiar with it in business. I am not the only one in the field, far from it. Just in our neck of the woods, between here and Castiglione del Lago, on the western side of the lake, that's a region about fifty square miles, I know of three other English-speaking project managers operating. It's a hard life out there, Milly. I sometimes wonder whether we couldn't all do a merger and pool our resources, but at the end of the day I am a lone wolf at heart.'

He watched the companion of his life brush her sheets of strudel pastry with beaten egg white and cut them into strips. 'I won't work with Esposito again,' he said. 'He has no finesse, none at all, he doesn't know the difference between deliberate and accidental wreckage. If he had played his cards properly we could have kept these people going for quite a while yet.'

'Well, that is human nature.' Mildred began to make the pastries, wrapping her rich mix of minced fig, spices, saffron and egg yolk into the strips and nipping the ends with a neat pinch of finger and thumb to seal in the mixture. 'I've had an idea for our medieval restaurant,' she said. 'I think it would enhance things if we had a minstrel.'

They discussed this new idea while they ate the pastries. Mildred fried these a few at a time in deep fat, afterwards basting them with warm honey and pressing them flat with her long-handled wooden spoon. 'It would have to be someone with a good voice, of course,' she said, glancing to see how her man was liking the sweetmeats. In their discussions Mildred generally provided the flights of fancy and Blemish struck a more practical, businesslike note and this seemed to them both to be perfectly in keeping with their true selves.

'He could accompany himself on a lute or mandolin,' Mildred said.

'It would cost quite a bit.'

'True, my love, but think how it would add to the atmosphere.'

'It would bring the punters in, there is no doubt about that.' Blemish was liking the idea more and more. 'We'd have to find someone we could trust not to dip his fingers into the till.' He blinked softly and his mouth shone innocently with honey. Milly was a real trump. Financial and sexual excitement possessed him in equal measure as he looked at her. 'Shall we dress up tonight?'

Ritter reached the stream in the afternoon of the following day. The weather had turned cloudy, with a milky haze lying over things and the sun occasionally striking through, dazzling the eyes. Before him he saw the running water, dark against the earth of the banks, with shifting glints where it fell in a series of small plunges to lower levels in the bed. Beyond these glinting splashes the far slope of the gully, thickly overgrown, rose to a line of oaks along the crest. That side he had no intention of clearing – he had wanted only to reach the water. He turned and looked behind him at the canes he had freed, stiff and motionless now in this milky light, at the dark mouth of the cave and the hacked and devastated slope beyond it, the raw wounds of his clearance. Time would be needed to heal this passage of his.

As he stood there looking upward, feelings of loneliness and bewilderment came to him. Why had he spent this time, why had it mattered? The mystery of neglect, perhaps it had been that, the sense that on a holding of three hectares, among people clinging to the margins of subsistence, even the earth of this ravine might have been used to some productive purpose, and in fact had once been so used, as witnessed by the canes, the willows, the straggling vines.

But it hadn't been this that set him off; it had merely provided him with a motive he could accept as reasonable. A screened-off place, overgrown and steep-sided, a place where the traces of something had been covered over . . .

That was why, he knew it now. He had felt the need to clear the place, restore it to the generality of nature, remove its secretness, its difference. One element in the complex legacy of that March afternoon fifty years ago had been this, a picture in his mind of the quarried excavations where the hostages had been taken to be killed. Imagination and memory had worked together, translating that talk of Nordic Spirit and Civilizing Mission into a moving mouth, the crack of pistol shots and the sprawl of bodies, a picture of banks, deep-sided, a place where such things could happen, parallel somehow with the normal, acceptable life of humanity.

It had been as if by giving back this little gully to the rest of the land he could cancel out his father's words, or make them somehow true, undo what had been done to those unknown people and what might have been done to Giuseppe and his mother. All his life he had been troubled by not knowing the fate of these two people whom he had betrayed. No one had come after them to live in the basement. There had only been Kurt, the orderly in the glass cubicle, making model aeroplanes out of matchsticks.

Words have terrible power – he had learned it then. A few stumbling words of his and these two had vanished as though they had never been. The worst had always seemed to him the most probable. They had fallen into the hands of the SS and been taken to the cellars in Via Tasso for interrogation. They had been shot in the back of the neck like the other hostages and the earth exploded over them to cover the traces.

It was possible of course that they had lived on, in the chaos following the German withdrawal from Rome. He sometimes imagined them as part of the vengeful crowd that hunted out Fascists after the occupying troops had gone. The main culprits had already decamped, or most of them. Trials there were, however. In the September of 1944 Carlo Sforza, newly appointed Commissioner of Sanctions against Fascism, reported that 2,000 persons accused of Fascist crimes were in prison and that 750 trials were scheduled.

One of the first to come up for trial was Pietro Caruso, Rome's chief of police during the occupation. He was accused of having turned over to the Germans more than fifty of the hostages subsequently killed at the Fosse Ardeatine. The day before his trial was due to begin, relatives of the victims, joined by an angry mob, tried to wrest him from the authorities and hang him. Foiled in this, they turned upon a man called Caretta, who was not only completely innocent of any hand in the business but had actually helped Italian political prisoners to escape from the Regina Coeli prison, where he had been vice-director. In front of the Palace of Justice, in full view of 200 policemen, they beat him half to death, then took him and drowned him in the Tiber.

Symbolic sacrifice, Ritter thought – there had been many such. Caretta's only guilt had been his association with a hated prison. Relatives of the victims . . . Once again he wondered if Giuseppe had been part of that mob, taken part in that senseless murder. The victims making new victims while the guilty enjoyed lawful protection . . .

At this moment he felt a strange shifting motion, very brief, below his feet. The earth seemed to stagger for a second as if burdened too heavily. He felt an impulse to clutch for balance, then it was over and he was standing still and the sounds of the world came back, but the hush had not been one of peace but of something terrible, casual too, the nature of it receding already from memory like the recognition of an accident narrowly avoided, something that might have killed. He stood quite still for a while, breathing deeply, no longer sure whether the earth had moved or only himself. In this moment of doubt, glancing down, he saw a dull gleam, something metallic bedded in the bankside just above the level of the stream, where the earth and stones were darkened with wet – it was water on the metal that had caught the light. He bent down and prised the object out with his fingers. It was a cigarette-lighter, much dented and scratched, made from a cartridge case, of the kind he remembered seeing Italian soldiers use during his time as a child in Rome. Turning with this in his hands, he looked back at the slope, through the screen of the poplar trunks and the pale foliage of the willows, at the dark opening where the cave went into the bankside. From there one would be able to see the whole course of the stream as it ran between the trees. Something had happened here, Ritter felt suddenly certain of it, with a certainty that made the morning, for these few moments, seem darker and colder. Something had happened here, something had been witnessed.

The letter had reposed in Monti's pocket all that morning. There was no hint of appeal or apology in it but he knew his wife, knew the importance of dignity for her, knew that in her way and at some considerable cost, she had acknowledged a mistake, even made a kind of offer. Without some response from him she would be slow to do so again. But he could not decide what the response should be. His own sense of dignity, more fitful than his wife's, was nevertheless strong when there was a sense of injury to support it. To be too accommodating would make light of his wounds. He had suffered her leaving with a passivity that he felt to be shameful; was he to be similarly supine now that she hinted at return? Always to be acted upon, never acting. In this indecision moralism came to his aid: Laura should not be encouraged to think that for forgiveness it was only necessary to dash off a note.

In the stress of these feelings he had not slept well and he felt strained and restless, unable to settle down to work. He decided to drive to Perugia and revisit – yet again – the Rocca Paolina, have another look at the subterranean chambers and passages that were all that remained now of the vast fortress built by Pope Paul III on the ruins of the Baglioni houses.

He left his car in Piazza Partigiani and went up by the series of internal escalators, a triumph of civic planning, that take one steeply to the summit of the Colle Landone and the historic heart of the city. Piped music sounded faintly as he ascended – Mozart's Klarinett Concerto. He always enjoyed the ease and incongruity of it, this effortless passage upwards on the moving stairs through the bowels of one of the greatest monuments to tyranny and terror ever constructed.

Looking at the people passing on their way down, he was struck by the mystery of common humanity, the strange composure of the faces, each glimpsed briefly, then gone, sliding away out of sight and memory. His own face too would reveal nothing, in spite of the nagging pain of his indecision. There would be pains far worse behind some of these sleepy-looking faces. And terrible, unavowable thoughts . . .

He did not take the final flight of stairs, that which emerged on Piazza Italia and the open air, but turned aside, spent some time walking through the twisting, high-vaulted passages, where the poor remains of the Baglioni houses had lain buried since Paul's conquest of the city in 1540. There were not many people down here; some few occasional wanderers like himself he passed in the gloom of the place. From somewhere not far he could hear the droning voice of a tourist guide. His steps struck echoes from the stone.

Tracing the arches of bricked-up windows, the line of masonry where the stump of a tower had been left to stand, peering into the narrow recesses where gateways had been blocked off, he wondered again why the Pope had allowed these last traces of the hated family to survive in this limbo beneath the buttresses and battlements of his enormous stronghold. Perhaps he had merely wanted space for dungeons and storerooms. But for Monti the symbolic had always held a strong appeal and he preferred to think that Pope Paul had ordered his architect, Sangallo, to leave these last traces of Baglioni power and wealth as a reminder of his dominion, and of the fate awaiting all who opposed his will.

His wanderings ended where they always ended, before the marble portrait of the Pope himself, the Grand Proprietor, on the wall of the square chamber, perhaps originally a guardroom, which adjoined a steep passage leading down to the lower levels, the fearsome belly of the place, where dungeons were built into the walls, designed so that a man could neither sit nor stand in them.

Paul's cold profile hung on the wall just above eye level, carved in low relief on a disc of stone. Though life-size, it resembled a face stamped on a coin, austere, imperial, with a kind of harsh sagacity about the lines of the mouth. An official face, not really a portrait. But even a true likeness could hardly have offered an answer to the question uppermost in Monti's mind. Had it been this pontiff's long-standing plan to destroy the Baglioni or had they themselves, by their own heedlessness and arrogance, presented him with an opportunity he was quick to take?

The true likeness he had seen in the Farnese Collection in Naples, the Pope's true face, in all its lineaments of cruelty and greed, rendered with the force of genius in Titian's 1545 portrait of him. Five years after the destruction of the Baglioni and the demolition of their houses, he sits hunched forward in his scarlet cap and mantle, looking sidelong at the spectator, thin-jawed and evil-eyed, like an old ferret.

Plotter or opportunist? Two main types of humanity. Sometimes, of course, there was an intimate mingling. He thought suddenly of the letter in his pocket, requiring from him too the forming of a plan or the seizing of an opportunity. He distrusted himself as a man of action, knew he was not resolute, distrusted even his impulses. Perhaps this Pope had distrusted his. In the welter of blood and treachery that was the history of Perugia and the history of the world, the successful ones, those who came out on top, were always people with a consistent policy . . .

This one too, he thought, looking at the frozen nobility of the face in its medallion of stone. There seemed to him now some faint suggestion of sardonic humour about the lips. Nothing if not politic, this son of the Church. Once again he ran through the events. In the September of 1534 Pope Clement VII dies. Within a week of this the teenage Ridolfo Baglioni, with some choice associates, murders the Papal Vice-Legate, Cinzio Filonardi, and some other members of the papal party, by the usual method of multiple stabbings. The bodies, still warm and bleeding, are thrown by the gang into the *carnaio*, the common pit where the corpses of the destitute from the hospitals are thrown.

An affront not to be overlooked. Filonardi represented the Pope's authority in Perugia; effectively he was the governor of the city. But the new Pope, elected to the throne of St Peter in the name of Paul III, shows no immediate reaction. He waits a year, then comes on a visit to Perugia accompanied by 1,000 troops and fourteen cardinals. A show of power and pomp then, but the apparent purpose is to forgive the city this murder of his legate. True, the delinquent Ridolfo is sent away; but Paul makes the municipality a gift in perpetuity of 1,500 packloads of wheat a year, thus leading the people of Perugia to believe that in spite of everything they are his favoured sons.

After this he bides his time. He sounds out opinion, takes the measure of things. Then in 1540, when the city has suffered a series of bad harvests and poverty is widespread and acute, he publishes a bull increasing the price of salt. Since the purchase of a certain amount of salt was compulsory, this amounted to a tax.

Did he do it by express design, to bring the city to revolt and give him a pretext for full-scale invasion? Was it true, as he said, that he needed the money to combat the Lutheran heresy and provide for the defence of Christendom against the Turks? Or was it, as the Perugians believed and later chronicles hinted, that it was for the upkeep of his court and the advancement of his bastards? These were questions to which history afforded no complete answer and even less the face before him, which he scanned again now with a sort of obstinate attentiveness, as if the stone might soften into meaning if stared at long enough.

But there was nothing much to be learned from faces, even living ones. He thought again of the faces that had passed by him on the escalator. Laura's face would be unreadable when they met again, it would not be possible to know whether her leaving had been the maturing of a plan or the seizing of an opportunity. Which would I rather it was? he wondered, with a faint feeling of sickness. A plan was less impulsive, made the need for the lover seem somehow less urgent.

Paul's scheme, if that was what it was, had worked well. The people of Perugia rose in desperate revolt, the papal troops advanced on the town. Ridolfo, returned from exile, made a brief resistance with what force he could muster but he was easily defeated. In a matter of days it was all over, the city was in the hands of the Pope. He sent his relative, the Duke of Castro, to choose a site for the fortress and the work of demolition began at once. The pleasure palaces, the scented gardens, the costly furnishings of damask and cloth-of-gold . . .

Not that it had been only the Baglioni mansions. The whole of the Borgo San Giuliano had been swept away. Church after church fell beneath the assault of crowbar and pickaxe, the tombs were violated and the remains of the dead flung out and scattered. As the years passed and the Pope's paranoia kept pace with the number of his enemies, more and more buildings were destroyed. In 1543 Santa Maria dei Servi was pulled down because it was too near. Two years later the tower of San Domenico suffered the same fate because it overlooked the papal fortress.

Monti felt again the impact of fatality in this chain of events. Buildings demolished, new ones built. Human relations not much different, structures of affections. In the foundations there were always flaws, seeds of subsidence and decay, faults that needed attention if the house was to stand.

Sometimes, of course, collapse was preferable to repair; but this was something not easy to decide. The destruction of the Baglioni houses had signalled the end of the oppressive rule of that lawless and arrogant brood; but the government of priests that followed had been a tyranny crueller, more systematic, far worse. Forced labour, crippling taxes, torture as a customary practice, people shut away for the slightest offence, for no more than a wrong word, in the horrific cells below him, fashioned within the thickness of the massive walls, cavities hardly big enough to admit a crawling figure. The iron railings surrounding the Great Fountain in the Cathedral Square had been garnished continuously with decomposing heads.

For three centuries the Vicars of Christ in due succession ruled this once proud city state; and the symbol of this rule had been the colossal building in whose entrails he was standing. Symbols again, he thought – without proper attention to symbol there is no true history. No wonder the final demolition of the place had been greeted with such jubilation by the watching crowd. They had to wait for two years, even after the city was taken by the troops of Victor Emanuel and became part of united Italy. It was not until 1862 that the last of the walls were brought down and the great slabs of stone broken up to be transported. And so the rule of the Popes came to its symbolic end. Who lives by the bulldozer dies by the bulldozer, Monti thought – he would offer this for the consideration of his students when next they met.

He was looking at Paul's face still, though no longer in hope of finding clues in it. In the light of day above his head, where once had stood the towers of the Baglioni and then the ramparts of the fortress, civil servants parked their cars outside the offices of the provincial municipality in Piazza Italia. There was the little square with its palm trees and fountain and bus stops round the perimeter and across from this the imposing fronts of the Bank of Italy, the Palazzo Calderini, the Hotel Brufani. Some day all this too would be levelled to the ground. That was perhaps the condition we are all ultimately destined to, razed, blank, at peace – the peace of demolition with no walls left standing to shelter our illusions. Through the cloth of his shirt Monti touched the letter folded in the breast pocket. He was not ready for that state yet, though knowing that some day he might be.

This recognition of abiding need seemed like a sort of decision. He was in the act of turning away when he felt a sort of shuddering or wincing of things, so brief that he could not tell whether the tremor was within him or above or below, but lasting long enough for him to sketch a gesture towards the wall for support. The floor had seemed to shift under his feet but it was from above that the evidence came: a fall of white dust, mixed with some larger flakes, floating down from a corner of the ceiling and making a brief mist in the room.

As the morning wore on without incident, Cecilia began to think that the Checchetti might after all have summoned pride to their aid. She found herself quite fervently hoping that this was so, that in spite of the difficult and disadvantageous position they had got themselves into, in the teeth of threats of legal action and loss of cash, they would find within themselves the stern nobility to resist Mancini's ultimatum. Backs to the wall, fighting against the odds their folly had accumulated against them, the Checchetti might thus be redeemed, might rise above their own ugliness and meanness and petty malignancy.

It was not, she admitted to herself, on the face of things a very likely scenario. Nevertheless, as time passed and nothing happened, the hope grew. But it was not until she was making the mid-morning cup of tea for Harold and herself that she realized the true nature of this hope. She was standing at the rather primitive gas stove, which they were intending to change for a more up-to-date type of cooker. It was fed by a cylinder below and Cecilia kept this closed when not in use, fearing an escape of gas. Sunlight was streaming through the kitchen window and when Cecilia bent to loosen the cap at the head of the cylinder she moved into this shaft of sunlight.

She remained where she was for some time, leaning down into this sun-filled space, her hand resting on the neck of the cylinder. As she slowly straightened up again she was visited by one of those rare moments of pure knowledge, undiluted, untramelled, a shaft of insight straight and unfaltering. And in this moment she knew that it was not for the Checchetti that she cared so much, nor even for the symbolic redeeming, through them, of all those who toil and whose lives are of narrow scope but noble in simplicity. This was what she wanted to feel, what she liked to think she felt; but it was not the truth. She did not want Harold to win, that was the truth. Filling the kettle with water, setting it on the gas, she acknowledged it to herself: she wanted Harold to be thwarted.

She was at first, and typically, possessed by guilt at this visitation of knowledge. She was accustomed to think of herself as a guide to Harold, a kind of arbiter of the refinements of life. There were gaps in his education through no fault of his own – he had been obliged to leave school early and make his own way in life, unlike herself, who had had every privilege, whose parents had paid for private schools and extra lessons in music and art, and sent her to Italy to study.

Harold had been rescued from a toilsome life by discovering in himself a talent for buying things and selling them at a profit. He had started in a small way as a dealer in second-hand furniture and the scourings of obscure auction sales, then gone into property speculation in the 1980s, when the going was good. They were fairly prosperous now but she had always thought of her husband as somehow underprivileged – like the Checchetti, in a way. His dogged resolve to better himself, to acquire more knowledge and culture, had touched her from the beginning and appealed to the spirit of philanthropy, which was strong in her and which she tended to confuse with love.

A good deal of this feeling still remained as a habitual response but the heart had gone out of it over the years as she realized that Harold was not really seeking her help to unlock the door to finer perceptions and more elevated thoughts but was looking for enhanced status among the people he did business with. More credibility, as he would probably have put it.

She had known all this for quite a long time now. But somehow, since this business of the wall and the entry of Mancini into their lives, it had come home to her with starker clarity. Lately she had not felt able to talk much to Harold about feelings or impressions. She had even given up correcting his misquotations, a congenital tendency, she had always thought, like a form of dyslexia. It had aroused her sympathy once . . .

It was true, she thought, as she poured hot water into the teapot, Mancini had inaugurated a new phase, he had brought something out in both of them. She thought of the lawyer again now. The gestures of his hands, his manner at once pontifical and humorous, her strange difficulty in imagining any time of life for him previous to this, any childhood or youth. It was as if he had, since time began, been seated behind that vast and shiny desk of his. Harold had become a disciple, there was no other way of putting it: hardly an hour went by without his uttering some words of praise, some reference to the lawyer's phenom-enal powers. Perhaps he addressed Mancini in his prayers . . . This was a sour thought, of a kind unusual with her, and she felt at once ashamed of it. All the same, it was as if Harold had been looking for a master and now had found one.

The tea made, she went outside, to the area behind the house, and called up to Harold. He came down from the hillside, his binoculars slung round his neck. 'No sign of activity yet and it's not far from eleven.' He looked downcast.

Cecilia handed him his tea. 'Does it matter, Harold?' she said. 'Does it really matter? If they don't come they won't be able to claim the money and we can use some of it to have the wood brought down and stacked by someone else.'

'Someone else?' Chapman set his cup down very carefully, always a sign of strong feeling with him. '*Someone else*? You don't understand anything, Cecilia. This whole thing has been worked out by Mancini, it has a dynamic shape. It is not a question of money, it is a question of justice. If I had to pay someone else, it would mean I had come off worse.' A sort of baffled rage began to rise in him at this further evidence of his wife's lack of understanding. He looked with hostility at her sun-freckled face – she was too fair-skinned to tan deeply – and her unbecoming summer dress with its overall pattern of strawberries or raspberries. 'They tried to blackmail us,' he said. 'You who are so high-minded, don't you see there is a moral principle involved here?'

It was almost a sneer and Cecilia felt wounded by it, by the dislike she felt in the words. She was a little frightened too. She lacked aggression, had always been alarmed by Harold's promptness to it, by the harshness that sometimes came out in him, though in earlier days when it had come in the form of desire for her and protectiveness, it had not seemed unattractive. She made a conscious effort now to overcome her faint-heartedness and return his gaze. 'Now it is us blackmailing them,' she said.

'What are you talking about?'

'Well, I don't know what else you would call it. And let me tell you this, Harold, you talk about justice but it seems to me that all you want to do is humiliate these people.'

'Humiliate them? For Christ's sake, Cecilia –'

At this moment they both clearly heard the chugging of an ancient engine. This ceased and in the silence that followed, from somewhere at the front of the house, a voice was raised in a shout.

'It's them, they have come after all.' Chapman spoke these words very quietly, as if afraid of being overheard. 'We'd better go and talk to them,' he added in a louder voice.

Cecilia hesitated for a moment. It was going to be embarrassing, dreadfully so. She would have liked to refuse, to dodge the issue altogether, but the habit of falling in with Harold's wishes was too strong. 'Yes,' she said, 'I suppose we'd better.'

The Checchetti were standing together in front of the house in rough arrowhead formation, the father in the lead. They had left the tractor fifty yards off. This, and the presence of the daughter, was proof enough that they had heeded Chapman's terms as relayed by Mancini.

After some moments of total immobility the father took a few paces forward and spoke. 'Where do you want us to put the wood, *signora*?'

The amazing thing, to Cecilia, was the complete matter-of-factness of this question. The Checchetti were behaving as they would have behaved in any ordinary circumstance of the day. Looking at their faces as they waited there, Cecilia felt hot with shame for them. She glanced at her husband and saw that he was smiling broadly, openly. 'Tell them where the woodshed is,' he said. 'Tell them we want it stacked neatly or they'll have to come back and do it again.'

Cecilia was to remember this moment, the sunshine, the waiting figures of the Checchetti, Harold's vulgar display of triumph. All her life she had found it difficult to go against what was expected of her. There was a dizzying sense of release in doing so now. 'No,' she said. 'No, Harold, *you* tell them. Or better still, go with them and show them the place, show them exactly how you want the logs stacked. Watch them grovel. Then you can enjoy their humiliation to the utmost.'

Chapman turned towards her a face divided between anger and surprise. 'You are talking absolute rubbish. All they want is the money. They don't feel humiliated at all, it isn't in their range.'

He was perfectly right, of course, she recognized that; these people had no idea of dignity, none at all. But his rightness told against him more than the grossest blunder could have done. 'Harold,' she said, 'this dreadful abjectness after all their bluster and threats . . . don't you feel some shame for them, or some embarrassment at least?'

But he didn't, she could tell, not a scrap. If he felt uneasy now it was because she was behaving emotionally in public view. 'You don't feel anything for them because you can't,' she said. 'And the reason you can't is because you are just like them.' She was aware that her voice had begun to quiver and she made an effort to control it. 'You are made of the same stuff.'

'For God's sake, woman, get a grip on yourself.'

This exhortation set her in real danger of weeping. '*You* tell them,' she said, and she turned away from him and went back to the house.

She went through to the kitchen and out by the door that led to the area behind the house. Her vision was blurred now. Without much noticing where she was going she began to walk up the hillside, following the rutted track that bordered the terraces of olives. She passed the place where shortly before her husband had kept watch with his binoculars and went on higher, walking steadily, looking straight ahead, until she had left the cultivated land behind and was in the wilder country beyond it, a region of thorn and aromatic shrub, bare rock everywhere thrusting through the surface.

Here she stopped and turned to look back the way she had come. The sun was high overhead. She was aware of the heat on her face and the blaze of the flowering broom all around her and the strong, sweet scent of it. A sense of the fierceness of this place came to her, dispelling her tears. The day was cloudless and the air very clear; she could see the roof of their house below her and the road and the broad valley with its fields of sunflowers and maze. Beyond this, the gentle wooded hills and the blue shapes of mountains behind them.

She had loved the landscape of Umbria ever since first seeing it as a young girl. It was she who had wanted to have their house here. Warm in colour, at once fertile and spare, old in its connection with man, it had always seemed to her a place where she could be happy. Now, on one of the nearer hills, she could make out the walls and bell-towers of Corciano, with its thirteenth-century castle at the summit. She imagined making her way up there, as she and Harold had once done together, up the winding road, through the great stone gates, into the main square. There was a church just off the square, built on the remains of an Etruscan temple, and a little museum alongside with scraps of frescos by Umbrian artists of the *trecento*; and another church, lower down, Santa Maria, with a painted standard by Benedetto Bonfigli and an altarpiece by Perugino. When they came out of this church the whole town had been glowing with light, the radiant Umbrian light that came in early evening, and the sky had been full of swifts, wheeling and shrieking.

A small hill-town, a place of human resort since time im-memorial. There were scores of them within twenty or thirty miles of where she was standing. The names of some passed through her mind now, like a litany: Bevagna, Montefalco, Cortona, Bettona, Spoleto, Spello. The ancient stones of their houses and streets, the sense they gave you of having an eagle's view, with great sweeps of landscape falling away below – and even in the smallest, sleepiest place at least one wonderful building or sculpture or painting that by itself made the trip worth-while. Where else in the world could you have a combination like this as a common fact of experience?

She had thought that she and Harold would visit all these places together. Now, dry-eyed and curiously dispassionate, she faced the fact that their house in Umbria, designed to bring them closer, had in fact brought them too close for their re-sources of mutual tolerance.

At this moment, in the midst of these sadly ironic thoughts, Cecilia felt the ground suddenly pitch under her feet like the deck of a ship struck by a cross-wave, staggering and righting itself all in a second. There seemed to be some accompaniment of sound, something like a single note from a massed choir or a snatch of prefabricated studio laughter.

She stood still for some moments, then took a few steps to the side as if in search of a safer spot. That had been an earth tremor, no doubt about it. She was still looking at the hills. All was as before, land and sky unchanged. No running figures, no apocalyptic flames. Corciano was still there, raising its pale towers in the sunshine. She saw herself mounting stone stairs to some church or sanctuary or ruined citadel, scent of wild thyme and summer dust in her nostrils, hat on head, sensible shoes, guidebook and sketchbook ready to hand, full of expectation. And quite alone.

'Mr Green, Mrs Green, on no account must you give these people any more money,' Mancini said. 'Money once paid is extremely difficult to recover. This is true anywhere of course, in some degree, but in Italy particularly so because here the means of claiming, the legal means, are either atrophied or they do not exist. No, that is not quite true, the means exist in the same way that speed limits exist or the Italian Constitution, but like them they do not produce the desired results. There are procedures open to you. You can make your complaint, you can claim re-imbursement for losses suffered at the hands of either the state or private individuals. But in the overwhelming majority of cases you will receive no reply. Italians know this, they have known it for a very long time now, they have no belief that the law or the police or the public administration exists to serve them. These institutions do not themselves believe that they exist to serve anybody. People avoid official dealings when they can. When they can't they become easily frightened. "My God," you will hear someone say when he has become involved with official-dom, "Hannibal at the gates!" So people try to find unofficial ways of dealing with their problems, they develop *furbizia*, cun-ning, and this is more admired among us than honesty. It is a climate of feeling that works against you in your present situ-ation – the fact that you have paid will be taken to mean that you were fully satisfied with the work. No, please take my advice, withhold all further payments and ignore any threats that might come your way.'

The Greens sat side by side facing him across the large and

darkly shining desk, and Mancini was struck, as Blemish had earlier been, by the almost heraldic symmetry and similarity of these two elderly Americans, with their clear blue eyes and silver hair and delicacy of bone. Their expressions were closely similar too at this moment, not so much anxious as guarded, as if they were struggling to stay in a bad dream for fear of a worse awakening.

'Threats there have been already, of a certain kind,' Mrs Green said, and she went on to tell the lawyer what Blemish had foretold. 'He said it would cost us a fortune in compensation, he said the work would be suspended for years while the thing went through the courts and we would not be able to sell the house or live in it or anything.'

'That is a standard type of intimidation. It is not to be taken seriously. Do you think a man like Esposito would wait so long for a judgement that might not go his way? He will want a new car or a speedboat or a platinum watch that lights up and tells you what time it is in Bangkok. Men like Esposito always want a lot of things and they always want them now. Esposito will take what he can get. This other one, this Blemish, he knows it perfectly well.' Mancini paused, tapping softly with a pencil on the desk before him. 'This Blemish will almost certainly be operating without a licence,' he said. 'He will be receiving payments of one sort or another, commissions and so on. I would be surprised to find that he was declaring these sums for tax purposes. It is also possible that he has no current residence permit. A word in the ear of an acquaintance of mine in the *questura* may cause this Blemish some embarrassment.'

Mrs Green watched the lawyer's hand as it tapped with the pencil. The fingers were broad and well shaped, but rather wax-like in appearance. The nails were immaculate, brittle-looking, a uniform shade of dark pink. Mancini's hands looked as if they had been made by some skilful artisan and then attached. He caught her eye and smiled and nodded slightly as if he had registered this impression of hers. 'It will not put a stop to his games of course,' he said. 'Only time will do that. Even wickedness runs out of steam in the end. In individuals, I mean, not as a force in the world. Besides, he will have been careful to put nothing in writing.'

'There is the contract,' Mr Green said.

'The contract is with the builder, not the agent. Besides, it is quite legal.'

'Legal?' Mr Green sat forward and pressed with thin fingers at the edge of the desk. 'How can it be legal? My wife and I have talked it over and we think now that they set out to rob us from the start.'

'Quite so. That is more or less what I meant. Without a legal document, it would have been much more difficult for them. You have been the victims of a kind of confidence trick. This Blemish knew or guessed how much you were prepared to spend and that was the figure he advised Esposito to give as the estimate. Then they make the house difficult to live in, impossible to sell, cutting down your options. You go on paying in the hope that all will be set right in the end. But they have no intention of finishing the work. Why should they? Instead they make you into a kind of money factory.'

Mancini made the gesture of someone playing a barrel organ. 'Turn the wheel and money comes out.'

'They have made these great cracks everywhere,' Mr Green said, speaking at a tangent in pure self-defence. 'New ones keep opening up all the time.' Mancini's office overlooked the Corso Vannucci and from where he was sitting he could see a corner of the Cathedral Square, a section of the splendid marble fountain made by Nicola and Giovanni Pisano in the thirteenth century and part of the great curving façade of the Priors' Palace, built in the days of the city's greatness, when she was still a free republic. This partial view of famous beauty seemed to symbolize all they had been hoping for from Italy, all they seemed likely now to lose. He glanced briefly at his wife. She met his eyes and smiled a little and he knew that she understood what he was thinking and shared his feelings. 'A money factory?' he said. 'How do you mean? We knew we would have to pay extra for the *imprevisti*, anything unforeseen that came up in the course of the work.'

'My dear Mr Green, who can say what is foreseen? In the courts, in the absence of anything in writing, how could we establish what was agreed beforehand? No, you see, anything, anything at all, can be an *imprevisto*.' Mancini laid down the pencil and made a wide, spreading motion with his hands. 'Anything in the wide world,' he said, and smiled as if in pleasure at this universality of application. 'All the details of the work must be specified in the contract. Anything not specified can be an *imprevisto*, you understand? And in your case nothing was specified, nothing at all. That is what I meant by saying that they made you into a money factory.' He made the motion of turning the wheel again. 'Whenever they want some money they find an *imprevisto*.'

'And of course it always has to be paid right away, before the work can go on.' The bitterness of the cheated was in Mr Green's voice now.

'Of course, yes.' Mancini's smile faded as he watched the Greens struggling with this concept. They were people who would always find it difficult to absorb the idea of dishonesty. Just as the man Blemish would always be a fraudster, so these two would always be trustful, always believe. Two aspects of the human story that had never changed and never would. 'The drama of deceit and belief goes back to the Garden of Eden, and lawyers have been living on it ever since,' he said. 'The first great advocate was Satan. My main pleasure these days is in patterns. When I was younger I saw things singly – single threads to follow. Now it is . . . What is the word? *Ragnatele*. The things that spiders make.'

'Webs.'

'Thank you, yes. Now it is webs. I do not mean as traps so much, but more as structures.'

The two Greens regarded him for some moments with a complete absence of expression. Then Mrs Green, with a visible effort of politeness, said, 'I can see that might be interesting, Mr Mancini, but it is kind of abstract for us just at the moment.' She wasn't sure she liked this lawyer very much. He sat philosophizing there in the wreckage of their hopes. But he didn't give an impression of not caring. He didn't seem quite real to her, as if he were occupying some other kind of space. She was a mild woman and well disposed, but it was annoying, in their misfortune, to be regarded as simply illustrations of the human condition. 'What we would like to know,' she said rather tartly, 'is how to get ourselves out of this interesting web.'

'We cannot contest this, so much is certain.' Mancini picked up the contract by one corner and held it before the Greens. 'It has been signed by both parties and witnessed by a notary. It would not be legal in some countries, probably not in America – that is to say, it would not be valid without details of the work to be done – but it is legal and enforceable here in Italy.'

Mr Green turned towards his wife. 'That is what he meant, that is what Blemish really meant when he talked about mediating between cultures, bridging the gap.'

'Quite so,' Mancini said. 'It is in these margins that people like Blemish operate. Wherever there is a boom in building, wherever foreigners are flocking to buy property, you will find the same thing. Today Umbria is such a place. Laws differ from one country to another. The differences may seem hazy but they can get very sharp. In the region of Perugia alone there are a number of these project managers, some British, some German, some American. Italians are there in strength also, it goes without saying. Often they combine the function with that of estate agent, which is a useful way of making first contact with their unfortunate clients.'

Mancini paused and after a moment sighed and shrugged a little. 'Yes,' he said, 'they are all busy bridging the gap.' It was incredible, what lengths people would go to, what money they could be persuaded to part with, for the dream of a house. It was unlike any other dream of ownership – a way of life went with it. He sympathized with these two people more personally than usual. In general his clients represented interests which he saw it as his function to serve. But these two had lost more than money; they had been dispossessed of a vision. 'I will do what I can for you,' he said. 'We will have to bargain with them.'

Mr Green sat forward rather tensely. 'How much will it cost? If this Esposito is going to ask for a large sum in compensation . . .'

'He will ask for a large sum and then come down. Each time he comes down he will intensify his threats. The art of it lies in not forcing him so far down that he thinks he will be better off going to law. In short, it is the usual process of blackmail and bluff that goes under the name of negotiation, whether legal or political.'

'And your fee?'

'These days I like things to be interesting. I will ask you for 5 per cent of what I save you. If he started by asking for 50 million and came down to 10 my fee would be 2 million lire.' Mancini paused, smiling a little. 'This will be an incentive for me.'

'What line shall we take with Blemish and Esposito?'

'Do not enter into discussion with them at all. If they appear, show them the door. But it is not likely that they will.' Mancini made fists of his hands and rested his large head on them. 'Excuse me, I will think a moment,' he said.

There was a brief period of silence which the Greens occupied by making faces of resignation one to the other. Then Mancini raised his head. 'This is what we will do,' he said. 'We will first of all obtain the services of a reliable *geometra*. I know of one who is *ben introdotto* here, in the courts. How do you say that, well introduced?'

'You mean someone with pull.'

'Exactly. We will ask him to make a full report on the state of the building. He will want money for doing this of course, but if he thinks you are going to take him on as your *geometra* for the rest of the building work he will not ask for so much.'

'It is unlikely now that we can go on with the building work.'

'I know that and you know that. But there is no need for the *geometra* to know it. I understand from you that the work has been badly done?'

Mr Green nodded. 'Dangerously so.'

'We will make a counter-claim for damages. The house is in a seismic zone, it is almost certain that this Esposito has not observed the precautions officially laid down. And there will probably be infringements of *permesso* for the volume of the space permitted. The authorities are going through a phase of strictness just at present, you need a friend in the right place before you can even have a pergola.' Mancini smiled again and placed his hands flat on the desk before him, his usual way of indicating that the interview was coming to an end. 'I will keep you informed,' he said.

The Greens began to get to their feet. 'Well,' Mr Green said, 'we leave things in your hands, Mr Mancini.'

'Mr Green, Mrs Green, you could not, and I say this in all modesty, leave them in better.'

It was at this moment, as the Greens were turning towards the door, that the world seemed to lurch for a moment or two, not long enough to make it necessary to clutch at anything or stagger. The whole building seemed to undergo that brief shudder that swallowing a bitter drink might produce in the human frame. Mrs Green saw Mancini's hat, a rather stagy-looking, broad-brimmed black affair, like that of an old-fashioned conjuror, swing on its peg on the hat stand as if in a sudden wind.

Blemish and Milly did not notice the earth tremor, as they had taken a sort of holiday that afternoon, after a light lunch of medieval oatcakes and quince jam, and were dressed up in their medieval gear and scampering excitedly round their bedroom when it took place. The bedroom was of large proportions, having once been the monks' refectory. There was still a stone pulpit there, with worn steps leading up to it, from which the designated monk had read works of a devotional nature to his brothers as they ate.

Blemish and Milly had spent quite a lot of money – part of the proceeds of a previous piece of project management – on an antique four-poster, which they had set in the centre of the room. Milly planned to make a medieval canopy for it but in the meantime its fluted mahogany posts stood bare and served as supports for her, keeping her on her frantic course as she ran squealing round the room in her tight bodice and voluminous petticoats, hotly pursued by Blemish in his doublet and codpiece and lovat-green hose.

He was almost there, he was within an ace of grasping her amidships and heaving her on to the bed. That deep shudder of earth came and went without either of them having the faintest inkling of it.

When the world was still again, Ritter turned away from the stream and clambered up the slope of the bank. His mind was vacant; he had no sense of having made a decision. He began to walk along the track in the direction of the village, passing his house without a glance. As he came towards the point where the track began its long curve towards the public road, he saw the figure of a woman descending the hillside. It was the English-woman, Mrs Chapman. At the same moment that he recognized her she waved to him, sweeping her arm from side to side in a gesture that seemed too exuberant, out of character. He raised his arm in reply and smiled but she would have been too far away to make out any expression on his face.

When he reached the village, obeying a sudden impulse – it seemed the first independent movement of his mind since setting out – he went into the small bar and asked for a *grappa*. His entrance caused a certain tension of awareness among the four men playing cards in there. He had never been in the bar before and it came to him now that he must cut an odd figure, bearded, dishevelled, his clothes marked with the clay of the gulley. He wondered if these people had felt the tremor but a kind of shyness prevented him from asking; it seemed a question too eccentric for a stranger to ask. He finished his drink quickly, paid and went out.

Adelio was alone in the small house near the church where he had a room – the house belonged to his daughter and son-in-law. Roberto was at work, the daughter was visiting friends in Badia. Adelio explained these matters as he led Ritter into the kitchen.

He had been sitting here; there was a glass of wine on the table and a bottle half-empty. He had shown no surprise at the visit though it was the first Ritter had ever made. Moving with the deliberateness of the infirm, he reached down a glass from a cabinet above the sink and without asking poured out wine for his visitor. 'Our own wine,' he said. It was intended as a recommendation. 'Roberto has a small vineyard, eighty plants.'

'Where is that?'

'Here behind.' Adelio moved his head in the perfunctory way of one who expected these things to be known.

'It gives you enough?'

'Four hundred litres it gave us last year.'

Ritter widened his eyes and nodded, as politeness required, but he was impatient to come to his question. 'There was something I wanted to ask you,' he said, and he began at once to tell Adelio about his clearing of the gulley. 'I knew,' he said, 'from the time of uncovering the mouth of the cave, I knew this was something I must ask you about.' Perhaps not so much something that happened, he thought suddenly, in the pause before the old man's answer, but something that needed to be covered over. 'I thought it was strange,' he said. He had not mentioned the finding of the lighter.

Age and pain had made Adelio's face stiff and immobile; the wine he drank did not slacken it. The face, like the body, seemed guarded against suffering, so that the movements of the eyes and the mouth were alarming almost, as if they set the whole man at risk, somehow imperilled him. When he began to speak it was slowly, with long pauses clearly habitual; but he showed no reluctance, seemed in fact resigned to the telling. He might have been sitting here, waiting for this visit, this question. It is because I am the proprietor now, Ritter thought. I have acquired the right to knowledge along with the land.

214

'It goes back to the war,' Adelio said, and he drank and refilled his glass. 'You were hardly born then.'

'I was a child.'

'We knew Italy could not win. Some knew it from the beginning but most knew it by the summer of 1943, when the English and Americans landed in Sicily. No one wanted the war to go on, only the Fascists . . .'

Ritter nodded. The general circumstances of the time he knew already. The story was one that many Italians of Adelio's age could have told. With loss of belief in victory, resistance to the Mussolini regime had intensified. In a matter of weeks the Duce had been deposed and arrested. In September Italy signed an armistice on terms of unconditional surrender. When this was announced almost all the Italian units in the peninsula, as well as those in France and the Balkans, were either disbanded or transferred to the Germans. The country was thrown into confusion. The north was still under German occupation. Mussolini was rescued by German paratroopers and taken north. The Italian Social Republic came into being as an ally of Germany. The anti-Fascist parties became active and the underground resistance movement grew stronger and bolder. In the areas still controlled by Germany large partisan formations began to emerge and there was effectively a state of civil war.

'You did not know who was your friend and who your enemy,' Adelio said, with a thin smile that seemed illusory, difficult to believe in, in that immobile face. 'I was not Fascist or anti-Fascist. I wanted to have my life again.' He made a light gesture, opening his hands before him. The life he had come back to claim had been one of toil and privation but it was the reward of survival, it came accompanied by hopes of peace. 'You Germans were the enemy then,' he said. 'Now we give you our houses to live in.'

With the armistice he had done as many thousands of others,

abandoned his unit, made his way back home. 'They wanted us to take up arms again, join the Fascist militia. It was dangerous to refuse, they would shoot you if they thought you had sympathy with the partisans. They would shoot you as a deserter in any case. They came looking for us. I couldn't stay in the house, it was too dangerous.'

So he had made a den for himself, down there in the side of the gully where there was already a natural cavity caused by the arching growth of the tree roots. His hands as he described it made the shapes of smoothing and levelling, indicated the depth with a slow vertical movement of the arm. The entrance was screened off by canes his father had planted a dozen years before. Impossible to see from above, the slope was too steep, virtually impossible from below, unless one stumbled upon it. A perfect hiding place. Here, in that September of fifty years ago, with a blanket and provisions, he had been able to take refuge when they came looking for him. There was fighting in the hills around between the Fascist troops and local partisans. Then one day, early in the morning, a clear morning, that clarity of light between summer and autumn when the elements conspire to make you feel regret at the prospect of loss, the shooting had come very close. He was woken by it, there in his cave. It came from just beyond, on the neighbouring land beyond the gully, among the terraces and the rocky scrub.

He had stayed under cover, as far back as he could get into the interior of his cave, and prayed to escape notice. 'I was afraid for my life,' he said. 'Once I might not have admitted this so easily but now I am old I have less shame. There was a silence after the shooting and I waited for a while, then I came out to look.'

There were things he would always remember about that morning and in his halting way he was eloquent enough to make Ritter see what these were. The radiance of the light, the clarity of outline. You could see every smallest indentation in the line of the mountains that bounded the horizon. The leaves of the canes were motionless and stiff – there was no wind. There had been rain some days previously and a shallow flow of water tinkled in the stream bed. He had come crawling out of his cave, lain still among the canes for some time. There was no sound or movement anywhere. After a while he began to move cautiously along the slope. Then he saw the bodies, two of them, one at the side of the stream, the other high up on the further bank, lying outstretched on the sagging net of the brambles, his face turned up towards the sky. He had fallen from the edge of the bank above and been caught here and held. The other was at the streamside, face down, as if he had died in the act of drinking. 'I thought afterwards that this one must have been shot somewhere higher up and made his way down here. He was looking for a hiding place, he was hoping not to die. Like me.'

They were local men from Torricella, near the lake. One was in his twenties, the other – the one by the stream – was just eighteen. Their people had come for them the same day. There had been eight bodies altogether, scattered among the terraces and in the scrub country higher up. All but one of them were partisans; they had come down too far into country too open and been surprised at first light by a patrol of militia. 'We could have waited,' Adelio said. 'We could have settled the scores later, when you Germans had been pushed further north. It was only some weeks to wait.'

He had been shocked by the sight of these dead youths and, Ritter suspected, perhaps more by his own fear and sense of close escape. He had never wanted to set foot there again and he never had, not even to hide. The weed and the scrub had spread, covering everything over, clogging the canes and drowning the willows. The path that led down had been obliterated. 'My father, he never went there either,' Adelio said. 'It is an unlucky place. The earth is not good there and the slope is too steep.'

This verdict, at once superstitious and pragmatic, was the one that Ritter carried away with him. The old man did not rise to see his guest out, but remained seated there at his table with his wine – a second bottle now. Ritter uttered his thanks and made his own way out of the house, back on to the street.

All this was half a century ago, he thought, as he began the walk homewards. Time enough for resignation, for habitual reference to bad land and bad luck. The death Adelio had hidden from was close to him now again. But that remote September morning had still been clear to the old man's mind, the peculiar horror of it vivid as ever. As clear, he thought suddenly, as that March afternoon not much later has always been to me, my uniformed father in the white room. For a while, as he walked, the two memories were fused, his own and the one borrowed: sound of water, sprawl of death, the scatter of almond petals on the desk, the moving mouth. There were more ways than one of covering things over but however it was done the result would always be a sepulchre.

He had left the public road now and started along the *strada vicinale*. As he did so a car passed him with an elderly couple in it – he recognized them for the Americans whose house lay between the Chapmans' and his own. He waited some moments for the dust of their passage to settle. The surface of the road was dried out and hard, pale yellow in colour, chequered with shade from the poplars that ran along one side of it. Huge flaring poppies grew here and there along the edges. A chaffinch was singing somewhere, the same brief refrain, loud and full-throated. Ritter moved forward again, very slowly. He had opened a sepulchre back there in the gully. It was as if he had gone back to his boyhood and been permitted to stand there at the Fosse Ardeatine, and see the scattered bodies of the shot people before their executioners had blasted the earth to cover them . . .

These thoughts brought him once more to a halt. As he stood there, head down, he heard from somewhere ahead of him a strange roaring sound like a sustained explosion. It was followed by an aftermath of slighter muffled crashes, as if some metallic beast had begun by roaring and ended with sobs.

Monti heard the sound too, rather more distantly; but he was intent on his own purposes and did not think much about it. Some sort of decision he had come to already, though he had not been fully aware of it, as he stood there in the cellars of the Rocca Paolina, felt the place shudder around him, watched that descent of white dust.

He had gone back to his car and driven home. Now as he moved restlessly back and forth between sitting-room and bed-room, from inveterate habit he sought corridors of escape into the past, tried to wriggle free from the weight of deciding and acting through the contemplation of decisions and actions made by men long turned to dust. He thought again of the Pope's great fortress, built on the ruins of his enemies' houses, ce-mented with their blood. Paul had wanted, every day of his residence there, to celebrate the entombment of the Baglioni, stamp on their skulls, resurrect and kill them over again as he looked down from his terraces over the gardens that had been theirs. And all the time, very slowly, through obscure historical processes, the enemies were gathering who would one day de-molish this vast monument and raze it to the ground.

The same destiny awaited all habitations, whether brought about by human violence or the more patient violence of time and weather. But we can hope for temporary shelter, he thought. It is all that life offers. The past cannot give it to us nor the future, only the present as we live it day by day. He glanced for some moments round the walls of this rented house which had nothing of himself in it but his loneliness. All at once he was swept with pity for his wife and for himself and with need for her.

It was the first impulse of love he had felt since her leaving; and it was almost immediately followed by fear. He took out Laura's letter and read it again quickly. Nowhere in it was there any explicit statement that she would wait till she heard from him. It occurred to him now that all his assumptions might be wrong. She might not wait for a reply. She might decide to come and see him or she might change her mind again and go off somewhere. How could he have thought she would wait there tamely till he saw fit to answer? It would seem like waiting for permission.

Monti had never deluded himself that he was a man prompt to action; he had maintained a sort of passivity in the face of life, somehow existing in a place adapted to his shape, hollowed out for him. He had settled into the role of injured party as if in this way his merit might be recognized, his loss restored. But he knew now, with a force of conviction that seemed like joy, that one must restore one's own losses or confirm them for ever.

Whatever Laura decided, he must forestall her, he must get to her first. He would go to her now, he would leave now. Ten minutes to pack a few things. By eleven o'clock he could be in Turin. He would phone from a bar on the way to make sure she was alone when he arrived.

Not very far away Cecilia Chapman had also begun to pack, taking advantage of the fact that she had the house to herself. Harold had gone to report matters to Mancini. Nothing, it seemed to Cecilia, demonstrated her husband's essential servility so much as his present devotion to this devious lawyer. He had not asked her to go with him.

As she selected the things she would most need, Cecilia was surprised to find herself so determined and methodical. The decision to leave Harold had come with the force of things long overdue, things that had been silently beseeching recognition for a long time. It had come with irresistible force while she watched the look of triumph deepen on his face at the crushing of the Checchetti. Small things lead on to great, she said sagely to herself, as she selected among toiletries. It was not these wretched Checchetti – still going ant-like back and forth in their long task of bringing in the wood – it was not they who had been the cause. They were merely the occasion. She knew now what self-distrust had prevented her from knowing before: it was dislike for Harold that all these years she had been trying to overcome. She had called it by other names, she had thought it other than it was: her own inadequacy, her problems of adjustment to the married state, her failure, after the first year or two, to be much roused by Harold in bed. With all the considerable store of humility at her disposal she had looked at her own shortcomings and found the blame there. Now, with an exhilaration she was never to forget, she acknowledged the truth of things. She disliked Harold, she found him oppressive. She disliked his feet in their shoes and his aftershave lotion and the shape of his behind. She disliked the crudeness of his desire to better himself. She disliked the manner and nature of his laughter. These things she disliked not only in themselves but because they seemed collectively the emanation of Harold's soul. And she knew that time would only serve to intensify this feeling.

She had welcomed the idea of buying this house in the heart of the Umbrian countryside. A beautiful, peaceful place, a kind of retreat where she and Harold could be alone together. They had been drifting further apart but this would bring them close again. Or so she had pretended to herself. The real motive had been that she might learn not to dislike Harold quite so much. It was strange that such a simple, elemental thing as dislike could go by other names, could elude the conscious mind for months and years. She had run it to ground here in this house, which was to have brought them closer. The house was the tomb of their marriage and the Checchetti were even now heaping the earth over. *The tomb of our marriage*, she repeated to herself. She felt a detached, dreamlike sense of liberation. She would leave a brief note for Harold. He had taken the car but there was a bus stop on the road below the village. Or she could phone for a taxi from the bar – Harold would never dream of looking for her in a bar. It would mean something of a struggle with her suitcase but she felt capable of anything, the spirit of enterprise coursed through her. Some suffering was only right, in any case; one had to pay one's dues. Passport, Visa card, enough cash for the moment. She would get to Perugia station, take the first train to Rome . . .

She pressed down on the suitcase so as to bring the zips round and close it. It was a small case and rather full and she had to press quite hard. Afterwards she was never able to be sure whether her impressions of the next few moments were the result of these exertions coupled with her unusual state of mind or whether there was some cause in the world outside. The suitcase was on the bed and her pressure forced the mattress down in a rather lopsided way, but she seemed to feel some extra instability not connected with her efforts. There seemed to be a sliding of light in the room, a stretching and contracting of sunlight and shadow, very brief. At that moment she heard a peculiarly protracted grinding crash from somewhere outside, not far away.

She went rapidly downstairs and out by the back door of the house – the sound had come from this side. She followed the curve of the road, glanced up the track that led to the Greens' house, felt for a moment that she had made a mistake, taken the wrong turning, because the Greens' house was a house no longer. All one side of it, including the main entrance, had collapsed, leaving the roof gaping wide and a huge heap of rubble mounded up round the well of what had been the stair-case. The great oak roof-beams which had been such a feature of the house lay among the ruins, together with the heavy stones of the lintels and the shattered window-frames. Puffs and wisps of dust floated over it all like steam over a rubbish tip.

Cecilia stood for a moment or two, coping with the shock of this devastation. Then there came to her the fear that the Greens might be lying underneath, crushed and broken. It would have happened without warning and they must have been at home – their car was standing at the edge of the road. But glancing less wildly she saw now that the American couple were in fact sitting quite still in the car, side by side, looking up at the ruin of their house. They must have arrived almost at the moment it happened, Cecilia thought with something like awe. They did not seem to have noticed her yet. She wondered whether she should steal away, giving the Greens the time they would need to absorb such a disaster. But then they emerged from the car in the stiff-limbed way of the elderly and came slowly towards her. They looked as if they were walking in their sleep. Neither of them said anything.

'I heard the crash,' Cecilia said. 'There might have been another tremor just now. I don't know if you felt it? Perhaps in a car one doesn't.' There was no reply to this and she hurried on. 'Well, in any case, the first one would have been enough. Then, just some little shift . . . Maybe just a single brick shifting. I heard this tremendous crashing sound and I came to see . . . I really am terribly sorry about what has happened to your house.'

She should go, she thought. They would want to be alone with their loss; they might want to start retrieving what they could from the ruins and that would be too terrible a thing for an outsider to assist in. The evidences of occupation were still pathetically there. A pink and white sponge-bag lay amidst the rubble and a brass scuttle stood beside the blackened shell of the fireplace. On an internal wall, still improbably intact, was the framed print of Verrocchio's *Baptism of Christ*, slightly askew. Perhaps she should take the Greens to her house and make them a good strong cup of tea. The trouble about this course of action was that Harold would be back before very much longer. The thought put steel into her. She would have to leave the Greens to it, neighbours or not.

This decision caused a clash of behaviour codes in Cecilia. There was the code of reticence in which she had been brought up: one simply did not speak to relative strangers about marital breakdown, one's own or anyone else's. On the other hand, there was the duty of proper apology for failures of kindness: the Greens must understand why she was proposing to just walk away from them.

It was the latter course that won the day. 'I shall have to go, I am afraid,' she said in her light, clear but somehow wavering tones. 'You see, I am just in the midst of leaving my husband and if I delay things much longer he'll be back before I can get clear.'

She had hoped for some response to this but the Greens maintained their stunned silence. 'Of course, if you want to come and use the phone, you are welcome,' she said.

Mrs Green spoke at last. 'Don't let us keep you, my dear. You must go to him with all speed.'

'No, I am leaving him,' Cecilia said. She looked from one to the other of the two old people and saw that they were only waiting for her to go. She said, 'I am terribly sorry, I really am,' and turned away from them towards her waiting suitcase.

Cecilia's departure was a relief to the Greens and Mrs Green relaxed enough to weep a little. Mr Green put his arms around her and held her close to him. 'We'll have to salvage what we can,' he said. 'Italy is finished for us.' Over his wife's shoulder he surveyed the ruin, saw their picture, hanging crooked on the bare wall, the reaching gesture of the Baptist, Christ's meek head, the beautiful, deferential angels. 'I wouldn't have the heart to try again, even if we had the money.'

As often, the protective embrace came from him, the words of comfort from her. 'We have got each other,' she said through her tears. 'We might have been inside there when it happened.' She managed to smile as she drew back and held up her handbag. 'We've got everything we need here.'

Mr Green looked from her to the still-smoking wreckage of their Italian future. 'What do you mean?' he said. 'Everything we brought with us is under there.' He paused. In the face of disaster we snatch at trivial consolations. 'Well, there is one thing about it. Those crooks don't get another cent.'

His wife was still holding up the handbag. 'Credit cards, chequebooks, driving licences, passports.' She had found a source of consolation more durable than his own. 'You always tease me for sticking so close to this bag,' she said. 'We can cut our losses, we can just walk away from here.'

'No claim on the builder, no further claim on us,' Mr Green said slowly. 'No legal process either way.'

'We can sell for what we can get. There is the land, nearly five acres, and the planning permission for the building volume already obtained.'

'It wouldn't be much.' Mr Green jerked his head towards the remains of the house, for which he was now trying hard to generate dislike and contempt. 'They would have to clear this mess away and build a new house.'

'We have our pensions and something still in the bank.' Mrs Green paused for a moment, then said bravely, 'We can still afford the apartment in Florida.'

'Yes, we can still afford that.' Tidewater Towers, Fort Lauderdale. They had gone to view it while still undecided. A place expressly designed for old couples. Thirty floors, 300 two-room apartments. Beach location, uniformed security man in the lobby, parking lot for residents marked out with white lines, open-air pool . . .

Mr Green remembered the pool well. He had looked down on it from the twenty-sixth floor, from the narrow balcony of the apartment they were viewing. He had come out here alone while his wife and daughter discussed points with the agent. Something like a keyhole in shape with white enclosing walls and stepped terraces and shimmering, electric-blue water. It was a January day, late in the afternoon, and as the sun declined a tide of shadow crept moment by moment across the terraces and across the tiled surround of the pool. Some of the residents were down there in the warm shelter formed by the walls, sitting with faces turned to the sun. As the creeping shadow reached them they got up and moved their chairs a few feet back, away from the water, towards the white wall behind. And each time this happened they were brought closer together. Slowly, relentlessly, the shadow was driving them into closer and closer proximity in the shrinking zone of sunlight. So geometrical the lines seemed from that height, drawn with ruler and compass on a flat plane, the sharp edges of the terraces, the semicircular curve at the shallow end of the pool. And the people themselves so dimin-ished, so docile. It had seemed to him that they would end all huddled together in the last shreds of light . . . He had never spoken of these impressions to his wife though they generally shared such things. It was certainly not the time to speak of it now. 'We'll need help before we can do much here,' he said.

'We can rescue the Verrocchio if we can get across to it.'

The courage of these words moved Mr Green deeply. He raised a hand and laid it against his wife's cheek. 'Honey, we'll go to see the original, we'll go to the Uffizi Gallery and see it like we always said we would. Why should we let those bastards cheat us out of that too? We said we would go when the house was finished and by God it is.'

Harold Chapman had said he was going to see Mancini but this was not really a settled intention. Mainly he had wanted to get away on his own for a while. He had been cut to the quick by Cecilia's words to him as they stood together witnessing the self-abasement of the Checchetti; and more wounding even than the words had been the scorn writ large on her face.

As he turned on to the road that led to Perugia he felt at first too unjustly treated even for anger. In front of other people too. The Checchetti didn't know any English but they would have understood the import of Cecilia's words well enough, would have had the satisfaction, even in the midst of defeat, of knowing that here was a man whose wife could insult him in public, abuse him, walk away and leave him standing there, stripped of all dignity. She had poisoned his triumph, that was what it came to. She had made him a laughing stock before that gang of evil peasants. Worse still in a way, she had sullied Mancini's majestic design.

Ahead of him he noticed a bar beside the road with an open space in front of it and a few tables and chairs set out among scattered pine trees. On an impulse he turned off, parked his car and sat down at one of the tables. It was afternoon, a quiet time – none of the other tables was occupied and he heard no sound from inside the bar. After a minute or two an elderly, grizzled man came out and Chapman asked for a double *grappa* and drank it rather quickly.

The sense that he was embarked on a course distinctly un-usual, drinking spirits on his own, in the open, before it was even tea-time, gave an edge to his brooding, a quality of bitterness and abandonment. This was, he felt, his real condition. He was alone in the world. No one so alone as a man with a wife who does not appreciate and understand him.

He began to review the whole course of events since the morning the Checchetti had come to report the collapse of their wall. Cecilia had been unhelpful from the start, she had not supported him, she had left the defence of their common interest to him alone. She had taken a negative attitude, that was the only way to put it. She could afford negative attitudes of course, and all manner of fine feelings – she always had him to fall back on. Good old Harold. Lacking in refinement, but a good thick screen when the going got tough. Her face when he had dared to make a joke about the Madonna's detached left tit in that picture gallery. As if I had let off a thunderclap fart in the middle of a sermon. That was what it was of course, that was what Cecilia went in for, sermons about art. Pig-sick of it, he thought.

The waiter must have had some way of keeping the outside world under surveillance because he appeared again now, almost as soon as Chapman's glass was empty.

'Another *grappa*. A double.' Chapman raised his hand, made a space between forefinger and thumb. '*Un doppio, per favore.*'

Yes, he thought, half-way through this second one, he could manage in Italian without Cecilia's help. She had never done a proper day's work in her life, that was the trouble. She had no idea of the real world. That job in the art gallery owned by one of daddy's pals, that could hardly be called a bloody job at all, just going round in sandals and one of those shapeless dresses or some kind of cardigan down to her knees, hair all over the place, talking about paintings. It was his work, his money, that had provided a roof over her head – two roofs now. And this was the loyalty and support she gave him. He would sell the house – it was in his name, by God, yes, I wasn't born yesterday. With the improvements he had made he would more than get his money back. I may not know much about Raphael but I know something about land values in Umbria. So watch out. That would teach her, that would bring her into line. Fine feelings depend on having somewhere nice to feel them in and that means money in the bank. What was that bit in Othello? Iago's advice to someone or other, *put money in the bank*, something like that. There was a man who knew the world.

After his fourth double the waiter seemed to stop watching and Harold had to go into the bar to get another. He was feeling light-headed now and full of vindictiveness. The waiter was standing behind the bar and somewhere a radio was playing softly, swooning strings from some remote palm-court orchestra. Chapman raised his hand and repeated the gesture with thumb and forefinger.

'*Grappa?*' The waiter nodded and smiled slightly.

'We can't communicate at any but a basic level,' Chapman said, 'but I want you to know that my wife, Cecilia, is a pain in the arse. *Mia moglie è un dolore in culo,*' he said laboriously. Seeing nothing in the nature of comprehension rise to the other's face, he gave it up and returned somewhat unsteadily to his table.

She didn't move, that was the other thing. When they made love she didn't move. Cecilia was not . . . what was the word? Ardent, that was it. Cecilia was not ardent, not in the physical sense of the word. Excitable enough in the first year or two, yes, he was not the man to deny it. But between excitable and ardent, he told himself sagely, there is one hell of a big difference, they are worlds apart. Nowadays Cecilia remained more or less motionless and let it happen.

He fell to thinking, not for the first time, about his new secretary, Miss Phelps. Shirley. Fifteen years younger than Cecilia and her opposite in every way, brisk and scented, with pearl-painted fingernails, concerned about the plight of characters in television serials. Heart in the right place obviously. Everything else in the right place too. Black tights with a design on them of butterflies. Narrow skirts that drew across the line of her thighs every time she took a step in any direction. Tight-fitting blouses that showed you where the hollow of her back was and where the curve of her bottom began, matters a man could not easily determine when looking at Cecilia. Miss Phelps was a woman who had the courage to look like a woman. She was probably a good little mover too . . .

At this moment, occupied as he was with thoughts of movement, the earth itself seemed to move beneath him, momentarily to pitch as if staggered by some massive sideswipe. The table felt precarious and he seized his glass as if it might slide off and fall. It was over in a second or two and Chapman was too drunk by now to be sure whether the threat to balance was personal or cosmic. But in the immediate aftermath perspectives seemed to shift, a brief clarity of focus came to him, he saw Cecilia's face before him with that do-gooder glow it had on it when she was telling him something about painting or poetry. She was talking now about Raphael. All these years, he thought, art rammed down my bloody throat. Fed up to the back teeth with it. If I want to make jokes about tits I will. Or bums, he muttered to himself. A woman who lay like one dead while he did his best to come up to scratch, who spent half the day arranging flowers in vases while he toiled to improve their standard of living. Lecturing him, correcting his quotations, constantly in flat-heeled shoes. Enough was enough, bloody twaddle, he would cross art off his list. He would cross Cecilia off his list if she didn't watch her step. Rabbiting on about Raphael. Raphael this, Raphael that . . .

'Fuck Raphael!' he said loudly.

Ritter made no attempt to investigate the sound he had heard. He went directly back to the stream side, taking the short cut that led below the road, out of sight of the houses. He noticed almost at once that the stream was silent; in this brief interval of time the water had dwindled, lost its voice.

He stood at the bank and listened to the silence. The impulse that had started him on this work of clearance had not been accidental, he knew it now – had known it back there in the village listening to Adelio's wine-thickened voice. He had not been guided or helped to it; he did not believe in any agency beyond the human. But some necessity of his nature had been revealed to him, looking down at that tangle of creeper and bramble and thorn, that slow suffocation of the hopes and designs of man. A thing planted is a hope expressed, he told himself as he stood there. A hope of continuing, if nothing more.

His impulse had expressed a kind of hope too. Through it he had found the place of execution, the ditch, the trench. His fellow countrymen with their dynamite, old Adelio with his neglect. Both seeking to cover the traces. But he had found a trace. His fingers closed over the cigarette lighter in his pocket. It did not matter who had dropped it there, or when. Fashioned in hope of life from the shell of a bullet, found on a killing ground . . .

At a distance of fifty years small differences of time are cancelled out. Giuseppe's tear-stained face, that strangeness of the empty basement, words that could not be true from the mouth of a loved father, these things had happened while that stumbling soldier came down here to die by the stream side. At the precise same time. And everywhere in the world such things were happening then, just as they were happening now while he stood there. Not only to me, he told himself, not only to the child I was then. The logic of the heart is strange. It was only the sense that he had not been singled out that brought Ritter now to a kind of peace.

Ideas can take some time in the fermenting, a fact that is well known, and it was not until some three weeks after the wrecking of the Greens' hopes that Stan Blemish gave voice to his. Sitting with a bottle of Pinot Grigio before him in the cavernous kitchen of their house, watching Mildred's motions about the stove, scenting the aromatic steam, he began to talk about the need to diversify.

He had been going through a period of gloom lately. No new clients had presented themselves, Esposito had not yet paid his commission in full despite numerous reminders. Moreover, he had been subjected to what could only be termed persecution in the form of requests by the authorities for details of his source of income and tax situation. 'If that is the way they treat guests in this country,' he observed bitterly to Mildred, 'no wonder their tourist industry is dropping off.' It would do him no real harm, he felt sure of that, he had weathered such storms before. There was nothing in writing anywhere, no proof that he had ever been gainfully employed in Italy. All the same it was depressing, it was inhospitable, it made a man feel unwelcome.

'All businesses have to diversify when they reach a certain point,' he said. 'It is a law of growth. The alternative is shrinkage. There is no standing still, Milly.'

'I am sure you are right, dearest,' Mildred said, stirring the pan with her long-handled wooden spoon.

She was making a medieval pottage of leeks and onions and chicken stock, using saffron to give the whole an authentic golden appearance. The movements of her broad behind, together with the odours of the simmering stew, worked their usual magic on Blemish. 'We have the estate-agency side and the project-management side,' he said. 'It is time to go into the property-development side and I know where we could begin.'

Milly turned to him, spoon in hand, her face in its usual damp glow. She saw Blemish stretch his neck and blink softly and she realized with joy that her man was his usual self again, all those doldrums forgotten. 'Where, dearest?'

'The Greens' house is up for sale. Seventy million lire, that's all they are asking. It is a great opportunity.'

'What a brilliant idea. We could do it up and sell it again.'

'Cheaper to build a new house on the foundations. A bijou residence affording ample views. We could clear 50 million at least. That is 20,000 pounds, Milly, quite a bit of *cotto*.' Blemish's face clouded a little. 'We would have to do it through a third party, that's the problem. It is so difficult in this country to find someone you can trust.'

Driving to Perugia, where he was due to consult Mancini, Fabio had again the sensation, frequent since Arturo's desertion of him, that nothing looked the same – or rather that in their very sameness things somehow looked different. He knew every metre of this road, knew the landscape that surrounded it on either side. He must have driven along it hundreds of times, perhaps thousands. He began to work it out. Ten years, an average of three times a week – not far short of 2,000. Multiplied by two for the return journey . . . And all that time Arturo had been a constant element in his life, never completely understood but deeply familiar, confirming the familiarity of everything else. It was this familiar world that Arturo had exploited and abused. The natural camouflage of treachery . . . He experienced a feeling of nausea. This is what he has done to me, he thought. This is what he has done. Out of the familiarity he fashioned a trap for me and watched me walk into it.

He naturally did not speak of these feelings to Mancini. It was not the lawyer's province, after all. Though Fabio, like all Mancini's clients, experienced a peculiar difficulty in determining where the limits of this province lay. What had brought him on this occasion was a written notice from Arturo's lawyer to the effect that he questioned the validity of the promissory notes and that he intended to subject them to the most stringent investigations that modern science could afford.

'In other words,' Mancini said, 'they will hire someone to test the age of the ink.'

'But that will ruin everything. Our whole case will collapse.' Fabio was aghast. 'Not only that, it will be seen that we have presented a false document.'

'No, no.' Mancini held up a large, pale, immaculate hand in the gesture of one stilling turbulent waters. 'No, you are mistaken, or confused rather. It is an error on your part to use the plural pronoun. It is not our case, it is yours. We are not presenting these promissory notes, you are. It is not my ink on them, but yours – used for your signature, not mine. I am merely your advocate. As far as I am concerned and to the best of my official knowledge, they are genuine documents. In any case, as you will remember, it is not I who will be presenting them to the court but the lawyer engaged by your friend in Carrara, who is suing you for repayment of the debt. If they were discovered to be other than genuine I would maintain that you had deceived me. This may seem harsh to you . . .'

'It does.' Fabio struggled to resist the hypnotically persuasive flow of the lawyer's words. 'I thought you had my interests at heart,' he said.

'So I have, so I have. All my professional resources are at your disposal. And they are considerable. But reflect a moment, my dear Signor Bianchi. It might be easier if you thought of it in terms of medicine. If the doctor were required to suffer the same fate as the patient how could he continue to function? It is not like the skipper who must go down with his ship. But this matter of the ink test is not so serious in any case. You must get hold of an ultraviolet lamp.'

'You mean the sort people use for tanning?'

'It simulates the sun's rays, yes. Better to buy it rather than borrow, for reasons I am sure you understand. It will involve you in some expense, I am afraid. But you can always use it afterwards.'

'Afterwards?'

'Yes, these lamps have an infra-red component very efficacious against rheumatism.'

'I do not suffer from rheumatism.'

'I am glad to hear that. However, time passes, one gets older. The area around Lake Trasimeno is very damp in winter.'

'Excuse me,' Fabio said, 'I am a man who likes to get things clear. What use will it be to me in the meantime, this sunray lamp?'

'In the meantime?'

'Before the dampness begins to affect me.'

'I had thought you understood. You will need the lamp in order to age the ink.' Fabio looked blankly across the desk. There was something ineffable about Mancini, a sort of absolute imperturbability, something that disarmed all power of reaction. He radiated a wholeness of being so complete that it defied question. *I am he that is*, he seemed to be saying. *Than me there is no other.*

'You will have to be careful,' he said now. 'If you make a mistake it will not be possible to put it right again. We can make things older but we can't make them younger. That is because ageing is in line with the natural tendency of the universe and the second law of thermodynamics.'

'How long must I do it for?'

'What is the date on the promissory note?'

'The tenth of April 1992.'

'Let me see now. That is three years, two months and four days ago.' Mancini extracted from a drawer a single blank sheet of writing paper and took from the inside pocket of his jacket a platinum fountain pen of impressive proportions. 'Bear with me a moment,' he said. 'A little elementary calculus.'

After a period in which the only sound was the faint scratch of the nib the lawyer looked up. 'At one time I would not have been so exact but these days I am a perfectionist. If you expose the documents to ultraviolet light for a period of thirty-four hours and twenty-six minutes, at a distance of one metre sixty-five, you will get it down almost to the moment.'

This at least was clear enough; but Fabio felt more fogged than ever as he rose to go. 'But surely,' he said, 'if you know this can be done, then Arturo's lawyer, the one who is proposing to carry out the tests, he will know it too.'

'Of course. And he will know that we know it.'

'Also the judge who hears the case, he will know it?'

Mancini nodded his large head. 'Certainly. All those professionally involved in the case will be fully conversant with the properties of the sunray lamp.'

'But in that case –'

'That is how the law works, Signor Bianchi, knowing and not knowing at the same time and always, under all circumstances, pursuing the tactical advantage.'

'To a man like me that is a nightmare,' Fabio said. 'I am a man who likes everything to be crystal clear and in the open.'

'Are you sure? Think about it carefully some time – when you find yourself at leisure. In my opinion you, and all mortal men, would soon be in a state of nervous collapse if everything were crystal clear and in the open.'

These words had little meaning for Fabio but he did not feel up to arguing the point. Mancini had not included himself in the ranks of mortality and this struck him as peculiar. He undertook to buy a sunray lamp and follow the instructions carefully. Then, with a certain feeling of relief, he took his leave.

It was time now for Mancini's mid-morning refreshment. This took an invariable form: mint tea made for him by his secretary and accompanied by a brioche from the pastryshop on the corner.

It was cool and quiet in the office and he felt at peace. He thought for a while of the interview just past, the business of knowing and not knowing, the total dependence on tactics. Looked at one way, it was a kind of elaborate game, designed to show that the letter of the law had been strictly adhered to. A game for the benefit of the ignorant. Justice of course was another matter, it rested on moral distinctions, not legal. Above all it rested on common sense. These two men had joined together in a fraudulent enterprise. They were equally guilty in the eyes of the law. But one had done it to evade taxes, the other as part of a treacherous plan to cheat and dispossess his partner and lover. There was, to any but an idiot, a distinction to be made here.

Mancini sighed to himself, brushing small crumbs from his lapels. Judges were not always notable for taking the common-sense view of things. Justice in this case would best be served if Fabio kept the house and land and the income deriving from them and Arturo received a sum of money substantial enough to mark his contribution of work and service. By private agreement it would have to be, since Italian law did not recognize the rights of homosexuals in property settlements. The best outcome, if it could be done quickly. But Arturo would want more, his lawyer would encourage him to press the false bill of sale. If the device of the promissory notes was not accepted, the case would drag on for years and in the end Arturo would get nothing, his lawyer would get it all. This was not justice either. He had behaved with outstanding wickedness, but moral turpitude does not cancel property rights – another distinction important to preserve . . .

He had finished his tea now. He rang for the secretary to come and take the tray. She informed him that his next clients were already waiting and he asked her to show them in.

A group of four – two married couples, all of them Italian. They sat in line abreast before his desk and told him a story of misfortune, interrupting one another frequently. Mancini listened, looking from face to face. It was his long-established habit to make mental summaries of what he was told, to extract the essence from the often stumbling and repetitive statements of those who came to him. These people, old friends, had combined together, put their savings together, to buy an abandoned *borgo* in the hills near Umbertide, four houses in need of restoration, a ruined church, various outbuildings, ten hectares of woodland. Their idea had been to have the place put to rights so that they could live in part of it and sell or let the rest – there would have been space for two more couples at least. The man from whom they had bought the property, also an Italian, had produced letters of guarantee and bills of sale, all apparently in order . . .

'Yes,' Mancini said, 'you discovered when it was much too late that this man did not own the property, not in any real sense, though no doubt he had legal title to it.' He nodded with his usual blend of dispassion and sympathy. 'It is a story I have heard before. It was all in mortgage to a bank, wasn't it? And this man, where is he now?'

The answer when it came did not surprise him. The present whereabouts of the vendor were unknown. He had decamped with their joint deposit, leaving them with a massive debt to the bank.

'Yes, yes, I see.' It was the same disastrous dream, the same haste to buy before another buyer came along and stole the dream away. But the real thief of dreams was generally not the one you feared but the one you trusted . . . 'You should have come to me before signing, not after,' he said. 'I will think for a moment. These days I like to study things. It is like a plan of campaign. You choose the ground that suits you best, you position your forces.'

He folded his large, pale hands into loose fists and rested his chin on them. For a short while silence reigned in the room.

242

Then he looked up and lowered his hands again to the desk, causing glimmering reflections in the lustrous surface. 'This is what you must do.'